The Necromancer's Rogue
Copyright © 2018 Icy Sedgwick
ISBN 978 1 9807 7357 3

Cover Illustration by Cat Hellisen.
Cover Design by Icy Sedgwick.

This paperback edition was printed by KDP Print.

An e-book edition of this title is also available.

www.icysedgwick.com

THE

NECROMANCER'S ROGUE

Book 2 of the Magic & Mayhem Series

by Icy Sedgwick

Other books by Icy Sedgwick

The Grey o' Donnell Series
The Guns of Retribution
To Kill A Dead Man

Short Story Collections
Checkmate: Tales of Speculative Fiction
Harbingers: Dark Tales of Speculative Fiction

The Magic & Mayhem Series
The Necromancer's Apprentice
The Necromancer's Rogue

BEFORE WE GET STARTED

If you enjoy this book, please take the time to leave a short review at whatever retailer's site you purchased it from. Reviews help other readers find good books!

You can also get an exclusive prequel story from my website – but more on that at the end of the book.

Buckle in, keep your arms inside the car at all times, and enjoy the ride!

For Eufame. This one is for you.

CHAPTER 1

The Almighty Crack, as the sound would be known in the days and weeks after the dust finally settled, was first heard by those waiting to petition the priestesses at Beseda's Shrine. Being in the catacombs below the Underground City, they were closest to the epicentre, and reported the noise as being like that of the Great Cannon of the City Above. Several visitors chose to remain in the shrine to claim Beseda's protection from the unseen foe they believed was attacking the city. When no pillaging forces appeared, the priestesses ushered out the petitioners.

The inhabitants of the Underground City heard it next, and later described it as a muffled roar that roused the sick and drunk alike from their beds. Many of the slum-dwellers believed it to be the gates between the cities finally rolling shut, and prepared to raise their voices in protest. Calm was restored when they reached the mighty Lockevar's Gate and realised it was still open, and they drifted away to return to their subterranean lives, the mysterious noise forgotten for the time being.

Those in the Canal District of the City Above heard the crack and thought the foundations of their homes had burst at last. They believed they would be flooded, and scurried around the lower storeys of their homes until they noticed no intake of water, and went back to their daily business.

The Almighty Crack was quietly observed in the Magickal Quarter, where the Academy's diviner ominously proclaimed the beginning of a period of mourning. The rest of the staff ignored him and instead blamed an experiment gone wrong in one of the classrooms, and the diviner failed to realise it was the only time in his life that his prediction had been right. The staff couldn't find the source of the noise and promptly returned to lessons.

Yet in a forgotten tomb below the Underground City, beyond the catacombs of Beseda's Shrine, a statue adopted a new pose. Long ago the figure had stood tall and proud, a warrior goddess enjoying the glory of her city, but now she pressed her back against the wall, stone arms clasped around cold knees. Her mane of hair curled in limestone tendrils around her forehead, hiding her fearsome face from view. Her discarded spear lay on the floor, its shaft split down the middle. A plumed helmet rested on its side near the door. Few would have recognised the fragments of chipped stone at her side as being a heart.

None would have remembered the name of this being, once terrible and formidable, yet they would eventually come to share her pain as the Heart of the City finally broke.

CHAPTER 2

Monte McThwaite sat at the table in the pub. A book lay in front of him, bound in leather so black it absorbed all of the feeble light that flickered in its direction. No name was emblazoned on the spine or cover.

"Seems like a pretty big book to be lugging around everywhere." He knocked back the last of his whiskey, winced, and put down the glass.

"Important things are no burden." The man across the table smiled, displaying ferocious rows of dagger-like teeth.

Monte shuddered.

"You won't find many down here wanting to read." Monte gestured to the pub's other patrons, a motley crew of drunks and fishwives back from the coast. A troll in the corner threw him a hard glare, and Monte looked away. His last encounter with a troll had left him without a sense of smell for an entire month.

"Good. The contents of this book are not for them." The man returned the troll's glare, apparently less worried about its strength than Monte.

"So why are you telling me about it then?"

"Firstly, you are familiar with death, and have a certain tolerance of it. This is helpful to my cause. Secondly, I get the sense you can actually read."

Monte tried not to beam with pride. He'd always wanted to be seen as an educated man and not the gravedigger he actually was. This stranger, this man, had noticed what everyone else ignored.

"I can read, but I'm not the only one in here – you see that guy by the bar?" Monte pointed out a tall, gaunt man with long grey hair and a matted beard. His hangdog expression told Monte that the four pints of Bezziwig's Broken Heart Basher had not yet begun to work.

"I do."

"That's old Crompton Daye. He's a wizard."

"Ah, a wizard will not suit my purposes. I need someone who can read but is not keen to use their mind unsupervised. Someone who will not think for themselves."

Monte scowled, his previous pride deflated.

"Oh don't look so piqued, my good man. I simply mean that wizards are too unpredictable and contrary. Their moods change on a whim. No, I need someone solid, and dependable. Reliable. The salt of the earth."

"What do you need this someone for?" Monte tried to recall how the conversation had started, but he could only remember arriving at the pub at the end of his shift, and then the book, that awful big black book. A gaping hole opened in his memory between the two events. Had the man approached him, or was it the other way around?

"I'm currently conducting what you might call an experiment, although it's also a bit of a quest, in its own way. Whatever you call it, it is vitally important, and could very well change the course of these delightful twin cities."

Monte raised his eyebrow in reply.

"You see, my strong friend, that is a book of last words, and I need someone to help me once I've heard the last words I'm listening for."

"Eh?"

The man leaned closer and lowered his voice. "I visit the dying as they lie on their death beds, and I collect their last words before they fade from the air and disappear into nothingness. My work is partly out of a desire to record for posterity the final statements of the dead. You could consider it a work of social history."

"But which ones are you looking for?"

"Excuse me?"

"You said you needed my help once you'd heard the ones you were looking for." Monte looked down at the book, wondering how many of those pages had been filled – and with what.

"Ah, my good man, you are sharper than you appear."

Monte beamed again. His smile widened when another drink appeared on the table before him. He looked around to thank the waitress but saw no one.

"Well, I need your assistance because I believe that among the citizens of this great city is one who knows the location of a certain artefact. It goes by many names, but the one I prefer is the Heart of the City. He who possesses the heart –"

"Possesses the City. Well, Cities," finished Monte.

"Exactly. You know the story, then?"

"Every child in the Underground City does, though I can't speak for Above."

"Indulge me." The man smiled again.

Monte forced himself not to look at his teeth. Why did a man need so many teeth?

"When the Underground City was first hacked out of the earth, a warrior goddess protected them from the things they awoke in the depths. She loved the city fiercely, and she died in battle, fighting a fearsome hydra. She killed it but she left her Heart to the city so that it may always be protected. My old mum always said if we need her again, we just need to find her Heart and she'll come back. But no one knows where it is anymore. I thought it was a bedtime story for children."

"Many men do, Monte. That is precisely why no one knows where the Heart currently rests – no one believes it exists. But I do." The man tapped himself on the chest with one long, skinny finger.

"So what has this got to do with your book?"

"I began my project in order to gain access to people on their death beds, which is ultimately the only place where man will speak the truth, and I'm yet to hear what I'm waiting for. Though I believe I shall, and soon, and I shall require your help once I do in order to locate the Heart itself."

"Say it does exist. What do you want it for?" asked Monte. Rumours tore around the Underground City about people disappearing from the street, the City Above Militia conducting beatings whenever they felt like it in the slums, and even wholesale demolitions near Lockevar's Gate. Surely things weren't so bad that anyone was looking for the Heart of the City?

"I told you, I'm a historian. An artefact like that should be on display. It shouldn't be hidden away in some cold hole somewhere. So, can I rely on your dogged determination and admirable assistance?"

"I've already got a job, though," replied Monte. He'd heard stories about the type of work men could find in the pub – and the trouble that usually followed. Besides, Myrtle would kill him if she found out he'd given up the grave digging for nothing. The work didn't pay well, but any salary was worth having in the Underground City.

"I realise that, which is why I shall pay you

more. How about a gold crown now, and a half crown for every week that you are in my employ?"

A flash of gold streaked across the man's pale knuckles. Monte's gaze followed its every movement.

"I'll do it." Monte agreed before he'd even made up his mind to do so. The man reached underneath the table to pass Monte the coin and he shoved it into his trouser pocket. Myrtle would be so pleased that she might even be nice to him.

"Excellent. My name is Mr Gondavere." The man held out his hand across the table. Monte shook it, feeling its cold, papery texture beneath his own flesh.

"When do we start, sir?" he asked.

"How about now? I do believe there's a man upstairs who won't be in this world much longer."

Mr Gondavere rose and headed towards the bar before Monte could ask him how he knew that. Mr Gondavere stopped to exchange words with the barkeeper, who widened his eyes and nodded. Mr Gondavere gestured with a nod for Monte to follow, and Monte passed through the hatch in the bar and up the back stairs, wondering exactly what he'd gotten himself into.

CHAPTER 3

Ground smog swirled around the feet of the traders as they set up their stalls. A clock chimed in the cavern of the marketplace to announce the early hour. Humans and trolls lurched back and forth, rubbing sleep from their eyes as they laid out their wares on grubby cloths. There was little gossip at this time of day, but the Crack would be the talk of the market when the customers arrived.

Vyolet lurked in the shadows at the edge of the vast vaulted space. The Flee Market was a tempting target for a Shadowkin, particularly at four in the morning. The so-called City Guard, in reality little more than local thugs collecting protection money from the traders, wouldn't arrive until five, and the traders were too distracted by setting up to notice a disappearing bread roll or hunk of cheese. Once they arrived, the City Guard would light the lamps, making shadows scarce, but until then, Vyolet could come and go as she pleased.

She stole through the shadows in the arches leading down to the wharf. Ferrymen carried crates up the steps from the canals, and a gaggle of fishwives trudged along the narrow quay behind them. Vyolet peered into the baskets they carried on their hips, but their treasure didn't interest her. It was mostly worthless detritus fetched by their husbands from the Distant Sea.

She passed an alchemist's stall and frowned. He wore a pin in the lapel of his threadbare frock coat, and the insignia was that of the local DWS group – Down With Shadowkin. Vyolet fought the urge to tear the pin from his coat as she passed, but instead, she filched a small bag of sleeping sand from his table while he looked the other way. Few in the Underground City had any love for the Shadowkin, but without their abilities, the spy network that kept the City Above at bay couldn't operate.

If it weren't for rogues like me... Vyolet began the thought, but she couldn't finish it. What was the use in being a rogue when she was forced to steal food from the market between jobs just to survive until the next assignment?

Still, the Flee Market was a den of opportunity. Named for its status as a haven for those fleeing justice, the vast square, with its vaulted roof and bright green lanterns, was Vyolet's favourite place in the city. When she was flush with money after a job, she often spent time browsing the stalls for magical trinkets. Obviously she needed to do so wearing a cloak and veil, passing herself off as a devotee of the Lords and Ladies of Death, and it irked her that she was treated better as a death worshipper than she was as a Shadowkin. At least people only passed rude comments when they thought she was a cult follower.

Vyolet spotted a disenchanter across the aisle and flattened herself against the wall beside his table. The shadow was narrow here and she barely managed to squeeze herself into the blackened rectangle. He removed the enchantments from cheap tourist wares, separating the imitation esoteric items from their magical sparks. The items ended up in a huge basket behind him, no doubt intended for resale elsewhere, but the sparks went into neatly labelled bottles on the table. One of the discarded items was a scarf, and Vyolet snagged it from the basket while the disenchanter busied himself with a wooden replica of the Abandoned Chapel. She tied it around her hair in the fashion of the worker women from the Trade District, but she knew her shifting skin colour and purple eyes would give her away.

Her stomach grumbled as Vyolet wandered among the stalls, sneaking from shadow to shadow, trying to spot a food stall. She passed stalls selling boots, fabric, magical equipment, broken furniture and even books, but no food. The clock chimed again to mark the half hour, and panic coloured Vyolet's hunger. She hadn't eaten since the day before, and she didn't have long before the city guards arrived. They were all card-carrying members of the DWS group, and would take great delight in ejecting her from the market – or worse, ejecting her soul from her body, and none but a necromancer could fix that mess.

Vyolet passed under the vast clock, the only way to tell the time underground, and saw she had merely five minutes until the guards arrived to patrol the market. She gazed across the sea of stalls and her heart leapt to see a baker reach his stall. He bowed under the weight of a large wicker basket on his back, while two goblins carried smaller ones behind him. She used the shadows between the cobbles of the floor to cross the open square in the centre of the market, and hid in the shadow cast by the awning of his stall. The goblins dumped their baskets and trudged off in the direction from which they had come, leaving the baker to set up alone.

Vyolet seized her chance and grabbed two fresh

rolls while the baker laid out long plaited loaves. She got three yards away from the stall when a large hand landed on her shoulder. The chubby fingers forced her to turn around, and she looked up into the heavy-set face of a city guard runner. He wore the enchanted goggles that allowed him to see her, even in the shadows, and a lopsided leer that brought an early winter to her soul.

"Thought you'd get away, did ya?" He leaned in towards her, and the smell of his breath turned her growling stomach. He tore her filched scarf from her hair, tossing it to the ground behind him.

Vyolet saw two more runners on the far side of the square. She twisted out of his grip and threw the rolls across the square, smacking the two goblins in the back of the head. They turned on each other, and the runners busied themselves with breaking up the fight. Before the runner could raise the alarm, Vyolet dipped her hand into the pouch on her belt and withdrew a fistful of sleeping sand. She blew it into the runner's face, and melted into the shadow cast by his vast bulk as he fell to the ground.

Vyolet streaked across the market, dipping and weaving through the shadows cast by early shoppers. Her heart thudded and her pulse roared like the rapids in the city sewers. Panic darkened the edges of her night vision and she fought to regain her focus. The distracted runners realised what had happened, and their shouts echoed between the stalls. She didn't dare stop to grab more food – escaping with her life seemed more important.

She reached the docks and skipped across the foetid canal in the long shadows cast by the wall of the marketplace. The sewers lay dead ahead, yawning black holes in the wall below the street. None but the bravest, or most desperate, ventured there, but the Shadowkin had few reservations about the dark or deep places of the world. Their elders told tales of their birth in the depths, harnessing shadows to gain mastery over the higher places. Vyolet didn't necessarily believe that, but she wasn't afraid of the dark.

Vyolet threw a glance over her shoulder as she darted into the mouth of the sewer, and collided with a tall, well-built body clad in leather armour. She froze, believing herself hidden in the shadows.

The hand that landed on her shoulder was not a hand at all, but rather a heavy paw topped with curved claws. Vyolet gasped. What manner of creature had the city guard employed? There'd be no getting anyway now. She dared herself to look up at the stranger.

A large wolf's head topped wide, muscular shoulders, but the expression in its black eyes was kind. Its deep russet fur disappeared under leather armour bearing the crest of the House of the Long Dead. Vyolet gulped. What could the necromancer general want with her?

The Wolfkin gestured with its paw and Vyolet gasped. How could a beast such as that know the secret signals of the Shadowkin? They often communicated through sign language as they hid in the darkness, a visual language only they saw. That a Wolfkin knew of it meant it wasn't as secret as they believed it was. Either way, the gesture was a greeting, and a friendly one at that.

"How do you know how to speak with me?" signed Vyolet.

"We Wolfkin know many things. We simply do not broadcast what we know. Not everyone needs to understand our ways."

Vyolet smiled. "You are from the necromancer general," she signed.

"Yes, and she needs your help. The whole Underground City needs your help."

"I think not, my friend. Most of the City is out to

get my kind, and they shun me whenever they can. They don't need my help." Vyolet scowled.

"They do not yet know that they need your help. Please. My mistress will pay you a great deal, and she is often in need of someone with your talents. She is not like the others of these Cities. She values difference. After all, she accepts the Wolfkin. She is one of two individuals in the whole of the Twin Cities that does."

Vyolet paused. The Wolfkin had a point, and it was the best chance she had of catching herself a meal. Besides, she didn't have to stick around once she heard what the necromancer general wanted. Her stomach growled, and she looked up at the Wolfkin.

"Okay. What does she need?"

Chapter 4

Jyx coughed and spluttered as his soul slammed back into his body. He'd lost count of the number of times he'd died and been resurrected since the first time. When was that? Days ago? Weeks? Months, even? He never saw anyone when he returned, and in the brief moments between life and death, he wondered how Eufame managed to fix the catastrophe he'd caused. She seemed to think his punishment would keep the Crown Prince happy, but what about the coronation parade?

Then he'd be torn from his body, and he stopped thinking about it. The world beyond the Veil defied logical thought.

He sat back against the bars of his cage and awaited the moment when his soul and his body would be ripped apart again. He counted backwards from ten. Nothing. He counted upwards to ten. Still nothing. He pushed himself forward as best he could, crammed as he was into the small cage, and peered out through the bars.

"Hello? Is anybody there?"

A Wolfkin appeared from the shadows to his right, followed by a second. Jyx recognised the first as the tawny Wolfkin that sometimes accompanied Eufame. The second wore plain black armour and a vacant expression. It must have been one of the ones Neferpenthe and her minions had killed.

"Hey! Hi! What's going on?" Jyx smiled at the Wolfkin, but it could no doubt smell his fear. The massive, wolf-headed men terrified him at the Academy, and they terrified him even more in the House of the Long Dead, where there was no Dean Whittaker to keep them in line. They scared him even more now that he'd caused the death of several of their number.

The Wolfkin shoved one paw through the bars, and fastened its claws around Jyx's head. He yelped, sure its grasp would crush his skull like the trolls that burst pumpkins at the Flee Market for coppers. The Wolfkin hummed, a sound midway between a melody and a growl, and sparks danced at the edge of Jyx's vision. An abyss opened up before him, warm and comforting in the way the space beyond the Veil was not.

"Can you understand me now?"

A voice echoed in his mind, and the paw, surprising in its gentleness, tilted his head upward. His vision blurred, and then his eyes refocused on the Wolfkin in front of him.

"Oh, it's you! You're talking to me!" Jyx's voice was thin in the vast chamber.

"Yes, it is me. You may call me Validus. That is not my true name, but you would not be able to pronounce the Wolfkin language. This is Ptem, though he cannot speak." The Wolfkin didn't smile but an aural grin warmed his voice, even when he gestured to the vacant Wolfkin. He certainly didn't patronise him when he mentioned the Wolfkin language. Jyx remembered the complicated series of barks and yips

Eufame performed with such ease and frowned. The Wolfkin released his grip of his head, and Jyx rubbed his temples.

"How are you doing that? How can I hear you? And why haven't I died again?" asked Jyx.

"We Wolfkin have magick of our own that men largely do not understand, but at present that is unimportant. I have interrupted Eufame's spell because you are more valuable alive than you are languishing in this punishment. I have granted you the privilege of Wolfkin communication because I need you to understand me." Validus's voice sounded the way Jyx pictured butter on hot toast – rich, creamy, and oddly comforting.

"Where is Eufame?"

"The House of Correction."

"What? Why?"

Ptem unlocked the cage and helped Jyx out. He stumbled and the Wolfkin supported him with a strong, muscular arm around his waist.

"Slowly, little one. Your body has become tired. It will need time to readjust," said Validus.

"Why is Eufame in the House of Correction?"

Jyx shuddered to think of the gargantuan monument to punishment at the edge of the City Above. It housed the worst dregs of society from both of the Cities, and few who entered ever returned. Those who did come back were never quite the same again.

"The Crown Prince grew suspicious. He did not think the destruction of the parade was as much of an accident as Eufame originally had him believe it was. Her enemies poured poison in his ears, and he had her arrested for treason. I do not doubt that his new advisor had much to do with that. Still, the punishment for most criminals would be death, but for a necromancer it is far worse."

"What will they do?"

"They will tear her soul from her body and leave

24

her as a shambling wreck of a person, incapable of independent thought or action."

Jyx scowled, unsure how he should feel about that. After all, Eufame had engineered his downfall and used him as the instrument of her vendetta against the Crown Prince.

"Why do you need me? I started all this, remember?"

"That is of little consequence to the Wolfkin. We need you to help us to locate her in the House."

"Why would I do that? She killed me! I made a mistake and she sent me beyond the Veil for it." Jyx flexed his foot to test his legs. His toes wiggled in response but his foot remained motionless.

"Will you not trust me?" Validus stared into Jyx's eyes. A spark of pleading burned in the Wolfkin's expression.

"You're not the problem. She is."

Validus sighed and even Ptem's ears drooped. Validus walked away from the slab on which Jyx sat. Ptem scooped him up in its arms and followed Validus out of the chamber.

"Where are we going?"

"To talk somewhere more comfortable."

Ptem carried him out of the chamber and along a short corridor. His heart sank when they came out in the vestibule that led to Eufame's chambers. Validus directed him to look out at the devastation in the vault beyond. Slabs that once held royal mummies stood empty, and broken tables were piled at the far end. Jyx felt a pang as he spotted the entrance to his own quarters in the gloom. He'd been so full of hope when he first came down here, fascinated by the necromancy process and so eager to impress his new mistress. If only he'd listened to her, and kept his ambition in check. Well, that wasn't a mistake he'd make again in a hurry.

Jyx looked around. The hairs on the back of his neck stood up to see the curtain that hid Eufame's library. Once, its rippling, changing fabric called to him and promised him mysteries. Nausea bubbled in Jyx's throat to think of the damage he'd caused as a result of what he'd found in that room. The room to the right was Eufame's study, another room destroyed through his stupidity.

Validus opened the door and Jyx squeezed his eyes shut. Ptem carried him over the threshold but the sound of crackling flames piqued his curiosity. Jyx opened his eyes. He recognised the tall bookcases filled with Eufame's personal collection along the wall. A woven throw covered an overstuffed sofa. No trace remained of her broken glass ornaments and vases.

Instead, plush armchairs stood in a semi-circle before the fireplace, and torches burned in braziers on the walls. Jyx spotted Eufame's cat, Bastet, curled up asleep on the armchair furthest from the door. Wooden panels on the opposite side of the room barely hid a box bed from view. A roaring fire blazed beneath the mantelpiece and the air smelled of wood smoke and bacon. Jyx couldn't remember seeing any of it the last time he was in here. It was hard to believe Eufame would have such a cosy room in a place like the House of the Long Dead. But perhaps his desire to wake the pterosaur blinded him to his surroundings. Before he could think about it any more, Ptem deposited him in one of the armchairs and handed him a bowl. He took the lid off a pot hanging over the fire, and ladled soup into the bowl. Validus sat in the chair beside his.

"Jyx, you must try to understand. You are alive now, are you not?" he asked.

"Yes, thanks to you, and I'm really grateful to you both, but why should I help her?" Jyx blew on a spoonful of soup to cool it. The soup was hot and thick, full of chunks of potato and ham. Ptem handed him a hunk of bread to dip in it.

"If she had meant you harm, would she have

chosen the Perpetual Death, a process which can be stopped at any time?"

Jyx paused, the bread halfway to his mouth.

"There are many reasons that Eufame did not want to give up her position, and these are reasons that go some way towards explaining why she did what she did. Believe me, she would not have engineered such a disaster for nothing. The man who seeks to supplant her position is not a kind man. He is interested in neither necromancy nor learning, only power."

"Is he the one who sent all the suitors?"

"The very same. He would return the Wolfkin to the full slavery we have worked so hard to leave behind, and no doubt end the quest for knowledge that Eufame instituted within this House decades ago. In all likelihood, he would sell what he could of the library that intrigued you so much, and burn the rest."

Jyx grimaced at the idea of so much knowledge going up in flames. Across the room, Bastet stirred, and lifted her head. She turned her feline gaze on Jyx, and he tried a weak smile in greeting. She stretched and climbed down from her chair, only to saunter across the room and climb up into Jyx's lap.

"You see? Even Bastet is pleased to see you, and you know how loyal she is to our mistress."

Ptem took Jyx's empty bowl from him, and Jyx petted the tabby cat, who purred beneath his touch.

"So he wants to ransack this place? What else can he do?" asked Jyx, thinking again of the precious library.

"Eufame holds a seat on various councils, and due to her influence, prevents many bad decisions from being made. Yet there is a secret motion being proposed within the council of the City Above to clear out the Underground City."

"Clear it out?" Jyx froze. In all of the excitement, he'd forgotten about his family. He didn't know what had happened to his mother or his siblings.

"Indeed so. From what I gather, it will be razed. Eufame had your family moved before her arrest to keep them safe from the Crown Prince's wrath, but she could not move them out of the City completely. If you help us to find her, we may yet be able to save the Underground City, including your family."

Jyx stared into the leaping flames in the grate, wishing he'd learned about fire divination at the Academy. He didn't know what to do for the best, and a pang tore at his heart when he realised he missed having Eufame telling him what to do.

"We've made up a bed for you, Jyx. Why don't you sleep a while, and see what your dreams tell you?"

Bastet climbed down from Jyx's lap, and Validus led Jyx on shaky feet across the room to the box bed. A warming pan lay between the luxurious velvet covers, and Jyx's mind dissolved into sleep as soon as he flopped onto his side.

Chapter 5

Vyolet followed the Wolfkin through the twisting streets of the Underground City, gnawing on a bread roll filled with cheese. People recognised the insignia on her companion's armour and shrank back, and Vyolet hid in his shadow. The flickering lamps on the buildings did little to dispel the constant gloom of the closes and alleys, and the Wolfkin's presence radiated safety. Even the occasional DWS agents they passed averted their eyes at the approach of the Wolfkin, and Vyolet wondered what other benefits an association with the necromancer general might have.

The Wolfkin stopped outside a narrow house on Edge Street, a long curving road that clung to the wall of the Underground City. The cliff disappeared into the darkness above, and the rock face marked the true boundary with the City Above, who had its own Edge Street along the cliff where it rose up into the mountains on the surface.

Vyolet tapped the Wolfkin on the shoulder, and

he turned round slowly, careful to keep Vyolet in its shadow.

"Aren't we going to Lockevar's Gate?" she signed. She swallowed the last of her sandwich. The bread and cheese were both fresh, and Vyolet wondered if the Wolfkin had brought it from the City Above. Fresh bread was one thing, but fresh cheese? Few could afford anything other than mould underground.

"No. It would not be safe for either of us to pass at the moment. The council of the City Above still sharpens its knives for my House and I could not guarantee your safety."

Vyolet raised one eyebrow. She knew all about what had happened at the House, how the necromancer general's apprentice had destroyed the royal mummies intended for the Crown Prince's coronation parade, and that the necromancer general herself had "gone missing". The gossip suggested certain members of the council were keen to assume her position, and associated deciding vote on various Boards, but Vyolet lost interest when politics became involved.

"We shall use another entrance. I don't doubt that it is also watched, although I would imagine it is watched less closely," signed the Wolfkin.

He knocked on the door, and a wizened crone answered. She said nothing but held the door open wide enough to allow the Wolfkin and Vyolet to pass. They entered a square, empty room with ancient beams holding up the low ceiling. The crone gestured to a narrow, crooked corridor that led into the darkness.

"Where does that go?" signed Vyolet.

"We shall find out." The Wolfkin couldn't smile, but the glint in his eye betrayed his amusement.

Vyolet followed the Wolfkin into the corridor. No torches lit their way but the Wolfkin saw perfectly in the dark, and Vyolet's Shadow nature made the darkness as comfortable to her as midday to a human. They followed the kinks and corners of the corridor until it opened out into another chamber, this one featuring a narrow wooden staircase that led into an opening in the ceiling. The Wolfkin ascended the stairs and Vyolet brought up the rear, her legs aching from the climb by the time they reached yet another room at the top.

Another wizened crone, a twin to the woman downstairs in all but dress, met them at the top. A coin passed from the Wolfkin to the crone, and Vyolet followed the massive Wolfkin along another corridor and out of a low doorway into a street.

Vyolet cried out as she stepped out into the morning sunshine. The bright light hurt her eyes, and she clapped a hand over them. Buildings leaned into the cobble-lined street, and the Wolfkin hurried her into the shadows beneath a bakery's upper floor. Passers-by cast curious glances at the massive guard that seemingly gestured at nothing in the darkness.

"Welcome to the City Above, Vyolet," signed the Wolfkin.

"The light hurts my eyes. I'm not used to daylight," replied Vyolet.

The Wolfkin handed her a pair of goggles, much like the ones the DWS wore to penetrate the shadows and see her kind. She put them on, and the sunlight faded through the purple-tinted lenses.

"These should help. Now come along. We have much to do," signed the Wolfkin.

"Are we going to the House?"

"In a manner of speaking, yes."

The Wolfkin strode down the street, keeping close to the buildings so Vyolet could skip through the shadows and remain hidden. The inhabitants of the City Above were even more hostile towards the Shadowkin than those of the Underground City, seeing them as nothing more than rogues, thieves and spies. There were even rumours of a sister group to the DWS above, who made the activities of the DWS look like a children's picnic. Vyolet shuddered to think of encountering one of their members, even if a Wolfkin accompanied her.

The close confines of Edge Street gave way to the elegant Canal Quarter. Ribbons of blue-green water carved the Quarter into a grid, the waterways lined with white buildings that gleamed in the sunlight. The tell-tale scent of magick hung heavy in the air, and flashes of coloured light behind the shutters indicated the presence of mages. The Wolfkin pulled a dark tabard over its armour and Vyolet started to see the insignia of the Magick Academy emblazoned on its chest.

"I cannot be seen displaying the insignia of the House at the moment. It is not safe," explained the Wolfkin.

"Why not?"

"I will explain everything soon. For now, we must get through this quarter as quickly as we can. It is many hours until twilight."

They sneaked through the narrow streets, crossing more bridges than Vyolet could count, passing through wide squares and along leafy boulevards lined with grand palazzos. The Wolfkin did not sign at all, not wishing to draw undue attention, and once or twice Vyolet crept into the shadow between its back and its false tabard.

They paused for lunch in a garden square, where the Wolfkin bought sandwiches from a street seller who asked no questions. They lurked beneath the trees, watching the citizens scurry to and fro, until the noon sun shifted and the shadows lengthened.

Vyolet knew much about the layout of the City Above from her various assignments, and the missives she intercepted often mentioned names or places, but she couldn't remember ever visualising what it looked like. She was certain anything she had pictured wouldn't have looked like the city in which she now found herself. She'd never seen it during the day. The familiar city of shadows bore little relation to the bright world around her now. She tried to be observant and to remember as much as she could, thankful for the goggles that helped to indulge her curiosity.

She first realised they were not heading for the House of the Long Dead when the Wolfkin turned left along the border between the Canal Quarter and a severe neighbourhood made of sandstone named Giltville. The jewellers and goldsmiths of the City Above lived there, surrounded by the courtiers who snapped up their wares to buy favour with the council. Vyolet knew the long road to the House led north through Giltville, not west along its boundary. The Wolfkin paid her little mind, striding along the canal path, but she decided to ask where they were going when they reached the edge of Giltville.

A narrow park separated Giltville and the next district, the Justice Quarter. The only place that lay beyond the Justice Quarter was the House of Correction, a terrifying slice of hell that swallowed up rogues by the hundreds. Few Shadowkin ever ended up there, and those who did soon escaped as the dark, gloomy prison was not designed to hold beings essentially made of shadow. Still, Vyolet had heard the same tales as everyone else, and she didn't think it would be long before DWS found a way to incarcerate Shadowkin there.

Vyolet tapped the Wolfkin on the shoulder. He pulled into the shade beneath a vast oak tree and faced away from the path. There were a few couples in the park, enjoying the opportunity to promenade in the fading afternoon light, but they ignored the Wolfkin, too intent upon gaining the attention of their fellow peacocks.

"Where are we going?" signed Vyolet.

"I see you have guessed that we do not make for the House of the Long Dead."

"Yes, I have! The road to the House leads north.

We're heading west. So I have to ask again, where are you taking me?"

The Wolfkin sighed, and looked at the ground. Vyolet glanced back at the path, estimating how many shadows lay between her and possible escape. The buildings of the Canal Quarter cast their own shadows across the canal, and Vyolet could always make her way back towards Edge Street. She didn't think the Wolfkin could run across water like she could.

"I told you that my mistress needs your help, and she does. She has been arrested and taken to the House of Correction. I need your help to get her out."

"Why?" Vyolet frowned and planted her hands on her hips. Her smoky skin turned black with anger. An observant passer-by might have noticed a darker stain within the shade of the tree.

"Only a Shadowkin would be able to navigate the prison undetected, and remove a prisoner."

"The cells are enchanted. Lock-picking isn't one of my strong points."

"Don't trouble yourself with that. One of my kin has a magickal practitioner who will aid you. You merely need to cloak my mistress until she is out." The Wolfkin drew closer to the tree as another couple sashayed down the avenue towards the canal path. Most humans saw Wolfkin as little more than servants, but seeing one lurking in a Giltville park might give someone pause.

"Why not just wait until her trial and spring her from the House of Justice?"

"She will not get a trial. The Crown Prince will not allow one, and there are already members of the council who seek to move into her position of power. But that is not why we need to aid her escape."

The Wolfkin growled, and Vyolet turned to see a militia guard approaching. Unlike the city guard underground, the militia in the City Above didn't wear goggles to spot the Shadowkin, but they were armed with enchanted flintlocks whose bullets would seek her out with ease. She dissolved into the shadow of the tree, and placed her hand on its solid trunk to stop herself from shaking.

"Hey, you there, what are you doing?"

The Wolfkin turned towards the city guard and spread his paws in a gesture of defeat.

"Who do you work for?" The guard reached them and grabbed at the Wolfkin's tabard. He peered at the insignia. "What are you doing all the way down here?"

The Wolfkin produced a slip of paper and handed it to the guard. His brows knitted as he read the note, and Vyolet tried to peer over her companion's shoulder. All she saw was the insignia for the Academy before the guard crumpled the note in his fist.

"You're on an errand, eh? Well if Dean Whittaker wants something from the Justice Quarter, I suggest you hurry, instead of lingering here!"

The Wolfkin took back the crumpled note and nodded. His ears and tail drooped, and a tiny whine escaped his muzzle. He hurried away from the tree towards the avenue that led down to the canal path. Vyolet held her breath and pressed herself against the trunk – she couldn't leave the safety of the shadows until the guard was gone.

The city guard watched the Wolfkin leave the park, and head along the path. The trees on the other side of the avenue swallowed him up, and Vyolet suppressed a whimper. Surely he wouldn't just leave her here?

After what felt like a lifetime, a food seller at the top of the avenue called out a list of wares and the guard wandered off in search of a snack. Vyolet waited until he was out of sight, and passed from shadow to shadow until she reached the gates of the park. She thought again about the way the guard had spoken to the Wolfkin, and felt a surge of kinship towards the dog-headed creature. The human had treated him as badly as he would treat a Shadowkin, seeing nothing but a beast he didn't understand. Vyolet growled to herself. The necromancer general mustn't be like these humans if she inspired such loyalty in the Wolfkin. If she treated them so well, perhaps she could do the same for the Shadowkin.

CHAPTER 6

Monte stood at the back of the darkened room. A man lay on a narrow bed in the attic of the pub, his skin waxy in the flickering candlelight. His mouth hung open and his breath came in fluttering rasps. A woman sat to one side of the bed, clutching his hand and stroking his thin white hair. The man with the jagged teeth sat to the other side, his book open in his lap.

"Oh can't you save my 'usband, mister?" cried the woman, her eyes wet with unshed tears.

"I am not a doctor, my good woman, and I fear that your husband is far beyond the reach of mortal medicine."

The pub landlord had spoken to Monte before they entered the sick room. There was nothing wrong with the man, a retired stone carver named Phelps, except old age and exhaustion with life. The landlord asked in a low voice if the man with the jagged teeth meant to cure him. Monte replied that he didn't know, but he wasn't sure what cure there was for old age. He didn't add that the only cure came courtesy of the Lords and Ladies of Death – the pub landlord didn't seem like a fellow follower.

Mr Gondavere's blunt reply prompted another hysterical outburst from Phelps's widow-to-be, and he looked at Monte. Mr Gondavere rolled his eyes and shook his head. Monte knew his new employer felt no compassion or empathy with the dying man or his wife, yet it was not his place to tell him he should feel otherwise. Mr Gondavere had his quest, and Monte would be paid well. That's all he needed to know.

And yet...

Monte moved forward and knelt beside Mr Gondavere. He took the dying man's hand.

"Lords and Ladies of Death, I humbly beseech you as your loyal servant to be merciful in your treatment of this man. Help ease his passage, and comfort his spirit."

The words came unbidden to his lips, and while he didn't know where they came from, he knew it was the right thing to say. He stole a glance at the widow-to-be. She wore no outward sign of following the Lords and Ladies, but a quiet smile bloomed on her grief-stricken face. A combination of amusement and displeasure wafted from Mr Gondavere.

The dying man gasped twice, and his eyes swivelled to look at Monte. His mouth moved though no sound came out.

"Do you have any last words?" asked Monte.

"No...heading home...no broken heart." The dying man forced the words between his chapped lips, and the widow-to-be clutched his hand so tightly her knuckles turned white.

Mr Gondavere pursed his lips and wrote the last words in his book in a jagged, spiky script. The dying man took a final breath, squeezed his wife's hand then lay still. The room was silent, except for the scratching of Mr Gondavere's pen.

"Is 'e…gone?" asked the widow.

"I'm sorry, ma'am." Monte disentangled his hand from the dead man's grasp and stood up, resuming his post at the foot of the bed.

Mr Gondavere returned his pen and ink to a small black case and closed the book. "I am sorry for your loss, madam," he said, voice tight and eyes pinched shut, and left the room. Monte nodded once and scurried after his master.

He found Mr Gondavere downstairs in the pub. He stood by the bar, tapping his foot, and making a show of repeatedly checking his pocket watch.

"Was that useful?" asked Monte. The man had said 'heart', after all.

"Not in the slightest. Before we go any further, I must ask, what exactly did you think you were doing? Did I give you leave to speak, or to intervene in any way?" Mr Gondavere fixed Monte with a penetrating stare.

Monte gulped. "It just felt like the right thing to do, sir."

"Indeed."

"I won't do it again, sir." Monte stared at the floor, seeing the money he would earn evaporate into thin air. Myrtle would kill him, if he ever told her. He slipped his fingers into his pockets to feel for the coin he'd been paid earlier.

"On the contrary. I think that you lend my experiment a certain air of humanity, you might call it. Perhaps people will feel more comfortable around you than they do around me. They may be more likely to be honest in their final words."

Monte looked up at Mr Gondavere. His master ignored him to gaze at the drunken patrons of the pub with a mixture of disgust and fascination. Monte wondered how Mr Gondavere could be certain he hadn't already found the person who knew the whereabouts of the Heart, and that they'd simply not told him.

"Can I ask you a question, sir?"

"I have no doubt that you have the ability to ask a question, and therefore can, but what remains to be seen is whether you may ask me a question."

Mr Gondavere wrinkled his nose.

"May I ask a question?"

"You may."

"How do you know the person you're looking for hasn't already died? Wouldn't you need a necromancer to talk to them?"

"That is surprisingly a good question, my good man," replied Mr Gondavere, raising one eyebrow. "I have no real basis for knowing they haven't already died. I simply feel sure, and you are correct that I would need a necromancer to speak for them if they have. However the only necromancer in the City Above is currently held in the House of Correction, and is therefore useless to me."

Monte didn't know whom Mr Gondavere was talking about as he kept himself as ignorant of City affairs as possible. His master opened his small case, and lifted his book of last words into it. Given the tiny proportions of the case, Monte was shocked to see the large tome slide inside with so little effort. The clasps snapped shut and Mr Gondavere put on his hat, a simple creation of black felt with a large brim to hide his face.

"Come along, Monte. We have work to do."

Monte followed him out into the hustle and bustle of the street. He didn't think he'd ever seen the Underground City quiet. Even during the early hours of the morning, the alleys and closes rang with noise that echoed between the tall buildings. The eternal night that accompanied living underground made time a more abstract concept. Monte often suspected the inhabitants only kept up the pretence of time to make trade easier.

"Where are we going now?" asked Monte, trotting to keep up with his master's brisk pace.

"I believe we shall be needed at the temple."

Mr Gondavere didn't explain how he knew such a thing, and Monte didn't think he wanted to know. He simply followed his master.

Chapter 7

Jyx woke to find Bastet hunched on his chest, peering into his face. She mewed a greeting and sniffed his nose when she saw he was awake.

"Hey, Bastet. I'm glad you're not still mad at me." Jyx scratched the cat behind the ears, and she purred. "Are the Wolfkin still here?"

"We are indeed, Master Faire." The voice echoed in his mind but Validus's paw-like hand rested on the arm of a chair by the fireplace. Bastet climbed down from his chest and jumped off the bed, padding across the chamber to the fireplace. Jyx threw back the covers and rolled out of bed. A clean tunic and hose were laid out on a table near the bed, along with new leather boots and a belt.

"Are these for me?" Jyx ran his fingers over the soft wool of the tunic. The tunic and hose were both black to match the boots. He sank his hands into the rich fabric, a far cry from the threadbare garments he was used to. The new clothes bore no sign of having been mended, or passed from student to student.

"They are for you. We will have a busy day today, and you will need to be warm and comfortable, as well as properly attired," replied Validus.

The vacant Wolfkin busied itself with another pot

over the stove. This time the air smelled of porridge and fruit. Jyx threw off his old clothes, dropping them on the floor when he realised he'd died repeatedly in them, and pulled on the new outfit. The tunic and hose fit perfectly, and his feet breathed a sigh of relief when he pulled on the boots. They were lined with thick, warm felt.

"These are brilliant," he said.

"We Wolfkin have many abilities. One of our number is a master leatherworker. Or should I call her a mistress leatherworker? I am unsure of the correct terminology."

"A girl Wolfkin?" Jyx paused. He'd always thought of the Wolfkin as being 'it', despite their masculine forms. He'd never stopped to question the existence of female Wolfkin. His ears burned as he turned red with shame.

Validus laughed, a rich baritone rolling around inside his head. It reminded Jyx of tolling bells at the temple.

"Yes, we have female Wolfkin too. Do not trouble yourself, Master Faire. Few if any humans ever see our beautiful female folk, so it is scarcely strange that you would be surprised to learn of them."

"Why have I never met one?" asked Jyx. He thought of the Wolfkin at the Academy, and the ones he'd met at the House but they were all male.

"Our women are scholars and academics. They guard our knowledge, our lore, and our legends. Few of the council recognise their existence because they keep themselves well hidden. Humans legislated us into servitude due to our size – can you imagine what they'd do to our females?"

Jyx shuddered in response. He ran his fingers around the delicate patterns tooled into the leather belt.

"Mara made those for you. She excels in the study of arcane lore but she enjoys practising crafts as well when she has the opportunity." Validus gestured to the boots.

"They're wonderful. You'll have to thank her for me," said Jyx.

"With any luck, you shall get the opportunity to do so yourself."

Jyx sat in the armchair beside Validus. The vacant Wolfkin served him a portion of porridge, studded with dried fruits and slices of lemon. Jyx wasn't used to fresh fruit, especially in the Underground City where any fruit that could be found was often soft or mouldy. Still, he wasn't going to question where Wolfkin sourced their food. They seemed to have an entire network of their own alongside the Twin Cities. Who knew what else they could do?

Or would do?

"I have to ask, why are you being so nice to me?" asked Jyx after the first spoonful of porridge. It tasted of honey.

"How do you mean?" Validus held a peg of wood in his lap and whittled it with a large knife.

"Well, it was because of me that some of the Wolfkin died, and it's my fault Eufame is in the House of Correction, so if we can't get her, it could be my fault the Underground City gets cleared out. But you're giving me new clothes and telling me all of this stuff that you probably don't want humans to know about you. You shouldn't be so nice to me," replied Jyx.

"I cannot speak ill of my mistress, Master Faire, but if she had not arranged events the way that they did, much of what happened would not have transpired, and the Crown Prince would have used the Coronation Parade to manoeuvre her into some form of marriage alliance."

"She would have had to give up her job."

"Exactly, Master Faire. While many in the City Above would have rejoiced at her removal from a position of power, those of the Underground City would have felt the loss of her influence most keenly. However, we did not expect Neferpenthe to act, and raise so many of her kind herself, and therefore we did not anticipate the deaths of the Wolfkin, so you cannot be blamed for that. It was chance, and nothing more," replied Validus.

Jyx ate the rest of his porridge in silence. Only the sound of his spoon scraping his bowl, and the knife carving the wood, could be heard in the chamber.

Eventually, Validus spoke again. "It is fair that you should feel suspicious. You did indeed make many mistakes through your over-ambition and inexperience. However, my mistress did think well of you, and she expressly told me to take care of you before she was arrested."

"She couldn't stand me," replied Jyx.

"She hid you from the Crown Prince, as well as your family. My mistress does not act unless she has a reason for doing so, even if we do not always know, or understand, those reasons. Yet I must also be honest – we are nice, as you put it, because we need you."

"I'm nobody." Jyx gazed at the floor, thinking of the mess he'd caused in the vault. Visions of the blind pterosaur lurching around the room, smashing shelves and releasing rare enchantments into the air, swam before his eyes. He should never be allowed to use magick again.

"I told you yesterday that I need you to help me locate her in the House of Correction. When she set up the Perpetual Death, she left a tiny sliver of herself in you to keep the spell going without her needing to be present. That sliver will lead you to her."

Jyx stared at Validus. "You want me to go into the House of Correction?"

"I do."

"I won't do it."

"I'm sorry, Master Faire, but you really have no choice."

"What do you mean?"

"If you don't help me retrieve my mistress, then you are of no further use to me, and I can return you to the Perpetual Death."

Jyx gulped. Bastet jumped up into his lap and fixed him with a meaningful look. Jyx tried not to gaze into her eyes, but the warmth of her weight was reassuring. A purr rumbled in her throat, and Jyx's resolve softened at the edges.

"How can Eufame stop them from clearing out the Underground City? Surely if we get her out of the House of Correction, they'll just arrest her again. They won't give her all of her positions back on these boards you mentioned just because we helped her escape," said Jyx.

"A valid point," replied Validus, and Jyx thought he detected a sigh of relief in his voice. "However, there is an older force within the City which stands for different values, and my mistress holds more sway with that force than the council does. This force controls more than the council ever could. We need my mistress to remind them of that."

Jyx stroked Bastet and let his gaze roam across the carvings in the wood panelling above the fireplace. They depicted scenes in City history, but Jyx didn't know the stories. He'd never paid attention during history at the small school run out of the temple, and the Academy only taught history if it was applicable to magick. One carving caught his eye, of a beautiful woman holding a spear aloft, heading what looked like an army of thousands.

"Do not worry, Master Faire. You will not venture into the House of Correction alone. As we speak, one of my kin has found you a powerful companion, and I myself will go into the House with you. Your part in this will be brief."

"What happens once we've gotten her out?"

"We will defer to my mistress's judgment. I do not

doubt that she has already formulated several plans, and one of them will be based upon our effecting her escape. My only concern at the moment is securing her liberty."

"I don't like the sound of that," replied Jyx. For all he knew, Eufame would condemn him once more to the Perpetual Death, or she might just turn him loose in the Underground City, a once-promising magickian with no prospects and little future. Or he might end up in the House of Correction, never to see freedom again.

"We do not get to choose our path in life, young one. We must merely ensure we are properly prepared for the adventures that will happen as we walk along it. But time is of the essence. There was a sound earlier, something like a crack, and to my people such noises are rarely good omens," replied Validus. He left the chamber, and Jyx looked at Bastet.

"What am I supposed to do?"

Bastet gazed into his eyes. There was something vaguely human about her stare, and Jyx looked away. A sliver of his mind wriggled, and a voice echoed in his head. It was female, harsh and cold, yet indistinct. He couldn't make out the words, but the guttural cry was one of frustration – and desperation.

Jyx could not ignore a summons like that if it came directly from Eufame Delsenza.

Chapter 8

Mr Gondavere and Monte reached the temple after what felt like hours of aimless walking. Navigating the Underground City was hazardous at best, and they'd wasted a much time by doubling back on themselves or taking blind alleys to evade those Mr Gondavere was sure were following them. Monte saw no one suspicious, or at least more suspicious than usual, but Mr Gondavere saw assassins and thieves in every shadow.

The Underground City had no official religion, and as such, the inhabitants were free to pray to whichever deity best served their interests. Many citizens chose to worship nothing but commerce, others simply thanked "the universe" for freedom. Despite the poverty, poor sanitation and lack of sunlight, many believed the Underground City to be freer than the City Above. They had no council to rule their affairs, simply neighbourhood dons who regulated crime and imposed basic order.

Monte was not one of the 'godless masses', but

being a gravedigger meant he prayed exclusively to the Lords and Ladies of Death. Monte actually knew very little about them, and much of what he believed he'd invented to fill in the gaps. There were no priests to ask, and their temples had been destroyed years before. Still, he liked to believe that the nameless and numberless mass of spectres looked after the spirits of the dead. He thought they watched over the living, punishing those who took life, as it was not theirs to take. He suspected there was more to it than that, given the persecution of the cult if followers became too brazen. Hatred of the Lords and Ladies ran deep in the Underground City. Followers met in the sepulchres of the overcrowded graveyards at the lowest point of the City, and his association with them made him uncomfortable in the temples of other faiths. Beseda's Shrine, in particular, provoked a cold sweat and violent shudders if ever he ventured near it.

The temple that Mr Gondavere headed for was not that of Beseda, but rather a generic, catchall building comprised of a range of smaller chapels dedicated to various deities. It also housed a small school for the street urchins and aimless youth of the City. The faithless officials of the temple were the closest people to priests, but they served no deity in particular, preferring to dish out advice, comfort and hospitality to all who visited. Even hardened criminals hated to take advantage of these gentle, sweet souls managing the temple.

They entered the temple, and Monte shivered. The only faith not represented was his own, and he didn't think they'd have much space for the Lords and Ladies of Death, or their macabre congregation. He'd heard a rumour they once had their own chapel here, but if they did, he didn't know where it had been.

The central courtyard was a busy, noisy place, lit with vast yet ancient chandeliers, with a stream of clean, cold water running through it from east to west. The chapels led off the courtyard and stalls stood around its perimeter. Well-meaning folk from the trade districts dished out simple food and mended clothing for those in need. A tall woman clad in white led a lesson on the far side of the courtyard, surrounded by small children from neighbouring houses. Monte remembered those lessons and mentally thanked the temple for teaching him to read.

"Who are we here to see?" he asked.

"There is a devotee of Ethelburga who lies on his death bed. He hopes his patron might alleviate his suffering, but given the size of the growth in his stomach, he is not long for this world." Mr Gondavere peered at the names inscribed above the chapel doorways. Monte forced down the cold bundle of panic that blossomed in his stomach at such an intimate knowledge of what ailed a man he had not even met.

They spotted the name Ethelburga chiselled into a stone arch on the other side of the courtyard. Mr Gondavere plunged into the crowd and made his way towards the chapel. Monte trailed in his wake. He couldn't stop looking at the makeshift school. What had happened to his old teacher, Miss Babblethrop? Had she been swept up by the City Above's purges? Had the city guard bundled her into one of their sacks? Did she languish in poverty or worse – the asylum?

Monte tapped himself on the side of the throat, the automatic habit of a Lords and Ladies follower when thinking of a loved one in need. He'd reached the chapel, and stepped inside. It was less austere than Monte expected. Candles burned behind stained glass panes set into the wall, casting colourful paintings of light onto the stone floor. Devotees sat in small niches below the panes, their heads bowed in silent prayer. A statue of Ethelburga stood on a plinth at the end of the long, thin room, her stone hands clasped at her chest, her eyes facing towards the ceiling. Torches burned in braziers set around her so that fire blazed behind the statue. Monte stared at Ethelburga, expecting her to move.

"Excuse me, I am told that you have one who is not long for this side of the Veil?" Mr Gondavere stopped one of the chaplains who wandered around the room. She looked at him with large, wet eyes, and nodded. Without saying a word, she led him to the back of the chapel, behind the statue. Rows of wooden cots lurked in the darkness beyond the braziers. Nurses leaned over the dying, mopping foreheads and clasping hands, while chaplains said prayers over the dead.

The chaplain brought them to a cot near the back. An old man, more bone than flesh, reclined on the straw mattress. No family lingered to offer aid, so Monte knelt on the floor and took one of his hands. A weak pulse fluttered beneath the skin, stretched so thin it looked like paper. Monte bit his lip.

"Are you here for me?" The old man's voice struggled even to whisper.

"We are, sir."

"I'm not long for this world, am I?"

"I fear not, sir."

"I asked Ethelburga...she never replies." Tears welled up in the old man's eyes. Mr Gondavere produced a handkerchief and handed it to Monte. He dabbed at the old man's face.

"We are here to ease your passage," said Mr Gondavere, keeping his voice low. Monte had never heard it sound so soothing before. Maybe he wasn't so bad after all.

"I haven't got any family," said the old man.

"Tell me about your life then. Let us know about your history," said Monte.

"Before I go?"

"If you like."

The old man shifted on the cot, and Mr Gondavere

perched on the empty one behind him, balancing the large book from his case in his lap. Monte squeezed the old man's hand.

"I was a historian. Worked in the Archives. Oh, the things I knew!"

"What did you know?" Mr Gondavere had a sharp edge to his tone.

Monte threw him a dark look and nodded for the old man to continue.

"I specialised in old lore, forgotten things...fairy tales to most, but I knew they were true."

"I'm sure that was fascinating to learn about," said Monte.

"Oh, it was, it was. We did a lot of research for the House of the Long Dead. The necromancer general... she prizes knowledge."

Monte frowned. That didn't sound like he would be much help at all.

The old man chattered away about particular cases, reeling off names Monte didn't recognise. Mr Gondavere coughed, and Monte turned to him, shrugging. He couldn't tell the old man to be quiet, could he?

"You said you'd looked into a lot of fairy tales," he said, hoping to divert the old man back to something useful.

"I did, I did."

"Did you ever come across anything about the Heart of the City?" Mr Gondavere's tone was razor sharp now, and Monte even winced to hear it. The old man's expression didn't change; he faded so fast Mr Gondavere's impatience was lost on him.

"Oh that...once or twice. No one ever found it. If it did exist, it is well and truly lost by now," he replied.

"Do you think it really existed?" asked Monte.

"I always thought it was real, but there was no proof."

Mr Gondavere let out a short, sharp exhalation of

exasperation and Monte sighed. The old man's eyes rolled backwards, and he took a laboured breath.

"Sir?"

"I can hear singing."

"Rest now. The Lords and Ladies of Death will take care of you and ease your passage," said Monte, patting the old man's hand.

"They're here! I can see them!" The old man jerked in the cot, his gaze falling on Mr Gondavere. Fear burned in his clouded eyes, his mouth open in a silent scream. The old man pointed at Mr Gondavere, but Monte gently guided the pointing hand back to the cot.

"Do you have any last words?" Mr Gondavere leaned forward, anticipation shining in his eyes.

"The wizard knows, the wizard knows," whispered the old man, his voice cracking.

Mr Gondavere entered the words into his book. The old man's grasp on Monte's hand turned slack, and he rolled away on the cot. One of the chaplains squealed and scurried across to him. She shooed Monte and Mr Gondavere away from the body.

"Did that help?" asked Monte as they left the chapel.

"I need to ruminate on it. My, what a vexatious man. I really thought he might be useful," replied Mr Gondavere.

"What did he mean about seeing the Lords and Ladies of Death? He seemed terrified."

"Oh, he was dying. I expect humans see visions as their life leaves them," snapped Mr Gondavere. He hurried across the courtyard and Monte ran after him. What did he mean, humans?

Mr Gondavere waited for Monte in the crowded street outside. People veered around the tall man in the hat on their way into the temple, and Monte had little trouble making his way towards his new employer.

"I am most displeased, Monte. Most displeased indeed."

"I'm sorry, sir."

"It's not your fault. I just really thought he'd tell me what I needed to know." Mr Gondavere opened his case and slid the book back into it. "Come along, we need to regroup."

He walked away along the street and Monte followed. What might their next move be?

CHAPTER 9

Validus returned to the room, carrying the red robe of an apprentice. Jyx hesitated before putting it on, remembering the destruction he'd caused last time he wore it.

"Come along, Jyx. You must hurry. Time is not on our side."

"What's wrong?" Jyx adjusted the belt at his waist.

"I knew it would not be long before the council attempted to exercise their power. They are here," said Validus.

"Who's here?"

Validus frowned and left the room. Jyx looked at Bastet, but she simply mewed. He shrugged and hurried after the Wolfkin. He followed Validus through the vault, focusing on his flicking tail instead of the broken slabs on either side of his path. They reached the doorway and ascended the spiral staircase. Validus stopped him at the top and peered into the atrium.

"The coast is not clear," said Validus.

Jyx flattened himself against the wall and peeked around the edge of the archway. A veil of magick hung before the doorway, and looking into the atrium was like gazing through a window streaked with rain. The bodies had been cleared away there. No trace of blood remained, although Jyx's gaze lingered on the skeleton embedded in the marble floor, a sign of Eufame's displeasure with an earlier apprentice. More vacant Wolfkin lingered in the hall, wearing the insignia of the council on their leather armour.

Two overweight men stood in the centre of the room. One held a bottle of Eufame's midnight wine, and the other gnawed on a hunk of bread. Both wore the blood red uniform of the council guards, and armbands around their upper biceps marked them as members of the DWS group. Jyx shuddered. The DWS were virulent enough in the Underground City, but the excess cruelty of the City Above chapter was legendary.

"You see, Master Faire? Already the council attempt to oust my mistress. It won't be long before they attempt to bring the last of my Kin within this House under their sway."

"When will they take over the library?"

"So far they have been content to restrict themselves to simply changing the insignia, and bandy about talk of what they will do. We have placed strong wards on particular spaces of power, so they will not find it easy to access the archives. Indeed, they could not find the door to the underground vaults, hidden as it was, which is how my mistress kept you out of sight," replied Validus. "They took her from this very hall, but her spells were already in place."

"I've got a plan."

"Really." The Wolfkin couldn't purse his lips or raise his eyebrows, but Jyx sensed both movements in his tone of voice.

"Yes, really. It's something I definitely know how

to do, but I need you to distract them so they're not looking at me."

"No. There must be some other way."

Across the atrium, Ptem threw open the front doors. Both of the guards turned to face him. They gesticulated at the Wolfkin, shouting orders at him, but he ignored them. Jyx seized his chance. He darted out into the hall, careful to keep himself directly behind the guards. He paused several feet away. The light pouring in the doors cast long shadows behind them. Jyx stared at marble floor and visualised a glowing red net of energy.

"*Misit hoc rete, misit fortis, capere umbra, eam mea,*" he whispered.

The scarlet strands of power pulsed as they settled across the stones. The net snapped shut on both of the shadows, humming as it earthed itself. The guards cried out but slumped to the floor before they could turn around. The shadows rippled across the floor.

"No, no, you're not standing up. You don't need to," said Jyx.

The shadows lay still.

"You don't know what's happened to you, do you?"

The shadows shook in reply. Jyx took that as a no.

"You set off one of Eufame's defences, that's all. In about an hour's time, you'll wake up and all will be well, but you won't tell anyone what happened because you'll be too embarrassed to admit you weren't paying attention."

The shadows rippled in agreement.

"Good. I am the spirit of the hallway, and I shall leave you to sleep now." Jyx didn't know where the words came from, but they made sense as he spoke them. He glanced over his shoulder. Validus nodded his approval from the archway.

The shadows dulled to a faint stain on the floor. Hitching snores escaped from the guards. Validus left the doorway and crossed the atrium. He picked up the bottle of midnight wine, handing it to Ptem.

"See that is disposed of," he said.

* * *

They slipped outside into the early evening light and crouched behind a statue in the courtyard. No trace remained of the epic battle that had taken place between Eufame and Neferpenthe, the former necromancer who had raised an army of bloodthirsty mummies from the dead royals intended for the coronation parade. Coaches bearing the insignia of the council stood around in the courtyard. Two guards sat nearby, smoking and playing cards.

"We need to get through the archway. The horses will be waiting for us," said Validus.

"Won't they see us?" Jyx pointed at the guards.

"Indeed they will, though I fear your Shadow magick will not help us here. Can you throw sound?"

"I don't know, I've never tried."

Validus wriggled forward so that his muzzle was level with the edge of the statue. "I need you to throw my howl."

"How?"

"You will have to figure that out yourself."

A moment later, Validus opened his mouth. The howl formed in front of him, a smoky breath hanging in the cool air. Without thinking, Jyx scribbled a sigil with his finger.

"*Tolle hoc et illud, et ululate volant!*"

A gust of wind caught the howl and launched it across the courtyard. It shattered against the far wall, sending shards flying in all directions. Finally released, the long, undulating notes came from everywhere and nowhere at once.

"What's that?" One of the guards jumped up, his hand moving to the sword at his belt.

"It came from round there!"

The two guards ran out of the courtyard, following a narrow alley that eventually led to the kitchens. Jyx and Validus seized their chance. They clambered out from behind the statue and sprinted across the yard. Jyx darted through the archway onto the approach boulevard.

Two horses, black as jet, stood saddled and ready to leave on the road. Validus lifted Jyx into the saddle of the smaller mount, and Jyx held the reins so hard his hands turned white. He hadn't expected to see the sun heading towards the horizon, expecting it to be mid-morning, but living underground for so long had turned his body clock upside down. He peered around the pillar of the archway to look at the vast edifice of the House of the Long Dead. Bastet sat at the door.

"Will Bastet be all right?" he asked.

"Of course. My kin will take care of her, though Bastet has talents of her own," replied Validus.

"Will we be coming back?" asked Jyx.

"I am sure we will, should we succeed, but for now, our mission awaits."

Validus gave a signal and his horse burst into a gallop, clattering across the courtyard's cobbles towards the vast arch. Jyx's horse broke into a run, following Validus out onto the driveway that led to the main road. His horse needed no encouragement or guidance, and simply followed Validus.

* * *

They rode past the Necropolis, the huge city of the dead that lay between the House of the Long Dead and the City Above. Jyx couldn't remember seeing much of the landscape during his trip to the House from the Academy. When had that been? Weeks ago? Longer? Jyx didn't even know what day it was. Surprisingly, he didn't care.

The Necropolis seemed to stretch forever, a vast sea of headstones and tombs, sepulchres and mausoleums. The people of the City Above followed no religions at all, believing only in life and death, and the magnificence of their tombs spoke of their earthly wealth and status more than any spiritual significance. Eventually, its sprawl gave way to the most northern neighbourhood of the City Above. Jyx had a fuzzy grasp on the City's geography, knowing only the Academy to the east, and the Canal Quarter.

The horses ran so fast that Jyx had little time to take in the sights, but he was aware of a large district built mostly of brick. Villas lined the road, set back behind tall trees or neatly clipped hedges. The horses slowed when the buildings turned from brick to sandstone. The villas were replaced by tall terraces, and the street was narrower. Many of the shop signs in this district were brightly coloured, featuring paintings of jewellery or coins, and Jyx guessed this was Giltville. The people of the Underground City hated the idea of a neighbourhood dedicated solely to wealth, and Jyx shuddered to see so much money on display.

The sandstone buildings gave way to severe white monuments, their shades drawn against the fading light. Men in black cloaks and white wigs strode out of the buildings, gathering on corners or hailing horse drawn cabs. Jyx guessed this must be the Justice Quarter – he knew that the House of the Notorious Dead lay at the centre of the district, housing the corpses of the dead that no one wanted to speak to. They were dangerous folk, and Death-walkers kept the peace by maintaining the barrier between the souls of the dead and any spark of life that might guide them back.

They reached a tall, white wall, with black iron gates set into it. The metal curved into wicked points that gleamed in the twilight. Validus pulled up his horse in the shadows of the buildings opposite the gates.

Jyx's eyes adjusted, and he saw another Wolfkin, this one a deep russet with glossy chestnut fur. A figure lurked in the gloom beside it, but Jyx could make out no specific details.

"Validus! I was wondering where you were," said the other Wolfkin.

"Peace, Fortis. I am here now," replied Validus. "Have you found our other compatriot?"

"I have indeed." The other Wolfkin made a complicated string of hand signals to the figure beside it, and it stepped forward.

The girl was maybe two years older than Jyx, with skin the colour of gun smoke. Violet eyes stared out of a face too elfin to be considered conventionally attractive, but pretty all the same. Her wild mane of dark grey curls hung down her back, and she wore a leather jerkin and leggings the same shade as slate. Jyx knew he was staring but he didn't ever think he would be lucky enough to meet a Shadowkin face to face.

"I am Vyolet," she said.

"I'm Jyx, and this is Validus," said Jyx, gesturing to Validus.

"You can talk to it?" asked Vyolet.

"Him, and yes, I can. I hear him in my head."

"That's amazing! This one can talk in Shadow Speak!" Vyolet furiously signed something to the other Wolfkin, who signed in response.

"What did you say to him?" asked Jyx.

"I asked it what its name was. I just realised I didn't know it, but it just told me to ask you."

"Validus just called him Fortis. Please, call them 'he', not 'it'."

Vyolet frowned. She turned to Fortis and signed. Fortis nodded and signed back.

"I just apologised to...him," she said.

"It's okay, you'll get used to them. So, what's the plan then?" asked Jyx, turning to Validus.

"I will march you into the House of Correction, explaining that I have found the rogue apprentice behind the parade disaster, and I am turning you in, in exchange for a period of immunity for the House of the Long Dead," said Validus.

"You're going to do what?" Jyx backed away from the Wolfkin.

"Relax, Master Faire. It is merely a ruse to gain admittance. We will be accompanied by Miss Vyolet here, who will enter undetected. Once inside, you will locate my mistress, and Miss Vyolet will cloak you in shadow in order to effect your escape." Validus spoke to Jyx, and Fortis relayed the information to Vyolet through Shadow Speak.

Jyx allowed some of the tension to dissolve from his shoulders, but he kept a wary eye on Validus. He understood now why none of the plan had been disclosed to him sooner. The Wolfkin was essentially using him as bait, and there was no guarantee the Shadowkin would be able to protect him. She barely looked old enough to protect herself.

"How will we locate her?" asked Vyolet.

"Once inside, Jyx will be able to sense her location, and you should be able to find her relatively easily." Validus remained hazy about exactly how Jyx would know where Eufame was. Jyx tried to will away the cold ball of discomfort that had settled in his stomach.

"How do we get back out?" he asked.

"Vyolet will be able to take care of that."

"Hang on, so you want me to hide two people while we try to escape?" Vyolet planted her hands on her hips and frowned.

"It will be easier than you think. Remember that Eufame has power of her own and will be able to aid you, Vyolet," said Validus.

"This is a really bad idea," said Vyolet.

"I am sorry you think so, but it is the only way. My mistress cannot leave of her own accord, but she can if she is aided, and without her, I fear that the repercussions for both Cities will be great. The council may proceed unhampered in their plan to clear out the Underground City, thousands will be made homeless, and much of the knowledge preserved in the Houses will be destroyed," replied Validus.

"Clear out the Underground City?" Vyolet stared, her purple eyes wide.

"Indeed. Their plans have been blocked at every turn by my mistress, but with her safely out of the way, they may proceed."

"Why has she been blocking the plans?" asked Jyx. He couldn't understand it. Eufame had power, knowledge, and in all probability vast wealth, yet she rebelled against the Crown Prince and his council at every opportunity.

"She is not human, and therefore not subject to the whims and caprices of humanity." Validus's tone suggested he was unwilling to say more.

"Before we go in there, I have just one more question," said Vyolet. "Everyone has heard the stories of her amazing power, and the legends go back at least a couple of centuries. Everyone is terrified of her. So how on earth can they hold someone that strong in the House of Correction?"

Jyx nodded in agreement. Vyolet raised a valid point.

"My mistress is the youngest of five siblings. The eldest is Brigante, and she dwells somewhere beneath the Underground City, though we know not where. She has not been seen for many years. Two more reside far outside of the City Above and concern themselves only with the pursuit of knowledge. The fourth, Naiad, rules the House of Correction with an iron fist," replied Validus.

Jyx's heart sank. He knew all too well what Eufame was capable of, but to think of her with an older sister, who was in all probability stronger, more intelligent, and more ruthless – well, the plan was doomed to fail before they even started.

"So how on earth can I avoid the power of someone like that?"

"You must remember, I am not just sending in a Shadowkin, I am also sending in the necromancer's apprentice."

Jyx didn't know how he knew, but he could tell Validus was smiling at them. Fortis gave a short bark of approval.

Something tickled in the back of Jyx's mind, and the world slid sideways for a moment. He could see between and beyond all things, walls dropping away and doors becoming windows. A gate stood before him, and beyond that a driveway. At the end of the driveway he'd find a fortress, and within the fortress, Eufame waited. He saw her, superimposed over Vyolet and Fortis. She turned and smiled that bone-chilling smile.

"Come along, Jyximus. I'm waiting."

CHAPTER 10

Mr Gondavere sat at the table in the Nag's Head pub. Of all the pubs in the Underground City, the Nag's Head was the cleanest, which just meant that the barkeeper spat in the glasses more often. Monte couldn't find a table when he first went inside, but Mr Gondavere's appearance prompted a group of fishwives to abandon their seats and gather outside to cluck and gossip.

Monte didn't dare speak while Mr Gondavere studied his book. He'd read and re-read all of the collected last words, convinced he'd missed a clue. Monte stared into his watery beer, the heavy weight of death hunched across his shoulders. Normally he just buried them when they'd already left their earthly shells.

In his mind, he called to the Lords and Ladies of Death and asked for comfort. He'd never had much cause to directly petition them before, and he wasn't sure what to expect. Would he see an apparition, or feel a spectral hand clasp his own? He wasn't even sure what they actually were. He waited several moments, and his heart sank further when nothing happened. Maybe this work was dirty, and they'd abandoned him for it.

"Oh my!" Mr Gondavere sat back in his seat, the book open in his lap.

"What is it?"

"Do you remember the last words of the most recent unfortunate? About the wizard knowing something?"

Monte nodded.

"I had clean forgotten about it, but a woman some three months ago mentioned something similar." Mr Gondavere lifted the book onto the table, carefully avoiding the spilled beer and sticky puddles of whiskey, and showed Monte a page early in his book. He tapped the specific line with a long, skeletal finger.

"Wizards above and below, they know, they know," said Monte, reading the jagged script.

"Indeed!"

"Which wizards?"

"I took the liberty of consulting a colleague, and I have been informed that in many schools of thought, the wizards are the scholars of the highest merit, not the academics. It bears further investigation, does it not?"

Monte said nothing, wondering how or when Mr Gondavere consulted a colleague. They hadn't been apart since they'd left the temple. Monte wondered again to what sort of man he'd pledged himself, and what Myrtle might say if, or when, she ever found out about it.

"It certainly sounds a bit more promising that we thought it did," said Monte.

"We should therefore consult a wizard. I am just unsure how we can locate one."

The only place Monte knew to find wizards was in the library, but the Underground City had been bereft of libraries after the old ones were looted and turned into tenements. A thought struck him. He did know how to find one wizard in particular. Monte smiled.

"I know a wizard, and you won't believe his name," said Monte.

"What is it?"

"Crompton Daye," replied Monte. "He's the wizard I pointed out when I first met you."

"Then I do believe we should try to locate him. Do you believe he may be of some assistance?" Mr Gondavere closed the book and slid it back into the tiny case, apparently satisfied that he'd found all he was likely to at that moment.

"He might. I can't think of whom else to ask. Not a lot of educated folk down here, aside from the odd scholarship student at the Academy. The fishwives normally know what's going on, but they're often down at the shore, and you can't separate exaggeration from fact with them."

"It's a start, at least. Where might we find him?"

Monte looked around the room, but couldn't see Crompton anywhere. That ruled out the Nag's Head, at least.

"He's not here, so I'm guessing he'll be either at the Golden Lamb, or the Bloody Hand," replied Monte. "As he was in the Bloody Hand earlier, I'd say he's probably at the Golden Lamb by now."

Mr Gondavere smiled, revealing those dagger-like teeth again, and stood up. Monte drained the last of his beer, and took the glass back to the bar. The barkeeper nodded to him and raised an eyebrow at the departing form of Mr Gondavere. Monte shrugged and followed his employer back out into the street.

They made their way through the network of alleys and closes, this time ignoring those figures that Mr Gondavere believed were assassins. More than one street stood empty, their boarded-up windows bearing handbills for DWS or Petition Day at Lockevar's Gate. Monte shivered to see empty closes.

Where had the people gone? Something must have really spooked them to make them give up a tenement, even a cramped one. Mr Gondavere appeared not to notice the change in the atmosphere. Monte's employer paused to hand brass buttons to street urchins and smiled at a siren plying her trade on the corner. Monte stuck his fingers in his ears until he was well past the siren, and marvelled at Mr Gondavere's immunity to her enthralling song.

The Golden Lamb was in a lower district of the Underground City, surrounded by warehouses and workshops. The place was less frenzied than the rest of the City, being mostly only visited by workers or traders. Monte liked it down here; he was less likely to be accosted by the thriving packs of urchins, and everyone was too busy to bother anyone else. The canal, which led to the Great Sea, ran along the edge of the district, its insistent call drowning out the shouts of workers.

The pub was two blocks into the district, on the bottom floor of a tall building that housed sewing and weaving workshops. Some of the workers tried to refer to their workspaces as 'ateliers' in a fit of sophistication, but everyone knew the days were long, the lighting was poor, and the pay was bad. 'Calling a handful of crap a rose petal doesn't make it so,' his Myrtle sometimes said.

Monte entered the pub and nodded to the barkeeper before scanning the room. There were fewer patrons than in the Nag's Head, and everyone drank on their own in an atmosphere of funereal silence. No friendly banter or camaraderie existed there.

Crompton Daye sat in a booth near the window, although the thick layer of grime on the glass made it impossible to see outside. He tapped his fingers on the pitted table and stared into his pewter mug. Monte didn't know what had happened in his past to reduce him to an existence of drinking in bad establishments, but he didn't know him well enough to ask – if Crompton could even remember.

"Mr Daye?" Monte stood by the table and looked down at the wizard.

Crompton looked up, peering out from beneath straggling grey eyebrows. Clarity sparkled in his blue eyes, and Monte realised Crompton was not nearly as drunk yet as he wanted to be.

"Yes?"

"I'm Monte McThwaite and this is my employer, Mr Gondavere," said Monte, gesturing to his master. Mr Gondavere nodded in greeting.

"Nice to meet you. Now what do you want?"

"Why do you think that we want anything, my dear fellow?" asked Mr Gondavere.

"I saw you in the Bloody Hand earlier, and I can't think why you'd trek all the way down here if you didn't want something from me." No slur affected his speech, and Crompton regarded them with suspicion. Monte shivered. What would a sober wizard do if he got annoyed?

"Only information," he said.

"Oh. Oh well, I have that in droves." Crompton managed a smile, although it was lost among the grey bushes of his beard. The wizard gestured for them to sit opposite him. Monte slid onto the hard bench first, followed by Mr Gondavere, who set the case on his lap beneath the table, one hand gripping the handle.

"I am on what you could call a quest. Certain information has led me to believe that you would be helpful towards my success in this particular endeavour," said Mr Gondavere.

"Indeed. And what information is that?"

"It is a difficult tale to tell, however I could ascertain whether or not I would be wasting your time if I may first discover one thing. Have you ever been a scholar, sir?"

Crompton laughed, a loud guffaw from the depths

of his gut. Monte started, unaware that such a booming noise might erupt from such a skinny man.

Mr Gondavere raised an eyebrow, but the rest of his face remained as stone. "What, may I ask, is so funny?"

"Just the idea of me as a scholar. No, Mr Gondavere, I've never been a scholar. I do know several wizards who are, though. What school of thought would we be talking about here?"

"History, mainly. Archaeology, perhaps. Maybe ancient relics." Mr Gondavere strove to sound nonchalant, but Monte wasn't fooled. He wondered if Crompton was.

"That narrows it down. I know a wizard in the City Above who deals in the study of ancient relics." Crompton knocked back the last of his drink and gestured to the barkeeper for another.

Monte shivered. Apparently, the dying man in the chapel hadn't been speaking nonsense after all. Mr Gondavere must have reached the same conclusion from the way that he sat forward, tracing designs on the table with one finger.

"Could you tell me his name?"

"Why are you asking?" Crompton narrowed his eyes.

"An interest in history. I am not exactly from these parts." Mr Gondavere smiled that awful, toothy smile, and Crompton attempted to recover from an obvious recoil. Monte had to admit, he didn't actually know where Mr Gondavere was from, but the question hadn't exactly come up during the day they'd spent in each other's company. Monte gained the impression Mr Gondavere wasn't the friendly type.

"All right. Well my wizarding friend is old enough to remember the days before the squabbling between the Twin Cities, and he spent most of his days in the Underground City, foraging for relics from the time of its construction," said Crompton.

The barkeeper arrived with Crompton's drink, and he handed over a coin. Mr Gondavere ordered two drinks – a glass of port for himself and a glass of pumpkin juice for Monte.

Crompton resumed his story. "He had it into his head that there was something under the Underground City, though he could never pinpoint what it was, or where it might be, and being a man, he didn't make it into the Shrine of Beseda, which is the closest you're going to get to the lower levels without any real information. Eventually, the tensions between the Cities worsened and with the sacking of the main libraries, he moved Above to continue his work."

"Does he still look for relics?" asked Monte. He was fascinated, and wondered if the people of the Underground City had any idea that it might have once been an ally of the City Above.

"No. He mostly relied on the Shadowkin for their help when he worked down here, but they viewed him as a traitor when he went Above, and now he mostly deals in antiques. You can find him in Silence, just north of the House of the Notorious Dead. His shop is called Bucklebeard's Antiques."

"Interesting," said Mr Gondavere, tapping a long finger against his chin.

"Now I have to wonder what you could want with a chap like old Bucklebeard." Crompton regarded Mr Gondavere with a keen eye, and Monte wondered if the wizard ever got drunk.

"As I say, I am a student of history," replied Mr Gondavere.

"Fair enough. Though what's information like that worth?"

Mr Gondavere pushed a gold coin across the table.

"Not enough, I'm afraid," said Crompton. He kept his eyes on the coin, but made no move to take it.

"You want more money?"

"I'll take this, but I want a favour. An 'I owe you', if you want," replied Crompton.

"What could you want from me?" Mr Gondavere feigned surprise, but Monte would bet anything that there were plenty of things a wizard could get from someone like his employer.

"Oh, I have no way of knowing that yet. I just like collecting favours. Never know when they might come in handy."

"Very well. Call for me when you have need of this favour."

Crompton pocketed the coin and raised his glass to toast them. Mr Gondavere nodded and slid out of the booth, followed by Monte. They left the Golden Lamb, aware that all eyes followed their progress.

"What do we do now?"

"I'm not sure. If this Bucklebeard fellow has been unable to locate anything beneath the City then I fear he is of little use to us. However, there is a woman not far from here who is not long for this world. Perhaps she will tell us something of use."

Monte said nothing, and trotted after Mr Gondavere as he strode up the road. His fingers found the coin in his pocket, and he held its reassuring coldness in his fist. Surely this strange quest had to be worth a decent salary?

Chapter 11

Jyx followed Validus up the wide driveway towards the House of Correction, with Vyolet secreted in the shadows between the folds of Jyx's hood. Fortis had left them to return to the Underground City, where he would make more enquiries among the Shadowkin. Neither he nor Validus explained why, and Jyx realised he didn't really care. He just wanted all of this to be over with. He was just a tiny pawn in a monumental game of chess that could alter its rules at any moment.

The House stood before them, a vast monolith of dark grey stone. Narrow arrow slits served as windows, and purple flames burned in braziers along its façade. The scent of strong magick hung heavy in the air, and Jyx's head swam with the effort of remaining conscious. The Wolfkin seemed unaffected, and Jyx wondered again at the magickal constitution of the mysterious beings.

"Remember, when we reach the gate, allow me to do the communicating. I have no idea what we will see inside, but you two must stay together at all costs. Your mission is simple – find Eufame, and get her out," said Validus.

"What will happen to you?" asked Jyx.

"Do not worry about me, Master Faire. I am sure I will see you again before all of this is over."

They reached the doorway, a huge yawning mouth of black so pure it hurt Jyx's eyes to look at it. A pair of Wolfkin with golden skin and fur stood on either side of the door, wearing black armour bearing the insignia of the House of Correction. Jyx was surprised to see Wolfkin in such a place, but their subjugation apparently knew no bounds.

"State your name and business." One of the Wolfkin spoke to Validus, and Jyx realised they didn't know he could hear them too. He kept facing ahead and pretended not to listen.

"Validus, of the House of the Long Dead. I've captured the traitor, Jyximus Faire, the one responsible for the destruction of the royal mummies," replied Validus.

A cold knot formed in Jyx's stomach. He hoped he could trust the Wolfkin.

He and the golden Wolfkin nodded at one another, and they waved Validus and Jyx forward.

"Wait!" The second Wolfkin sprang forward, and handed something to Jyx. It was a glass tile, neither purple nor pink, and full of air bubbles. It caught the light but didn't reflect it back as he expected – it reflected back only shadows.

"It comes from a mutual friend," said the golden Wolfkin. He looked at Jyx and winked.

Jyx gasped. The Wolfkin knew he could hear them! And even more, he seemed to want to help. Validus nudged Jyx to accept it, so he slipped the square into his robes. Validus pushed him towards the doorway before he could say anything. Jyx closed his eyes so he wouldn't have to look at the painfully dark black.

The curtain of darkness showered over Jyx's shoulders like a waterfall, and he was shocked to emerge dry on the other side.

A lofty room soared above Jyx, the ceiling so high he could barely make out any details. Validus placed a hand on his shoulder and guided him across the vast lobby. Black-and-white tiles covered the floor in a chequerboard that made Jyx dizzy, and additional purple flames burned in braziers set into wall sconces. The atrium felt more like the entrance hall to the Academy than Jyx thought it would, with Wolfkin moving to and fro with shackled prisoners. He saw humans, trolls and even a siren being led across the atrium, their gaze fixed firmly on the floor. The same feeling of lethargy came over Jyx, and he fought the urge to yawn. He'd never been around such oppressive magick before, and it almost overwhelmed him. He didn't know if it was the work of Eufame's sibling or just the collective defensive magick used within the House.

Yet below it all was a thread of magick, icy white, where the atmosphere burned purple. That strong, almost magnetic pull tugged Jyx's attention to the right, towards a low black archway hacked out of the grey stone walls. He couldn't read all of the white sigils painted above it, but he recognised one or two. 'Danger', 'Maximum Security' and what looked like 'Enter at your own risk' appeared among the jumble. Two figures stood on either side of the doorway, taller than the Wolfkin and cloaked in black so dark it hurt Jyx's eyes. He couldn't see into the hood but he gained the impression of a skeletal face and hollow eye sockets. He pulled away his gaze.

"What are they?" he asked, keeping his question inside his mind.

"Dreadguards. Pray they do not speak to you. I should have known that they would stand guard over the entrance to the Maximum Security wing," replied

Validus, the mental answer sounding as a whisper tickling his inner ear.

"Where do we go now?"

"Only you can decide that, Master Faire. For all intents and purposes, I am guiding you, not the other way around. The limit of my instructions was to get you in here. Can you feel my mistress yet?"

Another golden Wolfkin stalked across the lobby towards them before Jyx could reply. It gestured at him and cocked its head to one side slightly.

"This is the apprentice?"

"Indeed."

"Very well. I shall take him from here. You are dismissed."

Validus nodded and gave Jyx's shoulder a squeeze so brief it was almost imperceptible. Jyx didn't know if he should attempt to speak, or just go wherever the Wolfkin took him. With any luck, he could give him the slip and head off to find Eufame. He placed a hand on his shoulder where Validus had so recently guided him, and turned him in the direction of the black archway.

"Am I considered a high-risk prisoner?" asked Jyx, immediately regretting the words. Should he have given away the fact he could read their sigils?

The Wolfkin said nothing and added a shade more pressure to his shoulder. Jyx's feet started moving and carried him across the chequerboard floor. He looked around, but none of the other Wolfkin gave him a second glance. No one came to greet them. Surely if he was that high-status a prisoner, someone would need to be notified? The thought flickered through his mind that the Wolfkin were keeping their cards close to their chests. Perhaps too close.

The Dreadguards inclined their heads towards Jyx as he passed, but they soon turned their attention back to the atrium without asking any questions – the presence of the Wolfkin was seemingly enough to grant passage. Jyx let out a long sigh of relief – he felt in better hands with a Wolfkin rather than one of the imposing cloaked figures.

They passed below the archway into a long corridor of black stone. Instead of darkness, invisible illumination turned the passage into an obsidian hallway of endless light. No shadows lurked anywhere. Jyx's heart sank. How on earth could Vyolet cloak him, or Eufame, in shadow if there were no shadows? If she couldn't get them out… Jyx wondered again if it had all been a ploy to turn him over, and rather than drag him kicking and screaming, the Wolfkin hatched a devious plot to get him to enter of his own free volition. He'd thought them a noble, honourable species, but maybe they were just as vindictive and malicious as humans. Perhaps it was payback for his part in the death of the Wolfkin at the House of the Long Dead.

Iron gates lined the corridor, each one shrouded in the same impenetrable blackness as the doorway to the House, the only darkness in the whole hall. Another tug came on his consciousness as the sliver in his mind twitched in the direction of the end of the corridor. Whatever Eufame had left inside him wanted to be reunited with its mistress. In a sick sort of way, Jyx realised he did, too. At least with Eufame around, he didn't need to be responsible for anything except for the tasks she set him. She might have used him to get back at the Crown Prince and condemned him to the Perpetual Death to further her own ends, but at least she knew what she was doing. Not for the first time that day, Jyx felt completely out of his depth.

"Jyx?" someone whispered from the depths of his hood.

"Sssh!" hissed Jyx, afraid the Wolfkin would hear her. Yet as he turned around, he realised he was alone in the corridor. The Wolfkin had gone.

Jyx rustled his hood and Vyolet clambered out, a

long trail of shadowy smoke that coalesced into her dark grey form. She slipped off the goggles she wore to protect her eyes from sunlight and hung them from their strap around her neck.

"Where did the Wolfkin go?" she asked.

"I don't know. Do you think they're all working for Eufame?"

"It's possible. This place creeps me out. It's so oppressive, like it's going to thunder at any point."

Jyx nodded, and on impulse, reached for Vyolet's hand. Her purple eyes widened in surprise, but she allowed him to lead her down the corridor.

"What were those things earlier?"

"Dreadguards. I've never come across them before, but they seemed happy to let us past. I don't know if they even know who I was," replied Jyx. "Come on, let's find Eufame."

More corridors lay beyond, all identical and devoid of shadow. Vyolet's gaze darted from side to side, her skin deepening to black as her discomfort grew.

"Are you all right?" asked Jyx.

"I'm not used to being so...visible. Where's the light coming from?"

"I don't know. Hopefully Eufame will have some way of dimming it."

"Do you know where she is?"

"Not really. I can't visually see where she is in here, it's just like...how do I explain it...when I get a splinter in my finger, I can use a charm to get the wood to act like a magnet to pull the splinter our, and it feels like that. There's a little piece of Eufame in my head from where she set up the Perpetual Death spell, and it's looking for her," replied Jyx. On cue, it gave another pull, and dragged him down a corridor to the right.

"Is she far away?"

"I don't think so. The pull's definitely getting stronger. She spoke inside my mind when we were outside, but I can't hear anything now we're in here. It's weird."

They walked on, hand in hand, marvelling at the silent corridors. Even their feet made no noise on the marble floor, and an image of the skeleton embedded in the tiles at the House of the Long Dead popped into Jyx's head. Apparently the Delsenza siblings favoured marble.

The sliver in his mind let out a squeal, and Jyx halted outside a cell at the bottom of the hallway. Dizziness clenched his stomach and threw a black curtain across his vision. Jyx reached out to steady himself against the wall. The stone was ice cold yet pulsed beneath his touch, and Jyx snatched back his hand.

"Yeuch, the wall feels like it's *alive*," he said.

"What?"

"It's like there are a million souls writhing around inside the stone. Oh no! This whole place...it's made of prisoners!"

Vyolet jumped away from the wall and planted herself in the centre of the corridor. She eyed the wall, as if expecting hands to reach from the stone and pull her into the fabric of the building.

"Come on then, let's go!"

"I'd really rather you didn't." A voice, both familiar and cold, floated out of the cell before them. The words skated along the edge of a rusty razor, leaving flakes of sarcasm in their wake.

"It's her!" Jyx hurried to the gate. Without thinking, he stuck both hands through the bars. The same waterfall sensation seized his forearms as they passed through the black curtain beyond the cell door, yet his hands remained dry.

"Greetings, Master Faire. You took your time but I'm impressed that you're here," said the person inside the cell. A cold hand grasped his own and shook it.

"Miss Delsenza! Validus sent us in here to get you."

"Us?"

"I'm here with Vyolet. She's a Shadowkin!"

"Oh really?" Genuine surprise coloured Eufame's reply. "Well send her in then! Let me get a look at her."

"I can't pass through the curtain, ma'am. There are no shadows on this side of the cell," replied Vyolet, still unwilling to approach the door or the walls.

"Nonsense, of course you can. I'm sure Jyx here will find a way. He's rather fond of commanding shadows." Amusement crept into Eufame's tone, and Jyx blushed to remember his experiments with Shadow magick. He'd managed to command the shadow of a Wolfkin back at the House of the Long Dead, and even though it proved fruitless in the end, he was still proud of the achievement. That same spell had gotten them out of the House, hadn't it?

"Is he now." Vyolet pursed her lips and a cold glare flittered across her face.

"There's nothing to cast a shadow, Miss Delsenza. It's like the walls themselves are illuminating everything from all angles," replied Jyx.

"Oh, for goodness' sake, Jyx, call me Eufame. I think we're past the point of formality now, wouldn't you agree?"

"I suppose."

"Urgh, remind me to teach you to develop some confidence when you get me out of here. Now think. Do you have anything with you that might cast a shadow? You don't need a lot, just enough to connect with the cell door so Vyolet can cross through."

"What about that square the Wolfkin gave you? If you held it just right, it might give me enough of a shadow," said Vyolet.

"What square, Jyx?" Eufame said.

Jyx took the tile from his pocket and turned it over in his hands. Its dull surface reflected no light, instead absorbing it within the bubbles inside the glass. He described it to Eufame.

"You're holding an *Umbra Quadratum*, Jyx."

"A shadow square! I didn't think they were real! But how does it work?"

"Try one of the incantations you know."

Jyx didn't know any specific incantations, so he flipped through the pages of the *Dominantur Umbras* that he'd memorised. He held the square in his hands and spoke aloud. "*Conjuro umbras Quadratum!*"

Nothing happened. The square continued to absorb the peculiar illumination in the corridor, but no shadows appeared.

"Try again, Jyx."

Jyx scowled. Of all the times that Eufame could choose to play the teacher, surely now was not one of them. He turned the square over and tried again.

"*Convertere lucem in tenebras, faciat quadratum tenebricosum!*"

The square pulsed in his hands, absorbing more of the illumination from the hallway and emitting it as thick black shadows that drifted like smoke out of the glass tile.

"It's working!" cried Jyx. A smile broke out across his face.

"Of course it's working. What else did you expect?" said Eufame.

Jyx positioned the tile to cast a shadow across the floor and the bars, the darkness bleeding into the black curtain beyond the gate. Vyolet stepped into the shade and disappeared.

"Why hello there, young lady. You must be Vyolet," said Eufame.

"It's a great honour to meet you, ma'am," replied Vyolet.

Jyx shuddered, feeling like the worse sort of eavesdropper.

"Never mind any of that. Do you know how to cloak others?"

"Sort of."

A rustling came from beyond the gate, and Jyx

thought of giant sails flapping in the wind. A moment later, Vyolet reappeared within the shadow in the corridor. She stepped out of it, and helped Eufame step out of it too.

Eufame flexed her shoulders and straightened, standing taller than Jyx and Vyolet. No bone held her long black hair pinned on her head this time, and instead her hair hung loose about her shoulders. She still wore her black robes and her usual expression of bored indifference. She was terrifying and fascinating in equal measure, but Jyx had never been so pleased to see her. She could take over now.

"Hello there, young Jyx. Many thanks for your help in springing me from that cursed cell," said Eufame.

"Was it really very bad?" Jyx had heard the stories of the torture chambers, and the awful dungeons in the depths of the House. Eufame didn't look gaunt, or injured, as he'd expected. She looked remarkably well, all things considered.

"Just boring. They gave me nothing to do, which I suppose is hardly surprising. But enough chit-chat, we must be away. What are the intentions?"

"Validus said you'd have a plan," replied Jyx, suddenly uneasy.

"Did he indeed. The closest we have to a plan for now is to get out of here. I do not doubt that my sister is aware that things are afoot, and I imagine she will want to act. Vyolet, we will need your abilities to cloak us," said Eufame.

"But there are no shadows, apart from the one Jyx made."

For the first time, Eufame seemed to notice where she was. She looked up and down the corridor and frowned.

"A Shadow Square requires someone to hold it," she said. "They won't let me walk out the front door, and they'll expect that Jyx is already in a cell. They certainly won't let you simply walk out, Vyolet."

Jyx swallowed the burning bubble of nausea growing in his throat.

"That must be why they put me in this wing, to prevent the use of Shadowkin. Oh, they've been very clever."

"There weren't even enough shadows in the atrium either," said Vyolet. "I had a tough time staying hidden in Jyx's hood."

"I wonder why their sensors didn't go off. They screen entrants for magickal concealment. I'm even surprised you managed to get the Shadow Square through."

"I wasn't concealed through magick. It's just what I do, what I am," replied Vyolet, a hurt tone colouring her words.

"Indeed," replied Eufame, raising one eyebrow. Jyx thought a suppressed smile hovered at the corners of her mouth.

"A Wolfkin at the door gave me the square," replied Jyx, to prevent Vyolet from making any more outbursts.

"One of the guards? Interesting. And they allowed Validus inside?"

"Yes, but then another Wolfkin told him to leave, and he brought us down here, but then he just disappeared."

"This simply gets more and more strange. I did expect that Validus might attempt a rescue, but from here on in it's up to us," replied Eufame. "Still, I don't imagine we can get across the atrium undetected. It was difficult enough for me to cloak my thoughts to speak to you when you were outside."

"They had Dreadguards too," said Jyx.

"Oh damn it all, really? Well we'll have to avoid the main atrium then, and we need somewhere with shadows so that Vyolet may be of assistance. If we cannot go through...then we go under."

"Under what?"

"The House itself. The dungeons are dark places that you should not wish to see, but where there is darkness..."

"...there is shadow," finished Vyolet.

"Precisely! Come along, this way." Eufame turned and strode away along the corridor. Even the inexplicable illumination shrank back from her presence, and she created a dark wave along the passageway. Jyx lamented that it was not dark enough to be considered a shadow, and broke into a trot to follow her. As much as he had no desire to enter the dungeons, it looked as if he had no choice.

CHAPTER 12

The dying woman lay on a narrow cot in a sick-room at the edge of the warehouse district. Mr Gondavere sat at her side, his book open in his lap, as usual. Monte stood at the foot of the cot. The silent sisters kept passing them, gliding instead of walking, and gazing at him with their large, black eyes. Monte knew of the existence of these strange creatures, part spectre and part wraith, but he'd never seen one before. Cloaked in black, they administered care where they could to the dying who didn't have the means to reach a specific chapel at the temple. The silent sisters represented no deity, only an ignominious end in a backwater sickroom. They took no payment for their services, though Monte wondered what became of the souls of those who died within their hall. *Is that their payment?*

"I wondered when you'd come," said the old woman. She peered at Mr Gondavere with rheumy eyes.

"You know of me?"

"We all do, sir. We all await your arrival." The

old woman tried to nod, and worked herself into a coughing fit. Mr Gondavere held up a cautioning hand before Monte could dart forward to help her. Monte stared at his employer, brows knit in confusion, and Mr Gondavere gave him an expression that seemed to say, 'She's dying, who knows who she thinks I am?'

"Good, good. Well I am here now. Do you have anything to wish to make known, any message to pass on to a loved one, perhaps? Something you wish you'd gotten off your chest?"

"There's no absolution here, sir. No, I know why you're here. I know what you want me to tell you," replied the old woman.

"You do?" Mr Gondavere frowned. He sat back slightly, as if the woman were possibly poisonous.

"You want to know where the Heart is."

"Do I, indeed."

"Yes. Well, you're in the right place," said the old woman.

"I am?" Mr Gondavere looked around at the shabby walls and damp floor of the sickroom.

"It's in the Underground City. It always was. It never left." She reached out and clamped her hand around Mr Gondavere's arm. Monte darted forward but the old woman turned a vicious glare in his direction, and he froze.

"Where is it?" asked Mr Gondavere.

"It's no use, it's broken. Did you not hear the crack? The Almighty Crack?"

"What has that to do with the Heart?"

"Her Heart broke, you fool."

"Why? What happened?" asked Monte.

"Neither of the Cities has turned out right. It's not what she fought for."

Monte's gaze travelled along the old woman's arm and he spotted a tattoo on her pale skin, distorted by the wrinkles in her skin and faded by time. The hairs on the back of his neck stood up when he realised the tattoo was that of an owl. The old woman was a priestess of Beseda.

"The Heart can't break, or it would be useless."

"Exactly. Far beyond the reach of your sort! You think I don't know what you are? Get out of here and stop preying on the dead and dying!" The old woman's ferocity scared Monte, and he backed away from her cot. She glared at Mr Gondavere and he leaped out of his seat as if she'd slapped him.

Two of the silent sisters drifted across the room, coming between the old woman and Mr Gondavere. Their peaceful black eyes glittered with animosity, and Monte turned to flee across the sickroom. He stumbled over a footstool and sprawled across the floor. His hand skidded across a stinking puddle, and he cried out when his nose made contact with the hard stone.

Mr Gondavere swept by him, hurrying towards the door. The silent sisters glided after him, and Monte noticed they ignored him in their quest to get Mr Gondavere away from the old woman.

Monte turned to look at her. She sat up on the cot, her face pale but defiant. Her hands shook where she gripped the edge of her blanket. She looked at him and her expression softened.

"I know you're just doing your job, child. While I'd rather you didn't, you'll follow him as long as you can, and it will be best for all of us. You have a part to play in this now, like it or not. You could try to leave, but you'd be sucked back in. Go to the City Above; get him away from here. He can't use the Heart anyway, but he's not the only one looking for it now."

Monte nodded, even though he'd understood little of what she'd said, and scrambled to his feet. He ran out of the sickroom without a backward glance.

He found Mr Gondavere standing outside, smoking a cheroot. Monte didn't know Mr Gondavere smoked, but given the way his hands shook and his lips trembled every time he sucked smoke into his lungs, Monte understood his sudden need. The silent sisters might have spooked him, but they'd genuinely unnerved Mr Gondavere.

"Did she say anything else to you?" he asked when he saw Monte.

"She told us to go to the City Above." Monte wiped his wet hand on his trousers. He pursed his lips when he realised the material was already damp. Monte didn't want to think about what that puddle had been.

"Why would she tell us to go there?"

Monte shrugged, not wanting to pass on the rest of the priestess's message. Beseda, the owl goddess and patron saint of wronged women, was not a deity to be trifled with, and nor were her priestesses.

"Hm. Well we would have gone there anyway, for we must locate this wizard friend of Mr Daye's. I suspect she does not realise that she is helping us on our quest," said Mr Gondavere.

"People keep confusing you with the dead –" The words slipped out before Monte could stop himself, and he clapped his hand over his mouth as though he could reclaim what he'd said, scrabbling at the syllables as they hung in the silent air between himself and Mr Gondavere.

His employer said nothing, apparently lost in thought. Monte heaved a sigh of relief and busied himself with straightening his threadbare coat, although he did wonder exactly what the connection was between Mr Gondavere and the dead. How was it that he knew when a person was lying on their deathbed, and why specific people might have something to tell him?

"I see that we have no choice. We must go Above."

"Crompton said his friend was at Bucklebeard's Antiques."

"Well remembered, Monte. You continue to impress me. Now, if this Bucklebeard has made a lifelong study of the Heart, then we can mine that knowledge for clues. It will be quicker, and perhaps less tedious, than collecting the last words of simpletons."

"That makes sense."

"Then we shall journey to the City Above. It is late now, and will take some time to cross the Underground City to reach Lockevar's Gate. Perhaps we should secure transport."

Monte nodded. His feet ached from all the walking, and the mention of transport made his sore knee sing. Maybe he'd even be able to sneak in a nap. He couldn't remember how long he'd been in Mr Gondavere's company but it must have been almost a full day, and he could do with some sleep, even if his employer apparently didn't.

They walked to the edge of the warehouse district, ignoring the workers who carried goods on hand carts up to the stations where drivers waited with carts and huge shire horses. Monte wondered if they would catch a lift on a goods cart, but Mr Gondavere took them into the lower reaches of the next district, the Rookery, a network of tenements and drinking dens. A cabman leaned against a wall, enjoying a brief break outside a suspicious looking doorway daubed with red symbols.

"Hello, my good man, are you for hire?" asked Mr Gondavere, gesturing to the hackney cab parked several feet away. The jet black horse snorted in their direction.

"Waitin' fer someone, in't I?" replied the cabman.

"I pay handsomely." A gold coin flitted across Mr Gondavere's knuckles, and the cabman's eyes lit up.

"Well 'op in, sir! Where are you two fine gentlemen goin' then?"

Mr Gondavere clambered up into the cab, leaving Monte to climb in himself.

"Lockevar's Gate, or as near as you can get to it."

"Very good, sir."

The cabman snapped the reins, and the horse set off, the cab lurching behind it. It swayed and bounced on its springs, clattering across the cobbles. Monte gripped the side nearest to him and fought the urge to be sick. It would be a long ride indeed.

CHAPTER 13

Jyx and Vyolet caught up with Eufame at a crossroads in the corridors. Within moments of stepping into the low atrium, Jyx realised he couldn't remember which corridor they'd followed to get there. All the passages looked the same, hewn from that same blank stone and lit with the same eerie illumination.

"Which way now?" Vyolet clung to Jyx's arm.

"There's only one thing to do when you get lost. Ask for directions," replied Eufame.

"From whom?" asked Jyx.

Eufame crossed to the next corridor and placed one white hand on the wall. Jyx's stomach churned as he realised what she was going to do. She whispered to the wall, her dark lips forming words Jyx couldn't hear. The wall erupted outwards in a sea of flailing arms and grasping hands. Eufame stepped back out of their reach.

"Now-now, behave yourselves."

The arms slowed their movement, but continued

to wave like fronds under water. A skull coalesced and pushed out of the wall, the enchantment of the building's fabric stretched across it like a skin.

"What do you ask of us?" The skull's lower jaw hinged back and forth, its teeth clattering in an approximation of speech.

"We need to know how to get down to the dungeons."

"Down? Oh, no one *goes* down there. They're *taken* down there."

"That won't work for me, I'm afraid. I need to know how to get into them." Eufame folded her arms.

"No, no, only taken."

Another skull further along the wall pushed itself forward, the grey enchantment straining to cover its rounded form.

"Of course you can get into them, you idiot," it shouted at the first skull.

"Don't tell them that! She will get so angry if she finds out, and then we'll never be free!" replied the first skull.

"We'll never be free anyway. Listen, pay no attention to him, he doesn't know what he's talking about. Take the corridor nearest your apprentice, and follow it until the sixth gate on the right. Walk through. It looks solid but it's an illusion. It's actually the top of a staircase," said the second skull.

The first skull shouted, trying to drown out the words of the second, but everyone ignored it.

"Are all of the gates illusions?" asked Jyx.

"No. Most of them are cell doors, but the occasional one hides more. That's the one you want. Don't stop on the first landing, none of those corridors lead you anywhere you might want to go. Go down again to the second landing, and follow your nose."

The second skull pulled back into the wall, the grey skin rippling before it settled back into place. The first skull shouted in annoyance but also retreated into the wall, followed by the arms and legs.

Eufame turned to Jyx and Vyolet. "See? It's amazing where you can find useful information."

"What were those things?" asked Vyolet.

"This entire building is made of the souls of the damned. One of my sister's more repellent ideas," replied Eufame.

Jyx gawked at her carefree tone. Did her advanced age make her so flippant, or would he too become so immune to suffering that it became matter-of-fact?

As instructed by the skull, Eufame went down the corridor nearest to Jyx. She counted the gates, stopping at the specified door, and walked straight through it, swallowed up by the curtain of black.

"Eufame!" cried Jyx.

"Should we follow her?" asked Vyolet.

"I don't think we have any choice," replied Jyx. "We can't get out without her."

They set off after Eufame, pausing outside the same door. Jyx stared at it, unable to believe it was any different from the gates to either side. These were the cells housing dangerous inmates – how could they trust the skull, and how did they know Eufame was safely on the other side? She hadn't called out to them to say it was safe to proceed.

"Is this the right one?" asked Vyolet.

"Sixth on the right, the skull said. So it should be. I just don't like this at all."

"Neither do I, but you said it yourself, we have no choice. Unless you have some magick that you can use to check it's the right one. Maybe Shadow magick." Vyolet wrinkled her nose and spat the last two words.

"Okay, I get it. You have a problem with me using Shadow magick. I don't do it for fun, you know. The first time...I just wanted to see if it worked."

"You've used it more than once?" Vyolet raised an eyebrow. Her skin darkened a shade.

"Yeah. I had to distract the council guards so Validus and I could get out of the House of the Long Dead. It was the only thing I could think of."

"Shadows have minds of their own, you know. They're not just there for your amusement. Neither are Shadowkin," said Vyolet. Her tone wobbled, but her skin returned to its normal colour. Her anger had passed – for now.

"Look, I promise I'll only ever use Shadow magick in future if I have absolutely no other choice, or Eufame tells me to, okay?"

Vyolet let out a long breath. "That seems fair."

The Eufame shard in Jyx's mind wriggled. It caught his awareness with a sharp stab.

"I think Eufame's waiting for us," he said.

Jyx gritted his teeth and reached out a trembling hand, pressing on the gate with his fingertips. His fingers disappeared clean through the metal and into the black curtain beyond. He moved forward until his whole hand was through the curtain, its strange not-wetness soaking his wrist.

"This feels so weird," he said.

Before he could move further forward, another hand, this one ice cold and smooth, grasped his own. Jyx yelped and the other hand yanked on his arm. He stumbled through the curtain, holding his breath as he passed, and came out in a stairwell, lit by flickering purple torches. He looked into the smiling face of Eufame Delsenza. The dancing light cast a mauve glow across the white streaks in her black mane and she let go of his hand to ruffle his hair.

"You need to have more faith, Jyx," she said.

Jyx turned around to see the cell door behind him. The curtain was transparent on this side, and Vyolet remained in the corridor, arms wrapped around herself, and glancing from side to side. Eufame stuck her hand back through the curtain. Vyolet reached out to take it and the necromancer general hauled the Shadowkin through the gate.

"Right. We should be a little safer down here in the sense that no one will expect us to go down – they'll expect us to try to make for the main atrium," said Eufame. "But that doesn't mean there won't be other dangers."

Behind Jyx, the rough stone steps disappeared into the gloom, the flickering torchlight casting a weak purple glow down the staircase. Vyolet smiled and stepped sideways into the shadow behind Eufame.

"Vyolet!" cried Jyx.

"I'm still here, Jyx. It's just I haven't felt darkness since we came in. I don't normally spend so long away from it," replied Vyolet, a disembodied voice echoing in the stairwell.

"Vyolet, I'm going to need a very long chat with you about shadows when we get out of here, but for now we have to get moving. We can't guarantee someone won't come up these stairs."

Eufame hustled them both down the stairs. Warmer air caressed Jyx's face as they descended, and he held his hand against a torch as he walked past. The flames gave off no heat, only light, and Jyx could only assume the warmth came from somewhere below. The words of the skull came to mind – what did it mean, telling them to follow their noses?

Jyx started counting steps as they descended deeper into the bowels of the House, but gave up after thirty. The Academy featured enchanted spiral staircases in the Forbidden Tower to catch out unwary or overly curious students, and the staircases kept adding steps to keep the students climbing until exhaustion forced them back down. Jyx thought of those staircases now, wondering exactly how many steps it would take to get to the first landing.

"Eufame, how far down do these stairs go?" asked Jyx.

"I'm beginning to suspect they go down as far as Naiad wants them to go," replied Eufame. Irritation bloomed in her tone, along with a note Jyx had never heard before – anxiety.

"Why did they bring you to the House of Correction?"

"Because my sister is one of only two people in the whole of the Twin Cities capable of holding me, and the only one who would actually want to."

Eufame stopped on the stairs, and Jyx almost slammed into her back. Vyolet caught him before he fell. She remained in the shadow, but the sight of her gun smoke hand wrapped around his wrist calmed his nerves.

"I may have made a mistake." A lead weight coated the bottom of Eufame's words.

"How?" asked Jyx.

"Validus should never have gotten either of you involved. He trusted me to be able to get us all out once you found me, but I don't know if I can."

Eufame sat on the step and gazed down the staircase into the gloom below.

"What do you mean? You're Eufame Delsenza, feared by pretty much anyone human in the Twin Cities. You can do anything." Jyx reached out to touch her but pulled back his hand at the last moment.

"Your confidence in me is reassuring, Jyx, but wholly misplaced, given our current predicament."

"Predicament...predict...do you think your sister has predicted what you'll do next?" asked Vyolet. She stepped from the shadow beside Jyx, her purple eyes gleaming.

"I don't doubt it," replied Eufame. "Why?"

"Because all we need to do is something she hasn't predicted."

Vyolet shoved her hand into Jyx's pocket and pulled out the Shadow Square. She hurled it down the stairs. Jyx cried out, but a comforting sound returned

– breaking glass. Eufame looked up at Vyolet, a smile in her wintery eyes.

"Clever girl!"

Shadows raced up the stairs to engulf them, extinguishing each of the braziers in turn. Jyx pressed himself against the wall, staring wildly into the complete darkness surrounding him. He opened and closed his eyes to reassure himself that they were indeed open. Vyolet's hand curled around his arm and she took his hand.

One minute Jyx's feet were planted on the stone step, the next he was weightless, flying downwards. Vyolet still held his hand, but Jyx swore she was beside him and all around him at the same time. Eufame whooped and hollered with childlike delight as the three of them made their way through the inky air. He wanted to shout but terror stole his words. He clamped shut his eyes and mouth.

Time passed quickly in the shadows, and two blinks of an eye later, solid ground met Jyx's feet, and his knees buckled under the sudden impact. He stood poised to run, arms held out either side of him for balance, and warm air ruffled his hair. Jyx opened one eye, expecting to see nothing but darkness. Instead, he peered into a long, curving corridor lit by fallen stars.

"Where are we?" he asked. He looked to his right and saw Eufame sweep Vyolet into a bear hug. He bristled. She'd never shown any appreciation for his efforts before. Then again, his efforts usually led to destruction.

"We're in the lower levels of the House, right at the edge of my sister's awareness. Vyolet here is an incredibly clever young Shadowkin," said Eufame, a genuine smile bringing warmth to her usually cold, severe features.

"What did you do?" asked Jyx.

"I figured that if we couldn't go to the landing,

then the only way to break the spell was to bring the landing to us. I don't have a lot of magick, but I can travel in shadow. That square absorbed a lot of light, so it stood to reason that it would unleash a lot of darkness."

Jyx nodded as though he understood, but his grasp on Shadowkin magick was tenuous at best. Until today, he hadn't even thought they were real. All he knew was Vyolet had applied lateral thinking and sidestepped the problem with a truly simple solution. He'd never have thought of that. Jealousy made his ears burn, and he turned away so they wouldn't see his face turn red.

"Come along. We've been lucky that our little trip down the stairs meant we've missed the dungeons entirely. We're at the edge of her awareness, but we need to go further before we'll really be able to get out of here." Eufame walked away, and Vyolet followed.

"Where are we going?" asked Jyx.

"Can't you smell them?" Eufame turned to look at him.

"No, smell what?"

"The sewers."

Jyx gulped. Now he knew why the skull told them to follow their noses. Eufame was going to lead them to freedom through the sewers of the Twin Cities' most abominable building.

He took a deep breath and followed.

Chapter 14

The swaying and rattling of the cab stopped, and Monte pitched forward. The sudden movement shook him awake, and he looked around in confusion.

Tall tenements rose on either side of the cab. Broken crates blocked further progress, and a pack of urchins played around them. The air was alive with the shouts of housewives and traders from the tiny market further along the street. The scent of rotting produce mingled with the smell of humans living in proximity to each other. Monte knew that smell – it was the same one that lingered in the close where he lived, somewhere to the east. He didn't recognise this street, so far away from his little cemetery.

"Where are we?" asked Monte.

"The nearest we can get to Lockevar's Gate. All of the streets appear to be blocked, so we shall get no further than this," replied Mr Gondavere. He clambered out of the cab.

Monte climbed down on shaking legs and he stamped his feet to return a semblance of feeling to them. He yawned and stretched, unable to believe he'd managed to sleep through his first coach ride. Gravediggers certainly didn't earn enough to hire them.

Mr Gondavere paid the cabman, and Monte watched him back his horse along the alley until he had enough room to turn around the cab.

"I believe that someone was on our tail, but the cab ride would appear to have given them the slip," said Mr Gondavere.

"Who is it that you think is following us?"

"I was originally hired for a particular job. I believe my erstwhile employer is attempting to keep tabs on my progress. Little does he know that I have deviated from that original job somewhat."

Mr Gondavere picked his way over the crates. Monte followed, scrambling to keep his footing on the splintered wood. Urchins swarmed towards Mr Gondavere, but he shooed them away. Once the squawking children had departed, he and Monte walked in silence, navigating the loud and busy closes in the direction of the Gate.

Their destination was a mammoth door between the two Cities. No one knew what material made up the doors themselves, but they were impervious to any force, both physical and magickal. Rumour had it that night iron was involved in their construction somehow, but no one was old enough to remember them being erected. Arcane symbols decorated the pillars, while sparks of magick flickered in the air on either side of the Gate. Low huts of ancient wood sat by the archway on both sides of the Gate, manned by armoured men wielding halberds.

A small crowd gathered by the hut beside the Gate, begging the sentries for entry to the City Above. The two sentries, both heavy-set men in their early forties, would not be moved, and held back the crowd. In order to prevent mass immigration into the City Above, the inhabitants of the

Underground City could not go Above without a pass, and they couldn't obtain a pass without a valid reason for being Above. In the interests of fairness, the council of the City Above also limited movement into the Underground City, in the attempts of stemming the tide of pleasure-seekers and criminals wishing to profit from the misery of the underground slums. A limited number of petitioners were allowed Above every day, and hundreds of City-dwellers waited at the Gate each morning in the hope that they would be fortunate enough to pass through. Monte didn't know what they thought awaited them Above, unless they thought they could make a better life for themselves. He'd never joined the crowd – Myrtle would never let him because he'd "just fail at that as well". He grimaced to think about his wife.

Mr Gondavere walked past the crowd, and up to one of the sentries. Monte followed him and cried out when he got closer to the man.

"Willum!"

"Monte!" The man broke into a wide grin full of misshapen, blackened teeth and clapped Monte on the back with one beefy hand. Monte grasped his free hand and shook it furiously.

"Do you two know each other?" asked Mr Gondavere. He pursed his lips.

"Yeah, I went to school with Willum's little brother. How's he getting on?" asked Monte.

"Got hisself a new job, din't he? 'E now works down in the Artist's Quarter, runnin' errands and whatnot," replied Willum.

"It's a small world, indeed," replied Mr Gondavere.

"What you doin' now, Monte?" asked Willum.

"This is my employer, Mr Gondavere. He's a social historian," replied Monte.

"My, that is interestin', yes indeed!" Willum smiled again. Somehow his lopsided, ugly grin troubled Monte less than Mr Gondavere's dagger-filled smile. Mr Gondavere gave a short, sharp bow.

"Yer'll be wantin' to go Above, then?" Willum returned Mr Gondavere's bow and gestured to the Gate with his thumb.

"That was our hope, yes," replied Mr Gondavere.

"Don't suppose yer have papers? Passes? Official sigils?

Monte shook his head but Willum simply shrugged.

"Normally I'd need to see 'em but seein' as how I know yer, I'll let yer through. Jus' don't let on, yeah?"

Mr Gondavere smiled and doffed his hat. Willum beamed, clearly unaccustomed to social niceties from well-dressed men. Monte shook Willum's hand, and promised to catch up with him again as soon as he could. Willum lifted a small portion of the vast barrier and allowed Mr Gondavere and Monte through, slamming it closed again before the crowd could surge forward.

"That was a stroke of luck, although I could have produced the necessary administrative items," said Mr Gondavere.

"I didn't know that," replied Monte.

"You never asked, and it was not your place to know. Kindly do not answer for me again, do you understand?"

Monte nodded in reply, too excited at the prospect of finally seeing the City Above to feel chastened by Mr Gondavere's rebuke.

It was night time in the City Above, and a vast canvas of deepest blue arced above Monte. He stopped in the centre of the thoroughfare, gazing up at the winking pricks of silver. He'd never seen stars before, except in his dreams, but they were even more beautiful than anything his imagination could have produced. He wondered what Myrtle would make of such a sight, but even that would probably fail to impress her. "I thought the stars would be brighter," she'd say.

"We must make for the district of the House of the Notorious Dead," said Mr Gondavere.

Monte's attention snapped back to the job at hand, and he followed his employer along the thoroughfare. Empty stalls lined the route, and Monte wondered what goods were sold in the small market. Was it food? Surely that would be cruel, selling the finest street food so near the Gate. He pictured the petitioners pressing against the barriers, their noses filled with aromas of food they'd never see, let alone taste.

They turned the corner. Whitewashed buildings lined the street to their left, and a canal cut its way along the cobbles to their right. Small balconies and terraces opened directly onto the water from the houses across the canal, and gondolas were moored at tiny jetties. Lights burned behind closed shutters, and flecks of coloured light drifted down towards the street. Monte wondered if Crompton Daye ever practised his wizardry in such a place before he ended up in the Underground City.

They came across a pier further along the street. Two gondolas bobbed in the canal, their gondoliers chatting in low voices as they leaned on their poles. One of them noticed Mr Gondavere and Monte, and stood to attention.

"It's a fine night, gentlemen! Have you a destination in mind?" he called.

"We do indeed. How far do these canals reach?" asked Mr Gondavere.

"The House of the Notorious Dead to the north, sir, and the Academy far to the east."

"Excellent. You are hired," replied Mr Gondavere.

Without another word, he handed his case to Monte, and clambered down the small steps into the gondola. The gondolier raised an eyebrow and looked at Monte, asking 'Is he always like this?' with his eyes. Monte replied with a shrug and passed the case back to Mr Gondavere. He climbed down the ladder and took a seat near the front of the gondola. He'd never been on a canal before, not even the one below ground, and he wanted to enjoy the view.

The gondolier pushed away from the jetty, and the gondola drifted along the canal. The street alongside the water gave way to more buildings, and soon they were gliding along a stretch of water so narrow Monte felt he could touch the houses on both sides if he stretched out his arms. Once out of earshot of the other gondolier, Mr Gondavere turned around and addressed his pilot.

"Could you take us as far as the House of the Notorious Dead? We need the streets just to the north, and I believe that is the nearest landing point."

"That it is, sir. Consider it done."

Monte turned away from them and peered out of the front of the gondola into the gloom. Only one in three of the oil lamps mounted on the buildings held light, and shadows stretched and swayed between the houses. The black water lapped against the sides of the gondola, and Monte resisted the urge to ripple his fingers in the canal. Who knew what lived in the dark depths, venturing forth only at night?

"We don't get a lot of commissions at this time of night, sir," said the gondolier, keeping his voice low. Even his whisper echoed off the walls.

"I don't imagine that you do," replied Mr Gondavere.

"But it's nice to keep busy," said the gondolier.

"Do you always converse so freely with your clients?" Mr Gondavere's words were black with warning.

"Just nice to know who I've got in my boat, sir. Have you been to the City Above before?" replied the gondolier, addressing his question to Monte. Mr Gondavere answered before he could speak.

"I have, but my associate has not. This is quite the excursion for him, I daresay," replied Mr Gondavere. Monte bristled at being discussed as though he were not present, although his pride swelled at the word 'associate'. That was better than 'employee'.

The gondolier fell silent, presumably having run out of conversation starters, and they drifted along, the only sounds being the pole and gondola moving through the water, and snippets of discussions heard behind the shutters they passed. Monte wondered if people kept the lower shutters closed all day to prevent passers-by from peering in.

The canal turned a corner and the gondolier steered them around the bend into a wider stretch of water. Their journey continued in a similar fashion, the canal cutting through the grid of the quarter, and the gondolier navigating the twists and turns.

Monte's eyelids grew heavy and he shook his head to ward off sleep. He slapped his face when he felt a yawn coming on, and tried to occupy himself with imagining what went on behind closed shutters. He gave up when he realised he didn't actually know what wizards did in their workshops. Grave digging was all he'd ever known, and it didn't equip him with much knowledge of other trades.

The gondola made another turn, and Mr Gondavere let out a long, low whistle of appreciation. Before them, a vast building rose seemingly out of the water, its black walls reflecting the rippling waters of the canals that encircled its small island. Niches cut into the stone took the place of windows, with small braziers burning in each.

Monte only knew of the House of the Notorious Dead through folklore. It housed criminals, and was a place intended to keep their bodies and their souls apart to prevent their resurrection. Most criminals were kept in the House of Correction, but truly heinous deeds warranted the further punishment provided by the House of the Notorious Dead. Still, Monte wasn't sure what to expect from the place.

The gondolier guided the boat below the drawbridge that connected the small island with the rest of the Canal Quarter. Seeing the canal as less of a canal and more of a moat, Monte wondered again what creatures lurked beneath the dark surface of the water. If he squinted, he thought he saw movement in the depths.

Guards stood either side of the portcullis, the metal grille locked in position at this time of night. Monte expected Wolfkin, but these figures were tall and hooded in long black cloaks. Their skeletal hands curled around the handles of scythes. Dreadguards. Monte's lips moved in a silent prayer to the Lords and Ladies of Death to watch over him in such a place.

Mr Gondavere motioned to the gondolier to pause just beyond the drawbridge, and he turned around to look up at the Dreadguards. One of them inclined its head in their direction and Monte shuddered, his fingers curled around the edge of the boat.

"Continue on your journey, friend. There is no reason for you to linger here," said the Dreadguard. Its voice was smooth and dark, like the water below.

"We have business in this neighbourhood, friend," replied Mr Gondavere. Scorn dripped from his lips as he enunciated the last word.

"Then proceed and continue with your business."

Mr Gondavere cocked his head on one side, and nodded twice. Monte strained to hear the voice of whoever spoke to Mr Gondavere, but he heard nothing. After a few moments, the Dreadguard stepped forward, bringing with it a blast of icy air and the scent of grave dirt. Mr Gondavere looked at Monte. He couldn't read his expression, but he braced himself for an outburst. Instead, Mr Gondavere said nothing, and motioned for the gondolier to take them to the nearest landing point.

The gondola pulled up alongside a rickety jetty around the corner from the House and Mr Gondavere paid the gondolier in silence. The gondolier shrugged at Monte and, once Monte had climbed free, guided the gondola away down the canal. Monte handed the case back to Mr Gondavere.

"What do we do now?" asked Monte. If he was honest, he wasn't sure what Mr Gondavere had hoped to achieve by stopping so close to the House of the Notorious Dead. Perhaps the old priestess had sent them here hoping they would be arrested for poking their noses into old business. Thinking of the old priestess dislodged a stray thought in his mind, but it flitted away before Monte could grasp it.

"Fear not, my good man, for I have it on good authority that we shan't need to spend too much time seeking our quarry!" Mr Gondavere smiled.

Monte nodded though he didn't understand. Who was this mysterious source that kept feeding Mr Gondavere information, and why had he never seen them? He thought of the way Mr Gondavere cocked his head on one side and listened to thin air. Monte shuddered and followed Mr Gondavere down the street, putting the canal behind them.

* * *

They stopped outside a tavern a few streets away. Monte spotted a sign hanging above the window of the shop next door. Its gilt script pronounced the shop to be Bucklebeard's Antiques. No lights burned in the window, and a padlock secured the front door. Monte wagered it wasn't just any old padlock, either.

"Looks like it's closed for the night," said Monte.

"I have little doubt that our mysterious Bucklebeard will not be found in his shop so late." Mr Gondavere smiled and gestured to the tavern. Like the pubs in the Underground City, the taverns Above appeared to open late. Light spilled into the street through diamond windows, and piano music drifted out of the door every time it opened. Mr Gondavere opened the door and stepped inside.

An open fire blazed in an ornate fireplace and copper pots gleamed on their hooks above the mantelpiece. Low stools clustered around empty tables and the barkeeper read a book behind the bar. A wooden automaton sat at the piano, its clockwork fingers picking out old tunes on the black-and-white keys. A single customer sat in a booth on the opposite side of the room, his hat pulled low over his face. Monte wasn't sure if the stranger slept, since he didn't move, and nor did his chest rise and heave. Was he dead?

Mr Gondavere ordered two mugs of tea and a glass of whiskey at the bar then made straight for the booth at the back of the room. As he drew near, Monte realised he couldn't smell the usual scent of death that clung to a dead person, so the stranger couldn't be dead. There again, Monte couldn't smell anything at all from him. It was as if he didn't occupy the same space as everyone else.

The barkeeper brought the drinks over on a polished tray. Mr Gondavere handed a mug of steaming tea to Monte and pushed the glass of whiskey to the stranger.

"Good evening, sir."

The stranger looked up and pushed his hat back on his head. A bushy grey beard hid the lower half of a kind face, and shaggy eyebrows almost covered his piercing green eyes. Despite the colour of his hair, the stranger didn't look that old. In fact, Monte couldn't see any lines or age spots on his face at all. If Monte had to guess, the stranger couldn't have been more than twenty-five. That was younger than him. Monte took solace in his drink, clutching the mug and sipping the sweet tea.

"Good evening, chaps. What can I do for you?" The stranger's voice was smooth and deep, though his words bore little trace of an accent.

"We've been speaking to an old friend of yours, and he thinks that you may be able to help us."

"Does he, now? Who is this friend of mine that would send you here at so inhospitable an hour?"

"Crompton Daye." Monte blurted the name before he could stop himself. Something about the stranger made him want to tell the whole story, and lay out all of the facts that he knew. He didn't know why, but this stranger would be able to set things right.

The stranger looked grave for a moment, until his face creased and he erupted with laughter.

"Crompton Daye, indeed! How is my old friend? Is he well?"

"He's well enough," said Mr Gondavere. He glared at Monte. "Am I to assume that you are Bucklebeard, of Bucklebeard's Antiques?"

"That I was, though my real name's Armitage Black. I got my nickname after a very ill-advised fashion experiment at the Academy. By, that must have been at least two centuries ago." The stranger fondled the pointed tip of his beard and Monte could just imagine him wearing silver buckles woven into his hair.

"Well then, Mr Black. I have heard that you are a student of history, much like myself," said Mr Gondavere.

"I am a student of history, that much is correct. Whether I am much like yourself remains to be seen," replied Black.

Monte fought the urge to snigger.

"Indeed, Mr Black. I am given to understand that your particular area of expertise is the Heart of the City," said Mr Gondavere.

"It was certainly a pursuit of mine when I lived in the Underground City. I looked for it for half of my life, but with the libraries gone and the Shadowkin pressed into service as messengers, I gave up and came Above. Why?"

"It is a relic that I feel deserves a place in the history of the Twin Cities, instead of merely a mythological footnote."

"Well I agree with you there. I've got no solid proof that it ever existed, but I always thought it would be below the Underground City, if it was anywhere. I never managed to find an entrance, though. Why? Have you found something?"

"An old priestess told us the Heart was broken. That was the Almighty Crack everyone heard," said Monte. He ignored the venomous look on Mr Gondavere's face.

Black's eyes widened. "That would be a sad fact indeed, my friend, although it didn't occur to me that the Heart and the Almighty Crack might be connected. Yes, the Heart would be useless if it was broken. I can only think of one person in the City who could mend it, but I can't see her lending a hand," said Black. He gazed into his mug.

"Who would that person be? I would love to interview her for my book," said Mr Gondavere.

"Let me think," replied Black. "How about you ask the bartender for another drink for me?"

Mr Gondavere smiled, stood up then made his way across to the bar. Black looked up and Monte followed his gaze. Mr Gondavere had his back to them.

"Look, you seem like a good sort, so you're going to have to keep an eye on him for me. I have to go and make some inquiries of my own, maybe see if I can't put a word in a certain someone's ear. But under no circumstances let him anywhere near the Heart, even if it is broken." Black winked. For a split second, time stopped, and the wizard opened a slit in the fabric of the world. He slid through and the tear sealed up behind him. Time restarted and Black was gone.

"Monte!" Mr Gondavere bellowed his name across the room.

Monte stood up and shuffled across the tavern to the bar. He blinked hard, hoping to erase the image of the world being unzipped so casually. His mind's eye clung to the sight of a man stepping through reality as though it was nothing but a normal doorway.

"Where did he go?"

"I don't know. He said he had to do some work and one minute he was there, the next he was gone," replied Monte. The lie sprang to his lips, but he fought the urge to bite his tongue. Any man who could control time like that... Black understood more of the world than he ever could. And if he said Mr Gondavere should be kept away from the heart, then that's what Monte would do.

"This is exceedingly vexatious, Monte. We needed his information so we could know where to start looking," said Mr Gondavere.

"I know, but I didn't know he was going to disappear like that," said Monte. The air felt somewhat colder following Black's departure, and Monte wished the wizard had taken him too. At least his smile was genuine.

"Did he tell you anything else?"

"No, sir." Monte tried to think of a way to follow Black's instructions, but he couldn't keep Mr Gondavere away from the Heart if they didn't even know where it was.

"Well, the night is still young. We may suppose that the Heart is not in the City Above, but rather in the Underground City, which I suspected all along. We may also suppose that some powerful magick will be required in order to mend the Heart before I may use it. Rather, before *we* use it," said Mr Gondavere, shooting a sly glance at Monte.

Monte adopted his usual expression of dopey obedience, but the slip of the tongue could not have been more obvious. Mr Gondavere had no intention of sharing the Heart or its abilities with him. No, he'd have to go back to grave digging, although at least that was solid and reliable work. He'd already lost a day's pay, but the gold coin was worth at least a year's work. Maybe he'd even pay Myrtle to leave him.

"So, what do we do now?"

"First, we finish our drinks. At least we have somewhere to start."

Mr Gondavere raised his mug and proposed a toast to hard work and success. Monte tapped his mug against that of Mr Gondavere, but like this entire endeavour, he found his tea very difficult to swallow.

"Will I have time to nip home and see the wife? Only she'll be beginning to wonder where I am," said Monte. He didn't think Myrtle would be particularly pleased to see him, but he did feel obliged to let her know what was going on. Besides, the longer he could keep Mr Gondavere from his inquiries, the longer Armitage Black would have to make his own.

"Indeed so. I am also aware that you must eat and sleep, and I have not given you sufficient time to do either."

Mr Gondavere smiled, and even though he was trying to help him, Monte still suppressed a shudder at the sight of all of those teeth. He returned a weak smile of his own while trying to ignore thoughts about what Mr Gondavere did for food or rest.

"Excellent. Well then, we have not an instant to lose. We must return to Lockevar's Gate at once."

Monte followed Mr Gondavere out of the pub, inhaling a final lungful of warm air before they passed into the chilly night beyond. His only real regret at heading back underground was losing the sight of the sky and the feel of fresh air on his skin. His fingers brushed solid gold in his pocket. At least the money made it worth it.

CHAPTER 15

Vyolet skipped ahead through the long shadows that undulated up the walls in the flickering light. Eufame fell into step beside Jyx, and the hairs on the back of his neck stood up to be so close to her. The shard of her inside his head sang a pure melody that Jyx didn't think he'd ever be able to replicate.

"I had your family moved, Jyx," she said.

"I know. Validus told me."

Eufame cocked her head to one side. The look she gave was full of both curiosity and suspicion.

"I hope you realise what an honour it is to be so bestowed with Wolfkin magick. It's not to be taken lightly, you know."

"Validus has been really nice to me."

"I don't doubt he has. He's a loyal associate. All of my Wolfkin are."

"You don't think of them as servants? Validus kept calling you his mistress."

"His own foible, but nothing I insist upon. The Wolfkin might be servants elsewhere, but I appreciate their unique talents. Naiad clearly doesn't, or she wouldn't have employed them as guards at the House of Correction. Dreadguards would have been a more obvious choice."

"Why?"

"You don't know a lot about Wolfkin, do you?"

"I don't either, but the one who came to find me knew Shadow Speak," said Vyolet, pausing to wait for them.

"That would be Fortis. He is fascinated by languages of all kinds – he can talk to most of the people who live in the twin Cities. He even tried to learn Troll, but that was beyond him, bless his effort," replied Eufame. "But for Validus to allow you to speak with the Wolfkin telepathically is a very big deal."

"He said I needed to understand him."

"And you obviously did, otherwise you wouldn't be here. Could you understand the Wolfkin at the door to this House?"

"Yeah. They knew I could understand."

Eufame nodded, a sly smile creeping across her face. Jyx shrank away, still unused to seeing any of her pleasant expressions.

"I'm not privy to all of the Wolfkin's plans, only those who work with me, but I wouldn't be at all surprised if they have some other plan of their own. I'm not going to rely on it, but we'll find out soon enough if I'm right."

A low moan, full of pain and wet around the edges, reverberated along the corridor. Jyx froze and Vyolet disappeared into the shadows beside him. Eufame drew herself up to her full height and pushed up her sleeves. A dull glow appeared in the arcane tattoos that snaked up her white arms.

"Show yourself, beast." Jyx would never have trusted himself to speak, but Eufame's voice was clear and steady.

The creature lurched forward, dragging one withered leg behind it. Jyx didn't know what it had been, but now it was a tangled torso attached to its limbs by tattered sinews. Yellow eyes burned in the wreck that was once a face, and its lower jaw hung open, displaying a mouth full of broken grey teeth. It groaned again.

"What is it?" Jyx hissed.

"I'd guess it's a former inmate," replied Eufame.

Jyx gulped. Would this have been his fate if he hadn't found Eufame? The thing lurched closer, and he resisted the urge to hide behind the necromancer general. She had power over the dead, but did that include this shambling mess?

"I think my sister knows where we are now. I suppose there weren't a lot of options from that staircase," said Eufame.

"What do we do?"

"This is barely a test, Jyx. You could beat it without even having to think too hard."

"How?"

"You worry me, you really do. All of those years of illicit study in the Academy, and that time spent working alongside me, and your first instinct is to hide behind me. Ridiculous."

The creature was close enough for Jyx to be able to smell its unique scent of grave dirt and rot. It opened its maw and howled, the tendons of its throat breaking free in the effort.

"I promised I wouldn't."

"I'm giving you permission to do so, and given the circumstances, I'm sure Vyolet does too."

Jyx checked the shadows behind the creatures. He flexed his fingers to quell the trembling in his hands and drew a deep breath. He ducked to the side of the creature, and visualised a glowing red net of energy across the scuffed floor in front of it.

"*Misit hoc rete, misit fortis, capere umbra, eam mea,*" he whispered. Scarlet tendrils appeared in the air, humming as they earthed themselves.

Eufame took two large steps backwards, and the creature lurched towards her. There was a loud snap as the red net flared into life and captured the creature's shadow. Its body swayed and fell to the floor with a wet thump. The shadow remained standing, its edges outlined with sparking lines of red energy.

"That was amazing!" Vyolet darted out of the shadows and threw her arms around Jyx.

"I thought you didn't like Shadow magick?" He blushed.

"I don't, but you've basically freed that shadow from its dead weight."

"Interesting perspective. It is certainly a basic practice, but an incredibly effective one. It's a quick way to arrest the approach of a foe, isn't it?" said Eufame.

"What do I do now?"

"Bring it with you. You never know when another pair of hands might come in useful. Besides, it's a lovely message to send to my sister."

"You don't think it might have just been a test, to check where we were? I mean, wouldn't she know you'd be able to handle something like this?" Jyx gestured to the collapsed heap of limbs behind them.

"My sister always underestimated me, just as she underestimates the Wolfkin. It's only natural that she'd underestimate an apprentice and a Shadowkin. She only knows to avoid shadows where she can, but she doesn't really know why. That, my dears, is how we'll get out of here, because she can't predict what she doesn't fully understand," said Eufame.

She ushered Vyolet and Jyx along the corridor, and Jyx gestured for the creature's shadow to follow them. It shambled behind them, faster now it was unencumbered by its decrepit earthly form. At least the shadow was silent and left the disgusting smell behind.

Moments later, another moan split the air, followed

by a second. Eufame rolled her eyes and cast her own shadow net on the floor. The two creatures dragged themselves into view, even more of a mess than the first. White bone glistened within open wounds and bruises flowered across their caved-in faces. The beasts sniffed the air and sidestepped the net.

"They've learned!" cried Jyx. He made a movement in the air, directing his shadow form to attack the two creatures, but it hung back, refusing to move. He repeated the movement, but still the shadow refused to attack.

Vyolet barrelled out of the shadows and the two creatures reached out their twisted hands to grasp at her. Their fingers almost closed on her black tunic, but when she passed them, they forgot themselves and staggered after her. A snap reverberated around the corridor and the red net earthed itself, capturing two shadows. The creatures fell to the floor in a heap.

"Excellent work, Vyolet," said Eufame. She directed the two captives to join Jyx's shadow form.

"I hope she doesn't send many more," said Jyx. He wasn't sure what would happen to the form he'd captured if he tried to create a new net.

"Do you like using Shadow magick?" Vyolet's voice trembled, and Jyx reached out his hand. She snatched her own hand away.

"I used to," replied Jyx. His hand fell and hung at his side.

"Do you like controlling shadows?"

"Only when they're shadows of something that's trying to kill me."

He stole a glance at Vyolet. She gave a tentative smile, and a spark of understanding tickled the back of his mind. He'd never thought of shadows as having their own minds or possessing any sort of independence. They were just something to control, and here was a being made of shadows scared that he might try to control her. He smiled back, hoping to ease her fears.

The corridor rounded a corner and ended abruptly, cut off by a chasm that stretched down into the depths. The passage continued on the other side, lit by blinking white lights. The three captured shadows swayed behind them.

"What do we do now?" Jyx clung to the wall with one hand and peered into the abyss.

"This is a little more challenging," replied Eufame.

"What's down there?"

"Probably nothing, and that's the worst of it. If you fall in, you'll eventually become nothing too."

Eufame tapped one finger on her chin, gazing across the chasm to the other passageway. She squinted and stared harder.

Jyx followed her look and yelped. "There are people over there!"

"What?" Vyolet leaned forward to look. Three figures stood in the passageway – a tall figure flanked by smaller ones, one of them blended into the wall. Something was behind them but Vyolet couldn't make out any details.

"Hi there!" shouted Jyx. He waved with his free arm.

His voice echoed across the space and the figure by the wall across the abyss waved back. Jyx wasn't sure if it shouted in reply or he simply heard his own voice reflected.

"Those aren't people who can help us, Jyx." Eufame grasped his arm to prevent him from waving again.

"Why not?"

"Because it's us."

Vyolet clung to Jyx, her skin turning inky. Eufame pursed her lips and glared at the figures. Jyx forced his eyes to refocus. The tall figure in the centre had white streaks in the black mane that tumbled around her shoulders. A black figure with purple eyes clung to the boy beside the wall. He recognised the confused expression on the boy's face, sure he would see it on his own if he looked in a mirror.

"What do we do?" asked Jyx.

"It's not actually us, just reflections of us," replied Eufame.

"What would happen if we got over there? Would they hurt us?"

"I don't think we can get over there."

A low moan rippled along the corridor, reaching around the corner towards them. Vyolet dug her fingers into Jyx's shoulder, and he winced. Eufame gestured and the three shadow forms shambled away around the corner to engage whatever came their way. They weren't fool proof, but they'd buy some time.

"Can you put out the lights on the other side?" asked Vyolet.

"Why?" Eufame looked at her sharply, the movement mirrored by the tall figure across the chasm.

"Well if we can't see them then they won't be there anymore."

"I can't see Bastet but I know she still exists," replied Eufame.

"Please, can you just put out the lights?"

"I can't remember the spell," said Jyx.

"That's just the atmosphere of this place. Use your Shadow magick. It's the only thing that'll get through."

Jyx made a gesture with his hand, drawing a sigil in the air with his finger. A trail of pale grey light appeared in its wake. Once he'd finished, he blew on it, and it drifted across the chasm. The puff of light stopped halfway and exploded into silver shards as it collided with an invisible field. The figures disappeared from the passageway and the lights on either side of the archway blinked out, casting the edge of the chasm into darkness.

"Oh, my sister is a clever one indeed!" cried Eufame.

"What?" Jyx stared at the shower of sparks that fell into the abyss.

"The chasm isn't actually that wide – there's a mirror enchantment on it so that it seems twice as wide as it actually is. Vyolet, you've seen where the light exploded – could you jump that far?"

"I think so," said Vyolet.

Another low moan sounded around the corner, this one closer than the one before. There was a scuffle and something snarled. The shadow forms had found the pursuers at least, but judging by the tearing sound and the fizzle of dying energy, they wouldn't hold them back for much longer.

Eufame clapped her hands together and held them up. The lights in the corridor dimmed as her hands glowed, until a pool of darkness filled the passage.

Vyolet didn't wait. She grabbed Jyx and Eufame by the hand and ran towards the abyss.

A hand snatched at Jyx's robe, tearing a patch from the hem as Vyolet hauled him across the chasm. Jyx didn't know if he was running across the chasm or through the shadows, but the darkness provided a comforting blanket across his vision. The shadows rippled around him, holding him safely. No more hands gripped his clothing and he allowed himself to breathe as his feet hit solid ground once more.

"As fun as it is, I don't think I'll ever get used to that mode of travel." Eufame straightened her robe and tucked her hair behind her ears.

"It's saved my life more than once," replied Vyolet.

Across the chasm, a cluster of shambling creatures gathered on the ledge they'd just vacated. The tattered remains of a shadow, outlined in red, hung from the clawed fist of the lead beast.

"What are they?" asked Vyolet.

"I dread to think. My sister obviously found them

among the very worst of the dungeon inhabitants," replied Eufame.

"Is she a necromancer too?"

"She's a sorceress, but she has dabbled in necromancy in her time. But, come on, we don't want to hang around here any longer than we have to. You must be able to smell the sewers by now."

The scent of sewage hung in the air, far stronger on this side of the chasm. Jyx realised he'd become accustomed to the smell and shuddered.

The three of them headed off down the corridor. It curved away from the chasm, the blinking white lights singing a peculiar melody as they passed. The tune wormed its way into Jyx's mind, prompting him to hum along.

"What are you humming?" asked Vyolet.

"Can't you hear it? The lights are singing," replied Jyx.

"That's ridiculous. Lights don't sing."

"These ones do. They're light sprites," said Eufame. "They only shine when they're asleep and they sing in their dreams. It's all rather sweet, if you like that sort of thing."

Vyolet grimaced. Jyx laughed and tried to peer closer whenever they passed a light. He couldn't see anything within, but he liked the idea of a tiny creature curled up inside it, singing as it slept. If it was true, it was the only positive thing they'd encountered in the entire House of Correction, apart from the Wolfkin.

The corridor led ever downwards and they listened for the sound of more moans or groans behind them. Jyx found it easier to be alert; the gauze drifting across his mind thinned as they descended and his thoughts didn't shy away whenever he tried to grasp them. Incantations and forgotten spells danced before his mind's eye, and his fingers itched to draw sigils in the air and bring magick to the tunnels.

"Ah! We're nearly there!" Eufame cried out and broke into a run down the corridor.

Jyx and Vyolet ran after her.

Eufame stood before an opening in the wall, blocked by a metal grate. Darkness lay beyond and the sound of dripping water echoed within the tunnel. Jyx wrinkled his nose at the terrible smell emanating from the opening. Eufame curled her fingers around the bars and pulled. Nothing. The grate didn't even budge.

"Can you use magick on it?" Jyx was surprised how little magick Eufame had actually used since they'd sprung her from her cell.

"Not if it's part of the building fabric. As much as it pains me to admit it, Naiad is stronger than me, Jyx. Though once we're out of here, it'll be no holds barred." Eufame ran her hands over the grate, searching for a weak point.

"I might be able to sneak through. There's a sliver of shadow on this side, and plenty on that." Vyolet pointed through the grate at the shadow cast by the bars.

"There will be no need for that."

A voice echoed inside Jyx's mind, both canine and human at the same time. Jyx turned around, expecting to see Validus, but instead he saw a Wolfkin with the golden skin and fur of a House of Correction guard.

Eufame smiled when she faced the newcomer, and Jyx was struck again by how alive Eufame's face became whenever she broke into a genuine smile. The Wolfkin bowed to her.

"Ah! Finally, someone with some sense. Do you have a way for us to pass through the grate and out into the sewers?" she asked.

Vyolet shrank back, away from Eufame, and Jyx realised Eufame had spoken aloud using the barks and yips associated with Wolfkin communication.

"I do."

The Wolfkin stepped forward and placed both of its paws on the grate. Golden light surrounded the Wolfkin's head, racing down its arms, through its hands, and into the bars. Jyx stared open-mouthed at such an easy display of magick. He longed for the day when he could access pure energy, without needing to use incantations or sigils. Maybe the Wolfkin would teach him. After all, they'd already given him the gift of Wolfkin communication.

The grate shimmered and disappeared from view. Jyx could still faintly see its outline, picked out in gold, but to Vyolet, the bars were gone. She hopped through and vanished into the darkness of the tunnel beyond.

"Come along, Jyx. This fine fellow can't hold the gate open all day," said Eufame. Jyx darted through the opening, followed by Eufame.

On the other side, Jyx lurched towards the wall and stared at the wet arch of brick above him. A huge weight was lifted from him and he smelled magick in the air. Pure energy hummed around him. On impulse, he scooped up a handful of moss from the wall of the tunnel and drew a sigil above it. He tossed it to Vyolet, her aura glowing purple in the shadows, and the moss dissolved into a handful of violet petals in her hands.

Vyolet giggled and clapped. "That was wonderful! Do it again!"

Jyx repeated the gesture, and Vyolet brought the handful of petals to her face. The violet of the flowers matched her eyes.

"Ah, you're free again. Very good," said Eufame. She reached forward to pick a stray petal out of Vyolet's hair.

"I had no idea the House was so oppressive!" said Jyx.

"That's why we didn't use much magick. Naiad has little time for Shadow magick, believing it to be below her, which is another belief she holds regarding the Wolfkin. She doesn't accept that they have magick of their own," replied Eufame.

The Wolfkin uncurled its fingers and the gate re-appeared in a flash of golden light. It stood on the other side, still inside the House. Jyx moved towards the bars and gazed up at the guard. It looked so much like Validus, except for the colour of its fur.

"Won't you come with us?" asked Jyx.

"I cannot. As long as I remain in this spot, Miss Delsenza's sister cannot sense her. I will return to my duties once you are safely away," replied the Wolfkin.

"Won't you get into trouble?"

"I am but one Wolfkin, Master Faire. Your mission is far greater than mine." With that, the Wolfkin turned his back on them, standing guard at the grate.

Eufame reached through the bars and squeezed his shoulder. He gave a small nod in reply.

"Come along, Jyx, Vyolet. We've got a lot to do, and not a lot of time in which to do it." Eufame plunged along the tunnel, away from the grate. She held aloft her left hand and conjured flames of silver light.

Jyx and Vyolet took each other's hands and followed.

Chapter 16

The tunnel led into the sewers, brick-lined corridors with vaulted ceilings like the chapels in the temple. Ledges ran the length of each wall to allow workers to keep their feet out of the bulk of the sewage. The trio walked along the ledges in single file, and Jyx curled his toes around the edge of the platform as he inched along behind Vyolet. Eufame took the lead, holding aloft her flickering silver light. The flames cast shadows up the walls that danced and twisted as she moved. Jyx wasn't sure what the spell was, but the flames also seemed to hold the stench at bay.

"Will your sister know we're gone yet?" Jyx's voice echoed around him.

"Undoubtedly, but unfortunately for her, she can't venture beyond the House of Correction. She's the only thing holding it together and, unless she wants it tumbling down, she'll stay there," replied Eufame.

"Will she send anything after us?" asked Vyolet, sounding small in the darkness.

"She may try, but her power is limited beyond

the confines of the House. Our biggest worry is if the City Guard are mobilised to re-arrest me, so we need to sort this whole mess out before that happens," replied Eufame.

Jyx thought about Eufame and her relationship to the House of the Long Dead. It couldn't be a coincidence that her sister was also in charge of a House.

"Eufame, why is it that your sister can't leave her House without it collapsing, but you can leave yours?"

"That's an excellent question, and one with a very simple answer. I had my House built out of actual stone, not souls."

"But the House of the Long Dead is really old!" replied Vyolet.

"So am I." Eufame turned and flashed a smile at Vyolet, and the stiffness eased in Jyx's shoulders before he even realised he'd been tense. Eufame's aura didn't feel as black as it normally was. Since leaving the House of Correction, her tone had been lighter. Maybe she'd felt as oppressed as Jyx had, and probably more so, since it was her sister who was in charge of the oppression. Jyx tried to picture an older Delsenza sibling, but his brain kept short-circuiting and focusing on Vyolet's hair bobbing in front of him instead.

"What's the actual plan now that you're free?"

"I might as well tell you, since you were good enough to get me out of that hole. Have you ever heard of the Heart of the City?" asked Eufame.

"Yes, every kid knows that story," replied Jyx.

"It's not just a story, though," said Vyolet.

"What?"

"It's real. It's somewhere beneath the Underground City. It's just no one actually knows where it is now."

"How can there be anything beneath the Underground City? I thought it was as low as you got," said Jyx.

"There are lots of things below it. The Shrine of Beseda, for one thing. The sewers. Tombs. But there are the ruins of a much older city below it too, and the Heart of the City is somewhere down there. I have to find it."

"Why?"

"Whoever controls the Heart controls both Cities. I don't want to control them, I just want to use the Heart to sweep the corruption out of the council."

"Is that because they're after your job?" asked Vyolet.

"I would never be that vindictive. No, I am fed up with having to block the asinine plans of the councillors who only want to line their own pockets. I've spoken with long-dead rulers, and they've asked me to do something about it. The council is taking the City Above in the wrong direction, and they can't be allowed to clear the Underground City. The two need to act in harmony if they're going to survive," replied Eufame.

The tunnel opened onto a wider sewer, with a river of waste rushing along before them. The ledges continued along either side of the larger tunnel, and a doorway cut into the wall across the river. A white mark had been carved into the brick behind them.

"Wait, I know where we are!" cried Vyolet. She traced the mark with her finger.

"You do?" asked Eufame.

"Yes, this isn't far from the Flee Market. It's known as Lost Dare Gap," replied Vyolet. "The urchins used to come down here and dare each other to jump over to here from that doorway." She pointed across the river.

Waste churned and bubbled within the black water. Nausea burned in Jyx's throat.

"Used to?" Eufame raised an eyebrow.

"There were a lot of accidents, so they found new ways to challenge each other that didn't involve anything so gross. The Shadowkin took over the sewers instead to hide in, but we don't often come this far into the network. I never knew why, but being down here, I can see it's too close to the House of Correction."

"Are you sure?"

"Yes, this is my brother Benjamin's mark. It's not new, probably about six months old, but we just need to get across there, and there's a ladder which'll take us up into the service tunnels above the sewers, and you can walk straight out of those into the City."

"I didn't know there was a link between the City Above and the Underground City," said Jyx.

"I'd hardly call the House of Correction a link, but there are passageways all over the place if you know where to look. Sadly, I don't, because geography has never been a strong point of mine," replied Eufame. "Now I think our priority is crossing this river."

"Jumping it isn't going to work," replied Vyolet.

"No, I have no intention of falling into sewage. I think young Jyx here should be the one to solve the problem," said Eufame.

"I don't know what to do! I can't conjure a bridge out of thin air," replied Jyx.

"No but try to think laterally. How else could you cross moving water?" asked Eufame.

"You could freeze it." Vyolet peered over the edge into the river and wrinkled her nose.

"I don't know how to freeze things. I didn't get to that at the Academy."

"But you do know how to un-freeze things." Eufame gave him a pointed look. A memory scudded across his mind's eye; he saw himself wandering into the Ornamental Garden in the Academy grounds, and leaning over a bridge to peer into the frozen stream. Faces looked up at him from beneath the ice, reflections caught by the water. He drew a sigil, and threw a stone, and the ice cracked.

"Does that work in reverse?" He didn't want to

know how Eufame knew about that. Her crow spy had probably told her.

"Give it a go." Eufame smiled.

Jyx practised drawing the sigil to unfreeze ice several times in the air then faced the torrent of sewage. It bubbled and frothed just inches beneath the lip of the ledge on which he stood. He drew the sigil in reverse, wondering if there was an incantation to go with it. He'd never used one to thaw ice.

Nothing happened. The river continued to roar past them.

"Try it again, and this time put some oomph into it," said Eufame.

"Is that a technical term?" Jyx muttered under his breath and pushed up his sleeves. He concentrated, visualising a cold wind blowing up the river towards them. He pictured the sewage coming to a standstill, the water becoming solid and freezing the river mid-flow. He drew the sigil again, and this time pushed it into the deluge.

A sudden blast of cold air roared up the tunnel, whipping Eufame's hair away from her face. Its wintry fingers plunged into the water, turning the river to ice. Solid clumps of matter paused, caught in the frozen embrace. Further upstream, the ice groaned where the oncoming river pressed against it, desperate to break through.

"We haven't got long," said Jyx.

Vyolet streaked across the ice so fast her feet barely touched the surface. She stood just inside the doorway in the opposite wall. Eufame strode after her, flicking her fingers as she walked. The ice crystallised into a fine powder of crystals so she wouldn't slip.

Jyx stepped down onto the frozen river. It shifted beneath him, and he swore under his breath. He tried to hurry, but water flowed beneath the thick crust of ice. A crack appeared to his left, and a thin trickle of brown sludge forced its way upwards, spilling onto the ice. Eufame reached the other side and stepped up beside Vyolet. Jyx focused on the crystal path left by Eufame, placing his feet inside her footprints.

"Jyx, it won't last much longer," called Eufame.

Jyx glared at her and considered using another sigil, but he didn't have time to pause on the ice. He broke into a run and got one foot onto the ledge when a huge crack split the ice behind him. The water roared beneath, springing up wherever it found room, and the ice splintered into small frozen islands. Vyolet reached out and grasped Jyx's hand pulling him onto the ledge. No sooner had his other foot touched the brickwork, the river overwhelmed the ice, and the remains of his spell disappeared away down the tunnel.

"Why didn't you do something to stop the water coming through?" Jyx glared at Eufame again.

"You may be my apprentice, Jyx, but I won't always be around to help you out. You need to learn how to do things for yourself. If you were truly in danger, naturally I would have stepped in, but you were not in any immediate peril," replied Eufame.

"Don't you care about him?" asked Vyolet, still clutching Jyx's hand.

"Of course I do, but Jyx will become a much more powerful mage when he learns to solve his own problems. I learned an awful lot through having to think on my feet," replied Eufame.

She swept through the doorway past Vyolet. Jyx followed. The dark anteroom led to a narrow, rickety metal staircase that ascended into the gloom above. Eufame's feet disappeared into the darkness. Vyolet let go of Jyx's hand and sprang upwards through the shadows. Jyx sighed and began the steady climb out of the sewers.

The smell subsided as they ascended, replaced instead by damp brick and moss. Jyx's eyes adjusted, and the dim outlines of the steps melted out of the darkness.

They climbed in silence and the staircase brought them into a second anteroom. A heavy wooden door occupied most of the wall opposite the stairs, with a second low door set into the larger gate. A familiar figure stood, half cloaked in shadows by the stairs.

"Validus!" cried Jyx. Without thinking, he darted forward and hugged the Wolfkin.

The Wolfkin patted him on the shoulder with a giant hand. "Master Faire. Mistress, and little Miss Vyolet. I am pleased to see you all." Validus's voice echoed in Jyx's head, and he disentangled himself to relay the message to Vyolet.

"My sister didn't make things easy, but as you see, we've made it," said Eufame.

"How did you know we'd be here?" asked Jyx.

"I heard from a mutual acquaintance that you'd entered the sewers. I guessed that you would emerge here."

"Very good. We don't have a lot of time to lose. Jyx, Vyolet, I must accompany Validus to the Wolfkin archives. I don't doubt that they have information that will be of use to the quest. Jyx, I want you to go and check on your family, and await my next instructions. Vyolet, I need you to be my messenger. You're the fastest of us, and you can evade detection," said Eufame.

"Where's my mother now?"

Eufame relayed an address, and Jyx committed it to memory. His family had moved to a new tenement not far from the temple – Jyx guessed Eufame had chosen it because the City Guard wouldn't be keen to cause a commotion near a house of worship.

Validus handed Jyx a new robe, this one purple instead of apprentice red. He hauled the red one over his head to swap the clothing while Validus passed his mistress a hooded cloak. Eufame tucked her hair out of view. The hood cast shadows across her face, and she muttered an incantation under her breath. Her features shimmered, and resettled in the expression of an old human woman. Wrinkles clustered around her eyes and mouth.

"This should keep me safe for now," she said. Eufame squeezed Jyx's shoulder, and followed Validus out into the street. Vyolet plunged after them, casting a final glance behind her before the doorway swallowed her up.

Jyx pulled up his own hood. He waited in the darkness for a few moments, before slipping through the doorway and into the Underground City.

Chapter 17

Vyolet tailed Eufame and the Wolfkin named Validus through the narrow alleyways near the Flee Market. So much had happened since her last visit here. She pressed herself against the walls, skipping from shadow to shadow. They passed city dwellers wearing DWS patches, but thankfully they didn't wear the goggles so beloved of the City Guard. Eufame and Validus might protect her, but she'd rather not test the theory.

Vyolet knew the alleyways and hidden passages of the Underground City well, a vast network of shadow streets that twisted and turned beneath the flickering gaslight, but she couldn't work out where the Wolfkin might keep their archives. Until recently, she hadn't known they even had archives – which was clearly the point. She couldn't work out why such a powerful and intelligent race wanted to remain enslaved by humans, though they probably had their own reasons. After all, letting humans think they were nothing more than guard dogs let them get on with their own endeavours away from any prying eyes.

They kept to the canal side of the Underground City, leaving the Flee Market behind them. Darting through the labyrinth, they reached the edge of the warehouse district, and Validus led them down through the narrow streets to the jetties that ran the length of the canal. The dockers ignored them, and Validus pointed out a raft moored in the shadows away from the hustle and bustle. A hooded figure sat on it, muscular arms protruding from the sackcloth cloak, and huge, paw-like hands curled around a long pole that disappeared into the dark water.

Eufame stepped onto the raft first, and sat down on the bare wood beside the figure. Validus helped Vyolet onto the raft, and stepped up behind her. The figure raised his free hand and made a familiar sign – 'Please sit'.

"Fortis!" Vyolet's voice broke the quiet, and her hand flew to her mouth as if she could grasp the name and pull it back before it was heard.

The figure signed a greeting, and Vyolet sat beside him, as close as she could get without sitting in his lap. At least now she'd be able to understand what was being said – Eufame and Validus communicated in a complex series of barks and yips.

Validus took the pole from Fortis, and used it to push the raft away from the jetty. They drifted along the canal, and Validus guided their course with nudges and prods from the pole. Vyolet kept her millions of questions to herself and snuggled closer to the Wolfkin, enjoying the warmth he radiated. They passed other vessels on the canal, but no one paid them any heed.

After a few minutes of silent travel, Vyolet studied Eufame. She sat on the other side of Fortis, her brow knitted in furious concentration. Both hands rested on her knees, the palms facing upwards, and a black haze hung above her fingers. Tiny sparks flittered through the haze, spinning up into the air to fall again like silver rain around them. Vyolet said nothing – she recognised a cloaking enchantment when she saw one.

Smaller watercourses branched off the main canal, disappearing into archways hewn from the cliff face that formed the boundary of the Underground City. Validus chose one distinguished only by the almost imperceptible sigil cut into the rock.

Once they were safely inside the tunnel, Eufame broke her concentration and clapped her hands. The black haze evaporated and the last of the silver sparks winked out of existence. Her disguise faded, and she resumed her usual haughty expression. She cracked her knuckles and held her hand aloft, conjuring the silver flames she'd used to illuminate the House of Correction.

The canal ran through a narrow tunnel only barely high enough to allow Validus to remain standing. Pick marks remained in the stone from the tools used to originally hack the tunnel out of the rock. Eufame's flames only lit the water for a short distance, but Vyolet could make out light further along. A warm rose glow grew brighter as they approached, until Eufame snapped her illumination out with a flick of her fingers.

The tunnel opened out into a large chamber hewn from the rock, before continuing on the other side of the room. A platform ran the length of the chamber and braziers burned at either side of the stairs leading up from the jetty. A white Wolfkin stood on the platform, wearing a black tunic and leggings not dissimilar from Vyolet's. The Wolfkin's body curved around the chest, honed to a fine waist before blossoming out into wide hips. A long white tail curled around the Wolfkin's right leg, resting on its knee.

Validus brought the raft to a stop, and the Wolfkin leaned down to offer its hand, thinner and more delicate than that of Fortis, but still markedly a paw, to Vyolet. She stepped up onto the jetty, followed by Fortis. Validus helped Eufame onto the platform.

"Vyolet, this is Mara. Mara, this is Vyolet, our Shadowkin messenger. You know everyone else," signed Fortis.

Vyolet smiled at Mara.

"I have always wanted to meet a Shadowkin! You are most welcome here," said Mara, forming the Shadow Speak with awkward hands.

Mara turned and led them up the stairs and into another corridor, lit by rose-coloured flames. Vyolet tried to count the number of corridors in which she'd found herself during the past few days and gave up.

"You should be honoured, Vyolet, few but Wolfkin ever see these archives. Even I've only been in them once before." Eufame's voice echoed around the low tunnel, and she fell into step beside Vyolet. The temperature dropped several degrees in her presence, and Vyolet longed for Fortis's warmth.

"What do they do here?"

"They guard their knowledge. Do the Shadowkin have archives?" Eufame gave Vyolet a sideways look, and Vyolet realised that the necromancer general didn't really know a great deal about her kind.

"I don't know. I suppose so. I've never really had much to do with the Shadowkin since I was little. My mother disappeared when I was young, so I grew up in and around the Flee Market, running errands and so on. I only see my brother occasionally."

"You don't just run errands now, though?"

"No, I have a wider skill set. I've been called a rogue, a thief, and a spy, though I usually just steal information. I've been a lot busier these past few weeks."

"I'm not surprised. Machinations against the Underground City have really stepped up a gear. I daresay you've intercepted a lot of important communications from the City Above."

Vyolet opened her mouth to reply, but the group stopped as the corridor ended in a pitted door of dark wood. Carved sigils covered its surface, and Mara held her hand against a whirled design in the central panel. She barked twice and the door swung inwards.

A huge, vaulted room opened out before her. Long tables ran down the centre of the room and bookshelves lined the outer walls. More cases formed aisles along either side of the tables. Vyolet and Eufame stepped into the space behind Mara, but Validus and Fortis stayed behind in the corridor.

"Aren't they coming in too?" asked Vyolet.

"The archives are the preserve of female Wolfkin," replied Mara.

Validus barked a goodbye to Eufame, and Fortis wrapped his hands around the simple sign for 'I will see you later'. The male Wolfkin turned and walked back down the tunnel, and Mara closed the door behind them.

"You'll have to be my interpreter now. I can talk to Mara in Wolfkin but you won't understand, so I'll speak to her aloud, and then you can interpret her Shadow Speak replies," said Eufame.

Vyolet raised one eyebrow but said nothing. Tales abounded about Eufame Delsenza, the dreaded necromancer general of the House of the Long Dead, but all of them described her as a cold, distant and somewhat cruel figure. None of them considered her to be in any way thoughtful.

"Mara, the Wolfkin were some of the earliest inhabitants of the Underground City. What drew you here?" asked Eufame.

"We once lived in the forests where the City Above now stands. There was a harsh winter and we descended into the caverns to seek shelter. We found the Underground City, still in its infancy, and at first, we were welcomed as both teachers and protectors," replied Mara.

She gestured to a vast fresco on the wall above the bookcases behind them, depicting female Wolfkin surrounded by human children, with male Wolfkin standing guard at the door. Vyolet scowled. She'd seen it before, on one of the chapel walls in the temple, with one difference – the Wolfkin had been replaced by smiling humans. Vyolet related what Mara had signed, and told Eufame of the copycat painting. A dark cloud settled across the necromancer's face and a spark of fear flared in Vyolet's gut.

"Had you ever heard stories of an earlier City, below this one?" asked Eufame.

"Yes. Many of my ancestors searched for it. Some of our number continue to do so."

"Why?" asked Vyolet.

"Many reasons. We are a curious race; we like to explore. We like to know things. We like to study the people who have gone before. How did people live in a City so much further underground? What happened to it? It is also said to house many treasures."

"Like what?"

"The Heart of the City is rumoured to be down there." Mara got up from the table and disappeared among the stacks.

"Humans make me sick." Eufame kept her voice low. "They've completely legislated the Wolfkin into subservience. Imagine what they could teach the idiots that live in both Cities."

"Can I ask you something?" asked Vyolet.

"You may."

"If you're not a human, what are you?"

To Vyolet's surprise, Eufame laughed. Her face creased in mirth and the severity of her sharp features dissolved. The giggle that erupted from the necromancer did not sound at all like a noise that a truly soulless being could make, and Vyolet found herself smiling in return. Some of the Wolfkin looked across at their table, but their expressions were those of curiosity, not annoyance.

"I'm descended from a race that evolved to look like humans. Millennia ago, I wouldn't have looked the way I do now. There aren't many of us left, but that's mostly because all but my siblings left to explore other planes of existence. We do so while staying on this one," replied Eufame.

"Is that why you can go beyond the Veil?"

"It's one of the reasons. Humans call my race banshees but it's a lot more complicated than that. We're a lot older than that term, believe me."

Mara returned holding a large book bound in deep red leather. She opened it and flicked through its yellowed pages. Vyolet inhaled the scent of ancient knowledge and old paper and smiled. Laughter sparkled in the Wolfkin's black eyes.

"Here," said Mara, laying the book on the table.

Vyolet and Eufame peered at the woodcut illustration on the open page. It showed a mighty female warrior, wearing a tall, plumed helmet and bearing a shield and long thin spear. She wore a long robe, clasped at the shoulder.

"This is the goddess of the First City, as we call it. You know her legend, yes?"

Eufame and Vyolet nodded.

"It is her heart that is the Heart of the City. The common belief is that whoever controls her heart controls the twin Cities, but this is a misconception. No one can control a warrior goddess. However, whoever wakes her can lay their case to her and she may protect the Cities."

"Ah, now that sounds more like what we need," said Eufame. "I didn't like the sound of trying to control a goddess who died fighting a hydra."

"Validus has told me of the problems with the City Council, and I think she would be most helpful in preventing the destruction of the Underground City. However, there are two issues that you must be aware of."

"Yes?"

"First, the Heart is broken."

"It's what?" Eufame stared at Mara, her wintry eyes wide.

Vyolet gazed at the woodcut in the book, trying to imagine what could possibly break the heart of a goddess, particularly one that had been dead for centuries.

"It is broken. When the goddess died, she turned to stone. The Almighty Crack was the sound of her heart breaking."

"Damn. That's a problem indeed. What's the other issue?"

"You're not the only one seeking it."

The dark cloud descended across Eufame's face for a second time, and Vyolet shuddered to think of the storm it might unleash.

CHAPTER 18

Jyx made his way through the alleyways of the Underground City, putting the Flee Market behind him. He'd loved it as a child, enjoying its hustle and bustle and diverse array of wares. He'd grown to hate it during his teenage years, seeing it as a pale shadow of the vast market of wonders in Monument Square in the City Above. So much of the Underground City disgusted him in comparison, yet he still called it home. Even if he managed to become a mage in the Autumn Gloaming, he'd never fit in Above. He'd always be "that boy who grew up Underground".

Validus walked tall and proud, and Jyx tried to emulate him. If he either ran or tried to hide in the shadows, he'd draw attention to himself, so he held his back straight and tried to move as Eufame did. No urchins approached him, and housewives veered out of his path.

The old tenement he once called home lay in Green Dragon Close, near the boundary thoroughfare of Edge Street. He didn't know the area around the temple well at all, and the unfamiliar street signs gave no clues as to the whereabouts of Holst Alley. He couldn't even ask anyone if they knew where to find Housewife Faire, since Eufame changed her name before the family relocated. He'd have to find the house itself.

Green Dragon Close stood in a network of narrow alleys, boasting grimy windows and gas lamps that flickered endlessly whenever they bothered to light at all. By contrast, the district near the temple was more well to do. Bow windows protruded into the street to advertise the wares of the shops. Metal signs hung high up on the walls to alert passers-by to the presence of craftspeople and their workshops in the neighbourhood. Gas lamps burned near the signs, casting clean white light into the street below.

A shop on his left caught his attention. Books crowded its narrow window, decorated with small clay figures and silk flowers. Gold paint picked out the name of the shop on a faded wooden sign above the window, advertising the bookseller as being "Mr PT Rosemary". A tiny sigil, representing 'Peace', appeared in the wooden lintel above the door and Jyx recognised the scratchmarks as the work of a passing Wolfkin.

He pushed open the door and a tiny bell jangled above his head. Books covered every available surface, crammed together on creaking shelves and leaning against the walls in piles almost as tall as Jyx. More clay figures peeped out from behind the leather-bound tomes, and Jyx recognised them as the same ibis-headed deity he'd seen in Eufame's library. Silk flowers stood in black vases between more piles of books on low tables around the room. White figures of animal-headed people drawn in profile decorated the vases.

An elderly man stood behind the counter. He wore

a tweed waistcoat and matching trousers, with red silk bands around the billowing sleeves of his white shirt at the shoulder and elbow. At the sound of the bell, he looked up from polishing his spectacles.

"Ah, good day to you, my young fellow." He smiled, his eyes twinkling behind the spectacles as he pushed them back up his nose.

"Hello. Are you Mr Rosemary?" asked Jyx.

"I am. And to whom am I speaking?"

"Markus. Markus Prady." The name of his old school friend, perhaps his only friend at the Academy, sprang to his lips.

"Master Prady, eh?"

Jyx nodded, but Mr Rosemary narrowed his eyes slightly, peering at a spot just above Jyx's left shoulder. Jyx swallowed hard and drew himself up to his full height. He'd had a growth spurt during the past few months and wasn't used to being almost six feet tall.

"Well then. Is there something I can help you find?"

"Actually, I'm after directions. Do you know where I can find Holst Alley?"

"And what do you want with Holst Alley?"

"Someone told me the finest seamstress in the City lives there and I've torn my Academy robes."

"Academy, eh?" Mr Rosemary eyed the House of the Long Dead insignia on the front of his purple robes, and Jyx mentally kicked himself.

"Yes, that's why I'm wearing these. I couldn't possibly disgrace the Academy by wearing the ones I tore. The rip is in a, ahem, delicate place," replied Jyx. Lying made him uncomfortable, but he didn't know if he could trust Mr Rosemary. Just because he had a sigil on the door and familiar statues around the room didn't mean he was safe.

"I quite understand. Then you need to simply continue along this street until you come to Grieg Close.

Turn down there, and Holst Alley is the third on your left."

"Thank you."

"Quite all right, and Master Faire, I'd see about applying a mirror enchantment if I were you," said Mr Rosemary.

Jyx froze by the door, his hand curled around the handle.

"Yes, I recognised you the minute you came in the door. Don't worry, few people would, but we have some mutual friends. They've got eyes and ears everywhere on your behalf, but there are other folk who are looking for you for other reasons."

"Who?"

"I'm not strong enough to detect that, but not everyone looks on you with a kindly eye."

"What should I do?" A bead of cold sweat trickled down Jyx's back.

"Here. There are plenty of mirror spells in here. Any one of them will help deflect attention away from you." Mr Rosemary reached below the counter and pulled out a thin leather-bound book. He pushed it towards Jyx.

"Wouldn't Shadow magick do the same thing?"

"Yes, but that's what you'd be expected to use. Always do the unexpected and no one will ever predict what you'll do next." Mr Rosemary stepped back from the counter and put his hands in his pockets.

Satisfied that the bookseller wouldn't grab his wrists and call for the City Guard, Jyx edged towards the counter. He picked up the book, and read the title. *Speculum fascinatio – Mirror Magick*.

"How much is it?"

"Don't worry, Miss Delsenza has an account here. I'll add it to that. She can thank me later. Hm, I think you should have this, too."

Mr Rosemary handed Jyx a small pouch of sand. He nodded once and bustled away into the next room, saying hello to someone Jyx couldn't see. Jyx hurried to the door before the unseen observer could catch him.

A cat mewed. Jyx paused, and turned around. Bastet stood in the doorway, twitching the tip of her tail.

"Bastet!" Jyx bent down, and Bastet trotted across the shop. She rubbed her head against his hand, purring as she curled her tail around his wrist.

"Is this guy all right then?" he asked in a low whisper.

Bastet mewed again, pausing long enough during the petting to stare into his eyes. That sealed it. If Mr Rosemary was good enough for Bastet, then he was good enough for Jyx.

Bastet flicked the book with her tail, and it fell onto the floor. Jyx read the spell on the open page, printed in neat black letters on the off-white page. The enchantment was simple enough and would reflect any gaze back to its owner. It was only temporary, but it should last long enough to get him to his mother's house.

"*Speculum mihi incumbit, ob auertat!*" Jyx pronounced the words with a flourish, drawing the appropriate sigil in the air in front of his face. The air around him hummed and tiny blue sparks flickered at the edge of his vision to tell him the enchantment was in place.

"I'll see you soon Bastet – I'll try to come back this way," said Jyx, giving Bastet a final scratch behind the ears. She mewed and sat on the floor. He made his way to the door and left the shop.

CHAPTER 19

Monte and Mr Gondavere reached Lockevar's Gate after several detours and backtracks through the streets of the Canal Quarter. Mr Gondavere again suspected pursuers and ducked into doorways every time a boot scuffed the pavement behind them.

"You never know who is watching, Monte. The City Above, more so than its underground twin, requires constant vigilance," said Mr Gondavere.

Monte grew weary of the delays – while he enjoyed the prolonged time in the fresh air of the City Above, he was impatient for the chance to eat and rest in familiar surroundings.

At last the gate loomed into view, and they reached the barrier. Willum remained on guard and opened for them from the Underground City side. He smiled and clapped Monte on the back.

"'Ere, yer wasn't there long, Monte!"

"I know, we got things wrapped up quicker than we thought." Monte shook his friend's outstretched hand.

"Many thanks for your assistance, my good man," said Mr Gondavere.

The gate closed behind him. A new group of petitioners clustered around the guard's hut, casting evil looks at Mr Gondavere and curious stares at Monte. His shabby clothes marked him out as an inhabitant of the Underground City, and Monte didn't want to be seen as a traitor to his home by going Above.

Willum grabbed his wrist. "Just be careful, yeah?" Willum looked from the group of petitioners back to Monte.

Monte nodded and followed Mr Gondavere along the cobbled road leading back into the Underground City.

"I must ask you, how far do you live from the graveyard that you service?" asked Mr Gondavere.

"I work in three different yards, sir, but I live in the outer wall of the Canalsditch cemetery," replied Monte.

"Then perhaps I may journey with you a little further after all. I require quiet in order to fully consult my sources, and there are surely few places as quiet as a graveyard, would you agree?"

Monte nodded. Who on earth could his sources be? He glanced at the petitioners by the gate, and two of them had broken away from the main group. They loitered nearby, but pretended to study the list of items that were prohibited from being carried into the City Above. Monte steered Mr Gondavere into the crowd.

"What do you think you're doing?" asked Mr Gondavere.

"Not everyone looks on us with a good eye, sir. The people waiting to see if they'll be allowed Above didn't look very friendly."

Mr Gondavere nodded then hailed a cart and paid a journeyman to allow them to ride in the back with his goods. Monte kept his eyes fixed on the crowd they left behind.

The two petitioners appeared. They started towards the cart but the journeyman cracked his whip and the horse lurched into motion. Four figures clad in blood red uniforms burst out of the crowd.

"Look! Council guards!" Monte pointed them out to Mr Gondavere. The guards surrounded the two men. One of the guards raised his baton. The cart trundled around a corner, but the wet sound of wood on flesh smacked in the air.

"I am scarcely surprised that the City Above has sent its own guards below. These vermin must be taught some discipline," said Mr Gondavere.

"Be careful what you say, sir," said Monte. He stole a glance at the journeyman, but he either hadn't heard or was pretending not to listen. Monte frowned. It seemed the rumours of council guard beatings were true, after all.

Mr Gondavere sat beside him and balanced his chin on one hand, lost in contemplation. They didn't speak during the rest of the trip across the City, heading ever downwards towards Canalsditch. The journeyman dropped them off at the edge of the district, and his horse clopped away down the street towards the warehouses.

* * *

Canalsditch was so named for its position alongside the mighty canal that disappeared into the cliff face, eventually coming out at the Distant Sea. Unlike the rest of the Underground City, its houses were individual dwellings, small cottages clustered together around crooked squares that provided meeting places for wakes or other funeral celebrations at the nearby graveyard. Monte's own cottage clung to the cemetery wall, swelling from the stone like a boil. A small iron gate set into the wall allowed access directly into the graveyard from Monte's house.

"Welcome to my home, sir," said Monte. He opened the gate into the small front yard, its hinges protesting at the movement with a whine. Night-scented stock and jasmine bloomed in the borders on either side of the brick path, with evening ivy clinging to the walls of the cottage around the front door. A candle burned in the front window.

"Your garden is delightful," replied Mr Gondavere. The note of genuine surprise irritated Monte. Just because he lived in the Underground City didn't mean he had to live in a hovel.

"It's all the work of my Myrtle," said Monte.

He opened the front door, but Mr Gondavere paused on the path, halfway up the yard.

"I shall refrain from coming in, Monte. I see a gate into the graveyard – I shall avail myself of the peace and quiet I shall find in there, and call back for you in a few hours. I have been searching for some weeks now, so I daresay allowing you time to rest will not make much difference."

"Are you sure? You don't want to meet the missus?"

"Perhaps when I come back to call for you." Mr Gondavere gave that dreadful smile then followed a narrow, slightly overgrown path to the gate into the graveyard. It swung open on silent hinges, and within moments he was swallowed up by the darkness beyond.

Monte passed through the doorway into the front room, where a set of steps led upwards to the bedroom above and a low doorway led through into the back parlour and kitchen. An indoor privy lay to his right, just off the front room. Of all the things in his home, the privy was his proudest achievement. Only two other houses in Canalsditch boasted indoor sanitation.

Myrtle sat in the rocking chair by the fire, her

knitting in her lap and her head resting on her shoulder. Gentle snores rumbled in her throat. The firelight softened the angles and planes of her face, and she reminded him of the pretty young slip of a girl he'd fallen in love with at the Grainger wake twelve years ago.

Monte smiled and picked up the blanket from the floor. He laid it across her knees, tucking it around her, and tiptoed across the room to the stairs. He climbed them two at a time, careful to avoid the fourth and eighth steps with their telltale creaks, and lay down on the freshly made bed. He fell asleep before he realised he'd still had nothing to eat.

* * *

Monte awoke to a dark room, the candle burned down to a stub in the holder beside him. He cursed in the gloom – candles weren't cheap. Thinking of money reminded him of the gold coin in his pocket, and he pulled it out, running his fingers over the images in relief on both sides. Myrtle would be pleased to see it.

Voices drifted up the stairs into the small room in the eaves. A woman – Myrtle. She was laughing. Monte frowned. Myrtle never laughed, unless it was at him. A man's voice – Mr Gondavere. He laughed too, a sound much like a saw dragged across rusted metal. Monte shuddered.

He hauled himself off the bed and made his way downstairs. Myrtle still sat in the rocking chair by the fire, with the blanket now neatly folded and lying on the table. Mr Gondavere sat in Monte's chair on the other side of the fire, his hands wrapped around a pewter mug.

"Ah Monte, you're awake! You all right now, love?" asked Myrtle.

"I'm feeling a lot better now," replied Monte.

"Good, good. There's some stew in the pot, if you're hungry." Myrtle smiled at him. Her face had fewer lines and her eyes carried a twinkle Monte had lost hope of seeing again, though he knew the twinkle wasn't for his benefit. It was for *him*. Monte returned her smile, though he knew it never reached his eyes. Suspicion of Myrtle's lusty intentions bleached any mirth from his expression.

Monte made his way through into the kitchen. A pot bubbled on the stove and Monte filled a bowl with the ladle. There was no meat in the broth, only vegetables, but it was hot and fresh, and Monte couldn't remember the last time he'd eaten. He sat alone at the table in the back parlour and shovelled the stew into his mouth.

More laughter erupted in the front room, though the voices were too muffled to make out any words. Tears sprang to Monte's eyes and he sniffed back his feelings. He'd wanted to make Myrtle smile with his gold coin, to earn her laughter, and maybe even approval. She'd barely spoken to him for the past six months, though Monte still didn't know why. He'd put a roof over her house, and given her that garden outside. Was it because he was still just a grave digger? Did Myrtle want more than that for herself? Monte choked back his stew. He'd tried so hard, and now here was Mr Gondavere, a total stranger with a mouth full of razors, and she was laughing and joking with him in the front room. What had he said to her?

He finished the stew and rinsed out his bowl in the sink. He left it to dry on the draining board. His heart hung low and heavy in his chest, and he stepped through into the front room.

"Mr Gondavere's been telling me all about your new job, Monte." Myrtle gestured for him to sit down, but with Mr Gondavere in his chair, he had to make do with a stool by the small table.

"Has he now?"

"Indeed he has. Who'd have thought it, my Monte the assistant to an 'istorian! I'm ever so proud of you, love."

"You are?"

"I have been telling your charming wife how indispensable I have found your services, particularly considering the very short time in which I have known you," said Mr Gondavere.

"Right." Monte eyed Mr Gondavere as a mouse might eye a cat that has become suddenly friendly and welcoming. What else had Mr Gondavere told her?

"He says you're to go away again for a bit, but I should expect you back in a couple of days," said Myrtle.

Monte nodded, unsure of what to say.

"I'll miss having you around the house, but he's given me your earnings so I can have a nice spread ready for you when you come back. A proper feast to celebrate your new job." Myrtle stood up and a heavy purse jangled from her belt. Monte grimaced. He knew he wouldn't see a penny of his earnings. His fist closed around the gold coin in his pocket. At least he'd been right. Myrtle didn't want to be married to a grave digger.

"I am sure you will have a lot to celebrate, my good woman." Mr Gondavere pushed himself to his feet.

Monte stood up as well, not wanting to be the only one left sitting.

"Anyway, you'd best be off, you've got a lot of work to do." Myrtle bustled across the room. Standing on her tip-toes, she planted a kiss on his cheek, and cupped his face in her hand. "Come back safe, yeah?"

Monte nodded, and Myrtle disappeared into the back parlour. Mr Gondavere straightened his coat and gestured to the door.

"Shall we?"

Monte pulled on his coat and followed Mr Gondavere outside.

"You have a very charming wife, Monte. I am

not surprised you wanted to return to share your good news."

"She's a delight, all right," replied Monte. His glare burned holes into Mr Gondavere's back.

"And you will have even more good news to share with her soon."

"Why?"

"I have a feeling we'll be returning with the Heart of the City." Mr Gondavere turned and smiled at Monte, but for once, Monte couldn't smile back. He had a very bad feeling about everything.

CHAPTER 20

Eufame and Vyolet pored over old books and maps in the archives. Vyolet couldn't read much of the text, written in Archaic Wolfkin or a strange form of the Common Tongue she didn't recognise. Eufame managed to find a handful of Shadowkin texts for her to translate. Vyolet tried to take an interest in the ancient history and culture of her people, but the authors were so dry. Even exciting folklore became dull and monotonous.

"Eufame, why do the Wolfkin have Shadowkin books?" she asked, eager for a break from a particularly boring book about early Shadowkin settlements.

"I expect they wanted to preserve the knowledge. Without knowing much about Shadowkin, anything else would just be guesswork," replied Eufame.

Mara sat down beside Vyolet. She pointed to the books and formed a Shadow Speak reply.

"There is a long history between your people and mine. Much trade in the past. Often your books for our protection."

"You protected us?"

"As best we could, but you learned ways to protect yourselves."

Vyolet translated the replies for Eufame. The necromancer closed her book and added it to the pile she'd designated as 'Useless for this purpose'.

"What happened?"

"The three races existed well in the Underground City and it was as harmonious as it could be," said Mara. "But then the City Above was founded and the Shadowkin could not venture outside into the daylight as it hurt their eyes. The new humans Above did not trust the Shadowkin and did not make space for them at their council. The Shadowkin remained in the darkness, forever on the outside."

"But why didn't they just live in the Underground City?" asked Vyolet.

"The humans took their lead from those Above. The wealthy merchants stopped trading with the Shadowkin, and soon the rest of the City followed suit."

Vyolet frowned. "What happened to the Wolfkin?"

"Humans could not understand us and they feared our power and knowledge. They used their superior skills of manipulation to legislate us into our current position."

"Wolfkin are massively underestimated, Vyolet," added Eufame. "It made far more sense for me to employ Wolfkin than humans."

"So why did you choose Jyx? He's a human, but you get on all right with him."

"Not all humans are bad. He has faults aplenty, his impatience particularly, but he could be great, if he allows himself to be guided in the right direction. I have high hopes for him. He performed so spectacularly in the role I created for him – perhaps too well." Eufame grimaced and Vyolet wondered exactly how much destruction Jyx's escapade at the House had created.

Mara gestured for Vyolet to continue reading, and Vyolet returned to her book. She flipped through the pages, skipping the old tales and folklore. Surely if information about an earlier ruined city existed, it would be in the archaeology books.

Vyolet didn't understand much of the terminology, but at least the archaeology books had illustrations. She recognised many of the locations in the woodcuts, or engravings in more recent books, and she read an entire chapter about the founding of the temple. None of the chapels were officially dedicated to their existing patron deities, and all of them belonged to earlier figures, long forgotten by the humans. At one stage, the Lords and Ladies of Death had a chapel of their own in a crypt beneath the temple, but it was abandoned when they fell out of favour. The next few sentences caught her eye.

"The crypt still exists, although its associations with the mystery cult belonging to the Lords and Ladies of Death meant that no new deity groups wanted to dedicate the space to their own needs. Its entrance lies on the far side of the temple, in the north-east corner, although the entrance has since been hidden by new construction work. It is believed that the crypt also marks an entrance into the catacombs below the Shrine of Beseda, far to the east."

Vyolet grinned. Hidden crypts? Secret entrances? Catacombs? Surely this had to be what everyone was looking for. She pushed the book across the table at Eufame. The necromancer frowned.

"I can't read this, Vyolet."

"No, but I can." Vyolet read the passage aloud.

"That has to be the place we're looking for. I knew there were catacombs, but I didn't know where they were – they're supposed to be part of the old ruins," said Eufame.

"Should we go and take a look?"

"Yes, and as luck would have it, Jyx's family is

lodged near the temple. Vyolet, I need you to find him and let him know where we're going. He's part of this now, and I think he should be with us when we go below."

Eufame wrote the address on Vyolet's hand, the quill scratching her grey skin. Mara took her back down to the jetty they'd used when they first arrived at the archives. The Wolfkin drew a sigil in the air, and the flickering lamps dimmed until they were little more than blinking lights in the darkness. Thick black shadows lay across the still water of the canal.

"Thank you, Mara. I hope I'll see you again sometime," said Vyolet.

"I hope so too. We have a lot to teach each other," replied Mara.

The Wolfkin hugged Vyolet then climbed back up the steps away from the platform. Vyolet shivered, alone at last. There was no Fortis to talk to her in the silence and no Jyx to hold her hand in the shadows. More importantly, there was no Eufame to back her up if anyone tried to follow her.

She took a deep breath and melted into the shadows beside the canal. She slipped along the tunnel, skipping through the thick shadow soup above the water. Once or twice she got too close to the lamps and her skin became visible in the dim glow. Her toes dipped in the water and she cursed beneath her breath, moving away from the lights and into the darkest shadows in the middle of the canal.

It was more difficult at the far end, where the tunnel opened out, and she raced across the main canal in a thin sliver of shadow cast by a tall pole. She only paused for breath when she reached the solid dock on the far side.

She gave herself a few moments then resumed skipping through the shadows to cover the ground back to the warehouse district. She drew closer to the docks and made her jumps smaller to avoid detection by the guards and dock workers. She spotted two tall hooded figures at the bottom of a street and her heart leapt. Vyolet ran towards them, streaking across open spaces between the shadows to reach Validus and Fortis.

Vyolet had almost reached them when one of the figures turned towards her. A skeletal face glowed in dim light from a gas lamp and emptiness burned in the eye sockets. Vyolet pulled up short and dived into the shadow cast by the two figures.

Dreadguards didn't normally venture into the Underground City. Were they looking for her, or Jyx? Eufame?

Vyolet's blood ran cold and she pressed herself against the wall. Death rattles emanated from inside the hoods of the two figures, although she couldn't make out what they said to one another. They must have tailed her and Eufame this far, but they couldn't know where the Wolfkin archives were if they were still here in the Warehouse District. Could they see her? Could they peer into shadows?

"Well, well, what do we have here?" The cruel voice to her left made her jump and Vyolet turned to find herself face to face with a squat man wearing goggles and a DWS sash. The second Dreadguard turned to look in her direction.

Vyolet pushed herself away from the wall and dived into the nearest shadow. She made her way up the street towards the City, darting through the shadows where the City was at its thinnest. Older Shadowkin could venture into a shadow on one side of the City and come out of another shadow in a different district, and Vyolet wished she knew how to accomplish such a feat. As it was, she couldn't use shadows as doorways, only corridors, each one connected to the last.

"I can still see you!" The voice of the DWS agent rang out behind her. Vyolet sneaked a glance over her shoulder. The squat man waddled up the street, though the Dreadguards remained in the ring of light from the gas lamp. Their empty eyes stared up the street at her, and their lack of movement scared Vyolet more than the DWS agent's pursuit.

The agent's goggles removed her advantage of stealth through the shadows, leaving only her advantage of speed. She threw herself into a side street and set off at a run, sprinting along the street. Tenements lined the alley and clean sheets and clothing hung from wires that ran above her head. She ran through the shadows cast by the washing. The curses of the DWS agent made her turn around. Sheets tangled around him, obscuring his face.

Thankful for laundry day, Vyolet took a right and ran up another side alley. A stitch niggled in her side, and she longed to stop to catch her breath. The cries of the DWS agent far behind her spurred her on, and she only resolved to stop when she knew she'd lost him. She couldn't think about the Dreadguards and what they might do. Did they run? Could they see into the shadows? Maybe they were made from the shadows, the same as she was.

Vyolet zigzagged through the Warehouse District, spicing up her route by taking left turns instead of right, occasionally heading back down towards the canal and then back up towards the City. She hoped the DWS agent would assume she'd simply gone straight for the City. His cries grew fainter until she could no longer hear him at all.

She slipped around the corner, streaking from one shadow to another, and slammed into the back of something thick and black, so dark it hurt her eyes to look at it. She looked up into a hood and a death rattle bubbled within its shadows. A skeletal hand grasped her wrist before she could turn and run in the opposite direction. The icy fingers froze her skin and she screamed. She slapped at the freezing white hand, prying at the fingertips, but it burned her to touch them.

"Let me go!"

She beat the cloaked arm of the Dreadguard, and it lifted her off the ground. It brought her face towards the black depths of the hood. She kicked at thin air, squealing from the pain in her shoulder as she twisted from its grasp. A patch of shadow lay across the wall to her right, and if she could just reach it, she might be able to slip away.

"'Ere! You let 'er go! She's mine!" The DWS agent appeared on the corner. The second Dreadguard moved towards him, gliding across the cobbles with outstretched hands. The agent ducked under the hands and made a grab for Vyolet's ankle. His fingers grasped the edge of her boot and he pulled. The Dreadguard swatted at the agent, releasing its grip long enough for Vyolet to kick out with one foot, dislodging the agent's goggles, and twist herself. She dropped into the shadow.

Pain blossomed in her ankle when she fell, but she forced herself upright, and pushed away from the wall. The DWS agent ranted and railed at the twin Dreadguards. With their attention fixed on the ridiculous little man, Vyolet broke into a lopsided sprint and left them behind.

CHAPTER 21

Jyx pulled his robe around himself and glanced from side to side as he hurried along the street towards Grieg Close. He couldn't sense any unwanted attention, and the sparks of his mirror enchantment still flickered in his peripheral vision. *So far, so good.*

The street rounded a bend and the Eufame splinter in his mind screamed a warning. Jyx threw himself sideways into a shop doorway without understanding why. He paused to calm his racing heart and he peered around the doorjamb. He muttered a curse under his breath. Two tall, hooded figures stood on the corner of Grieg Close, facing away from him. He might have mistaken them from Wolfkin in disguise if not for Eufame's warning. How could he get past them? No mirror spell would be strong enough to fool Dreadguards.

A siren stood a little way down the street, staring at the skeletal figures. Her red hair rippled across her shoulders like a river of copper and her wide green eyes sparkled in the gloom. Shoppers on the busy street cast her disapproving looks but she ignored their whispers and rude stares. She wore simple clothes of cream and brown, meaning her voice earned her more money than her looks did. She was perfect.

Jyx shoved his hands into his pockets and rooted through their contents for anything he could press into service as payment. His fingers closed around the pouch of sand. He pulled it out of his pocket and peered into the small purse. It would have to do.

He drew a sigil in the air over the purse, turning its contents into the most potent sleeping sand he knew how to make. He pulled its drawstrings as tightly as they'd go – he'd had an accident with sleeping sand once before, putting Bastet into a deep sleep in his room, and he had no intention of using it on himself.

Jyx positioned himself in the doorway so that the jamb hid him from the view of the Dreadguards should they turn around, but the siren remained in sight. He snapped his fingers several times, whispering an incantation over them while willing the siren to ignore the mirror enchantment and look his way.

"Respice ad me, oro te, respice ad me."

Her emerald gaze slid across the street and she locked eyes with him. For a moment, Jyx couldn't move, his mind held in her thrall, his body rigid and no longer under his control. Before he could move towards her, the Eufame splinter wiggled, and Jyx swore he heard her warning tone in the furthest reaches of his consciousness. Able to control himself once more, he beckoned to the siren.

She sashayed across the street towards him, naked curiosity stamped across her angelic features. Jyx knew of their fearsome reputation, and the sharp tongues they hid in those cherubic mouths, but he'd never spoken to one before. Jyx gestured for her to stand in the doorway with him. She linked her arm through his and gazed up at him.

"You don't look at me the way they do, but then they're not looking at you at all," she said.

"It's all right. No one ever notices me, but I'd like to avail myself of your services, actually," replied Jyx.

She took a step backwards, withdrawing her arm from his, and moved as far away as the doorway would allow her. A dark cloud passed across the siren's face, and lightning flashed in the depths of her green eyes. Shadows gathered behind her, and the temperature dropped.

"How dare you, I –"

"Not like that, my lady, honest! No, I need your singing talents."

The threat passed as quickly as it arrived and a wide smile broke out, turning the siren from a fearsome thunderstorm into a sunny summer's day. She slipped her arm back through his, and Jyx shivered to feel her cold flesh brush the back of his hand. At least Vyolet's hand wasn't cold.

"You do? Oh, that is marvellous. I do so love to sing. What would you have me do?"

"I need you to distract those two, and preferably lead them away so I can get down that close without them seeing me." Jyx gestured along the street to the two figures. They still held watch along the other end of the street. At least they didn't know he'd been to Mr Rosemary's yet, although Bastet might warn the old bookseller if they found out.

"They are Dreadguards, are they not?"

"They are."

"And why would you avoid them so?" The siren narrowed her eyes and cocked her head on one side, as though she could peer into the deepest recesses of his heart. Jyx suddenly wished he'd learned to use the mirror spell in smaller doses for specific targets.

"Well, I've made a few enemies in high places, but I've got a friend who's even higher, if only I can help her out." Calling Eufame a 'friend' after everything she'd done still felt strange, and the word sounded hollow in his mouth, but he couldn't think how else to describe her.

"That's all right, you have your secrets, and I shall have mine." The siren cuddled into him, nudging his side with her elbow. Jyx's face burned with the blush that spread upwards from beneath the collar of his robe.

"Thanks, but can you do it?"

"It won't be easy. Dreadguards are not so susceptible, but I have a song I think they will enjoy. But this is a difficult task, what is in it for me?"

"This." Jyx handed her the pouch of sand. She peeked inside and grinned even more.

"This is very strong stuff, Mr Stranger."

"I know. I don't care what you use it for, as long as it's not on me, but it's all yours, if you can get them away." Jyx peeked along the street again – the Dreadguards still weren't looking.

"Why not use the sleeping sand on them?"

"Dreadguards don't sleep."

The siren weighed the pouch in one hand and peered at him again. The Eufame splinter vibrated in his mind and a thin frost spread across the edges of his consciousness. The siren scowled and looked away.

"Very well. I will do this, but only as you have been so nice."

She pursed her lips and stalked away, hips swaying as she went. She made a beeline for the Dreadguards and positioned herself in front of them. Their hoods moved, inclining towards one another, but before they could stop her, she opened her mouth. Pure music poured forth, diving and swooping through a tumbling cascade of notes. The song was entirely tailored to the Dreadguards, and while

Jyx's magickal hearing gave him the ability to listen, the passers-by simply gave her a wide berth and muttered to one another about the "undesirables" of the district.

The siren took a step backwards and the Dreadguards followed. Her song altered their mood, evoking the melancholy of dusk, experienced even in the Underground City. She took two more steps backwards, mirrored by the Dreadguards' two steps forward.

Jyx watched the unlikely dance continue, with the siren continually adding layer upon layer to her mournful song. Her throat worked itself into a frenzy, issuing notes that bubbled and frothed as they hit the cool air. She kept walking backwards, leading the Dreadguards around the bend in the street until they disappeared from sight.

Jyx seized his chance and darted forward. He hugged the shopfronts as he edged along the street, hurrying into Grieg Close before the Dreadguards realised what was happening. He broke into a run and sprinted along the narrow residential street, keeping his eyes open for Holst Alley. Housewives watched his progress as he passed them, and he realised his mirror spell must have worn off.

He stopped running when he found the turn-off and pressed his back against the wall. He pulled ragged breaths into his lungs and pressed his hand to his chest to feel the thump of his heart. All of this exertion was no good – one of the attractions of magick was the low emphasis on physical exercise. If he'd wanted to run about the place he'd have become an errand boy, not an apprentice.

When his pulse slowed, Jyx consulted the address scrawled on his hand. He needed building number ten, three doors down to his left. If Eufame's directions meant anything, his mother and siblings occupied a flat on the third floor. He couldn't help but feel disappointed – while he'd hated his freezing garret in Green Dragon Close, he'd enjoyed being up high, looking down into the gloom from his lofty window.

A guard gargoyle perched on the wrought iron gas lamp above the black front door. No larger than a kitten, it fluttered down to hover in front of Jyx. Chips of obsidian served as eyes in its stone face and it pursed its rocky lips.

"You seem familiar to me." Its voice sounded like rusting metal scraping on pitted stone.

"I'm Jyximus Faire. My mother lives here."

A smile broke out on the gargoyle's face, and Jyx winced at the expression, so unexpected for a guard.

"That's why I know you! You look a lot like her. Go on up, Master Faire."

It moved aside, and Jyx opened the front door.

The hallway inside the building was dark and led to a central stairwell. Old oil paintings of Underground City luminaries, flickering candles in niches and small windows took up most of the walls. Jyx paused when he spotted a state portrait of Eufame halfway up to the first floor. Judging by her bored expression, she'd hated the experience of sitting for a painting. The windows cast barred shadows across the pale floorboards, but the glass was too dusty for Jyx to see into the street outside.

He climbed the stairs up to the third floor. Only one doorway led onto the narrow landing. His mother and siblings had the floor to themselves. He knocked on the door then tugged his unruly hair into some semblance of order. He just hoped his mother would be pleased to see him.

CHAPTER 22

Mr Gondavere led Monte to a cottage on the edge of Canalsditch. It clung to the crumbling brick of a tenement building in the neighbouring district, squatting in its shadow. A scrawny cat, more bones than fur, skittered away from the front door at Mr Gondavere's approach.

"I believe our final client may be of some definite use." Gondavere knocked on the door, and Monte bent down to pet the cat. It rubbed its head against his leg, turning its gaze away from Mr Gondavere.

"How do you know this stuff?" asked Monte.

"I have my sources." Mr Gondavere smiled and tapped the side of his nose. Monte looked down at the cat so his employer wouldn't see the naked distrust on his face. There was something very 'off' about Mr Gondavere, although Monte couldn't tell if his new-found dislike of the man was founded upon Myrtle's apparent acceptance of him.

The door opened, and a woman peered out into

the gloom. Pinched features and watery eyes dominated her thin face.

"Hello, my good woman, my name is Mr Gondavere, and this is my associate, Mr McThwaite. I believe your mother is unwell." Buttery tones slid from Mr Gondavere's usually sharp voice.

"She ain't just unwell, she's dyin', yer parasite, an' I've got no time fer the likes o' you!" The woman tried to slam the door shut, but Mr Gondavere stuck his foot in the way. She glowered at his shoe.

"We're not undertakers, nor surgeons, madam. We are here to console with her," said Mr Gondavere.

The woman looked up and narrowed her eyes. "Why?"

"We don't believe that anyone should fear the passage to the other side, and we would help ease her voyage, if we may," replied Mr Gondavere.

Monte stared at his employer. What had provoked such a change in approach?

"What's 'e for?" The woman jabbed her finger towards Monte.

"I provide comfort, madam," said Monte.

A rattling cough erupted inside the cottage. Mr Gondavere pushed on the door and nudged aside the woman. Monte followed him inside.

A pot hung from a hook over the fire. Its contents bubbled and frothed. A narrow bed stood on the far side of the single room and an ancient woman lay huddled beneath the threadbare sheets. Blood spattered the pillows beside her mouth. Monte frowned.

Mr Gondavere made his way across the room and took up a position on a small stool at the foot of the bed. Monte perched on the edge of the bed and folded one of the old woman's hands into his warm grasp. Her eyelids fluttered, and she peered at them.

"What are ye? Devils? Demons? Are yer 'ere to take me off?" She rasped the words, punctuating each question with a hacking cough.

"We're here to offer you comfort," replied Monte. He stroked her hand. Her pulse fluttered beneath her thin skin.

"I'll be dead soon enough," said the old woman.

"We know, that's why we're here."

"Am I to be dissected? Am I corpse bait?"

"Not at all. We merely wish to record your final words to preserve your memory once you are gone." Mr Gondavere tapped the cover of his book, now resting in his lap.

"I have no final words." The woman broke into a cough again and peppered Monte's hand with a fine red mist.

"I told yer to go!" The younger woman grabbed at Monte's arm and tried to pull him away from the bed, but her mother clamped his hand in her vice-like grip. Monte stared at her withered hand in amazement.

"They're 'ere to help me."

"They'll take yer away and sell yer to the necromancer."

"We have nothing to do with the necromancer, and as it happens, she is incarcerated in the House of Correction for her part in the treason against the Crown Prince." Mr Gondavere glared at the younger woman.

"No she ain't. Word is she broke out. She's somewhere down 'ere. How do I know yer ain't workin' for her?" The younger woman planted her hands on her skinny hips.

Mr Gondavere spluttered, his face red with fury. Monte hurried to reply before his employer could say something that would get them ejected from the cottage.

"I can assure you we aren't working for Eufame Delsenza, madam. We're just simple historians, and we'd like to make your mother feel comfortable and capture her last words. For posterity, and so on," said Monte.

"Yer bleedin' parasites." The younger woman

stomped across the room and flung herself into a seat in the corner. Monte bit his lip – after all, they were depriving this stranger of her final moments with her mother, all to pursue an archaeological artefact. He thought of his wages, left with Myrtle, and grimaced.

"You're 'ere about 'er, aren't yer?" The old woman coughed again.

"Who?"

"The Heart. When I was a novice for Beseda, me ol' mistress told me yer would come to ask questions," replied the old woman.

"Why did you not say so before?" asked Mr Gondavere.

"I was 'opin' you might leave afore then."

"Yer don't 'ave to talk to 'em, Mum!" The younger woman threw a disdainful look at Mr Gondavere.

"I might as well, now they're 'ere. See the Heart of the City had 'er own name once, only no one remembers it, and yer gonna need to know it if yer want to ask 'er for help. She knew ol' Beseda too, and it was my patron saint what hid 'er away when she died," said the old woman. "So yer might as well stop lookin' and start livin'. Especially you." The old woman tossed a meaningful stare in Monte's direction.

"Why would Beseda hide the Heart of the City?" asked Mr Gondavere.

"She's the patron saint of wronged women, ain't she? No more way to be wronged than gettin' killed defending a city wot betrayed yer," replied the old woman.

"Who betrayed her?" Monte had never heard that part of the story before.

Mr Gondavere spoke over him. "You'll tell me her name." His pen nib hovered above the page of his open book.

"I don't know it, and if I did, I wouldn't be tellin' you."

Mr Gondavere leaned forward, his eyes blazing and his brows furrowed. Monte held him back with one arm and shook his head. Mr Gondavere pursed his lips and sat back.

"Who does know the Heart's name?" asked Monte.

"I ain't sayin' nothin' more."

The younger woman stood up and bustled across the room. She reached out to grab Monte, but he rose, holding up his hands in apology. She narrowed her eyes and reached towards Mr Gondavere.

"You two need to get out!"

Mr Gondavere closed his book and slid it back into the case. He snapped it closed and got up, his expression grim. The temperature around him dropped several degrees, and the younger woman shrank away from him.

"I can assure you we are leaving, madam." Mr Gondavere swept across the room in a flurry of black cloth and wrenched open the door. The rectangle of darkness swallowed him up.

"You want to get away from that 'un," said the old woman. She nodded twice and Monte nodded in reply. He hoped she might give him an escape route of sorts, but she simply lay back against her pillow. Another coughing fit seized her, and the younger woman elbowed him out of the way. Monte slipped out of the cottage and closed the front door behind him.

* * *

Mr Gondavere stood on the doorstep. Monte expected him to be furious, or cold, but instead he grinned, displaying that mouth full of cruel fangs.

"Well I think we know where to go to find the Heart!"

"But we'll never get into Beseda's Shrine. We're men." As the patron saint of wronged women, Beseda inspired loyalty from few men, although Monte had heard rumours that she was popular among trolls, both male and female. Their perverse grasp of honour led them to see slights against them at every turn.

"You're right. We're men, but your lovely wife isn't." Mr Gondavere's smile didn't reach his eyes, which glittered like explosive diamonds. A threat laced his words, and Monte dropped his gaze.

"You can send Myrtle into the Shrine if you want, but how will we get into the catacombs? I don't think there's a back door she can go in and open for us."

"You would be surprised, my good man. We shall stop at your dwelling to collect her, and sally forth to the shrine." Mr Gondavere walked up the path away from the cottage. He cocked his head to one side, lips moving in silent conversation with an invisible companion. Monte stared at him. Exactly what manner of creature was his employer?

Monte set off up the path and joined Mr Gondavere at the gate. "How will you find out the name of the Heart?"

"I don't think that will be a problem. I sense that was a lie perpetrated by the old witch to throw us off the scent. It hardly surprises me," said Mr Gondavere.

They walked through the crooked streets and squares of Canalsditch, now bustling with housewives buying their daily rations, and shift workers either heading home or off to work. A handful of men shouted greetings to Monte, who replied with "Hallo!" or promises to meet up soon.

"You are popular here." Mr Gondavere didn't look at Monte.

"People know me. You get to know your neighbours. Plus, they prefer me digging the graves because I'm one of the few diggers that doesn't help himself to anything. But I wouldn't say I was popular, though."

"You would be missed."

"I suppose I would." Monte put an extra span of distance between himself and Mr Gondavere.

"That is good. It is good that people appreciate

what you do for them. We have not known that luxury for some time."

"We?"

"I meant 'I'. Forgive the slip of the tongue."

They walked in silence until they reached Monte's cottage. Again he bristled as Mr Gondavere insisted on speaking with Myrtle himself, leaving Monte standing outside his own home while he went inside.

He inspected the flowerbeds, enjoying the scent of the night-blooming blossoms. Myrtle had done a good job, putting plenty of effort into cultivating a beautiful garden. It was a pity she hadn't felt the need to put the same effort into her marriage. Monte ran his fingers through the drooping tendrils of a Night Fern and frowned. He'd bought her this plant as an anniversary present. He'd tracked down the seeds for the rare Moon Orchids at the Flee Market. The Star-Spangled Roses came from the City Above, smuggled in one year for her birthday. His gaze roved across the fecund beds and he scowled. He'd bought her every single one of these plants, in one form or another.

Laughter drifted out of the open window, and Monte fought the urge to crush the roses out of spite. Moments later, the front door opened and Mr Gondavere led Myrtle into the garden. She'd put on her best dress, a black crepe mourning gown, and added a black lace shawl she saved for special occasions. She smiled at him but Monte simply grunted in reply.

"Your darling wife has agreed to accompany us," said Mr Gondavere.

"Excellent." Monte didn't care what his employer had told his wife. A cold tendril of hatred wrapped itself around his heart, and he realised that he no longer cared what Myrtle thought. He no longer cared about her at all.

"It'll be such an adventure, sweetie!" Myrtle slipped her arm through Monte's, and wrapped her other hand around his bicep. Monte suppressed a shudder. She hadn't done that since the days of their courting. Hard to believe that was only eight years ago.

"I'm sure it will. We'd better get going, though. You heard what the old crone said – we're not the only ones looking for it."

"Your diligence is an inspiration to us all, Monte." Mr Gondavere smiled and made his way out of the garden.

Monte and Myrtle followed, and they headed back into Canalsditch. Monte tried to ignore the weight of Myrtle's hand on his arm, but she kept prattling at him about the feast she'd make him when they returned home. Monte had a strange feeling that he couldn't explain – and it said neither of them would ever return to the cottage.

CHAPTER 23

Vyolet ran for what felt like weeks, and her ears rang with the shouts of the DWS agent. She only stopped running when she reached Middletown, the central district of the Underground City. She passed other Shadowkin who lurked in doorways or pressed against walls to take advantage of the darkness, and their presence helped her relax. With so many of her kind in the district, the DWS agent would be hard pressed to focus on her.

Still, it wasn't the agent who worried her as much as the Dreadguards. She didn't know how they travelled, or if they could follow her scent. Perversely, her best option was to surround herself with humans to lose herself in their stench and travel to Jyx's address through the busy highways of Middletown.

Vyolet longed for company. Normally she did everything alone, apart from her occasional meetings with clients who needed her to steal information. Her time spent with Fortis, and then Jyx, and even Eufame, gave her an insight into how it felt to work with others. Perhaps her fear of the Dreadguards fuelled much of her current loneliness and paranoia.

Middletown was a sprawling mix of narrow alleys lined with tall, crumbling tenements, and wide shopping avenues lined with curiosity shops and small markets of varying themes. The housewives were out in force, shopping in packs and blocking streets. Those in the streets cast plenty of shadows, but Vyolet couldn't slip between them as easily within the crowds. She didn't dare walk openly – there were more Shadowkin, true, but that didn't mean they were accepted here.

She crouched at the entrance to an alleyway to ponder her next move. Suddenly something warm and furry brushed her hand. She looked down to see a small tabby cat sitting beside her, gazing up at her.

"Hello," said Vyolet. She petted the cat's head and it mewed in reply. She'd never stroked a cat before – normally they couldn't see her in the shadows, yet this one could.

"Do I know you?" she asked.

The cat mewed again and Vyolet swore she heard a 'Not quite' in the sound. She looked closer and saw a black velvet collar around the cat's neck. A small silver charm dangled from it. Vyolet reached down and examined the charm. She recognised the insignia – Jyx wore it on his robes.

"Are you from the House of the Long Dead?" she asked.

The cat mewed again, this time intoning its reply with 'Yes'.

"Did Eufame send you?"

The cat cocked its head on one side, as if to say 'Sort of'.

"I could certainly use Eufame's help right about now. I don't know how to get across Middletown without being seen, and it's too busy to get through the crowds."

The cat looked up, past Vyolet. She followed its

gaze and spotted a crude ladder a little way along the alleyway. Rough iron staples studded the wall in a vertical line.

"Nice idea, cat – if I can't go through Middletown, then I should go over it. I just don't know if I can jump across alleyways with this bad ankle."

Vyolet stretched her leg out and pointed to her ankle. It was slightly darker than the surrounding skin and a shade more swollen than her healthy ankle. The cat lay down across her lower leg, its stomach vibrating with the cat's purring.

"What are you doing?" asked Vyolet.

The cat's movements tickled, and she fidgeted under the weight of the tabby. The cat looked at her once or twice, as if telling her to keep still. Vyolet shrugged. If the cat had anything to do with Eufame Delsenza, then she guessed it knew what it was doing.

After five minutes, Vyolet's bad ankle was noticeably warmer than the other, and the cat clambered off her leg. Vyolet drew her injury closer to inspect it. The swelling and the darkness had gone.

"Oh you little genius!" Vyolet bent down and hugged the cat. She stood up and twirled several times on the spot using her previously bad leg. The ankle didn't hurt in the slightest. Vyolet hurried across to the ladder, marvelling at the lack of pain.

The staples were wide enough for her to place one foot in the centre, and she tugged on several to ensure they wouldn't simply come away from the wall when she put her weight on it. Vyolet looked back along the alleyway, but the cat was gone.

"Onwards and upwards, I suppose." Vyolet took hold of a staple and hauled herself up. It was slow going, since some of the rungs were missing in places, and she had to reach twice as high, but after a few moments, she found herself standing on the roof of the tenement building. Luckily, they weren't as tall as the ones in Green Dragon Close, where they soared several storeys above the alleyways.

Thick, syrupy darkness surrounded Vyolet, broken only by the dim glow of the streets far below. Vyolet skipped across the roof, enjoying the cool darkness, and she jumped from building to building with ease. The alleys below were narrow enough that she rarely had to leap more than four feet at once, and she ran through the darkness across wider spaces.

Middletown gave way to Nunnery Gardens, a badly named district of brick buildings and narrow offices. The older inhabitants of the Underground City remembered the old convent that occupied most of the site, surrounded by gardens filled with herbs and night-blooming flowers. Dedicated to the Order of the Black Nuns, the convent fell foul of an obscure piece of City Above legislation and was pulled down. Bookkeepers and scriveners now occupied the offices at street level, with more affluent clerical staff taking the apartments in the tenements above. From what Vyolet had heard, more buildings would be going the way of the convent.

Vyolet took her time, no longer racing from building to building. She peered down into the streets to get her bearings and took a diagonal route across the district. Chimney pots littered the rooftops, belching thick smoke into the air. She allowed herself to dissolve into shadow to pass through more easily. She passed another Shadowkin among the chimneys, but they ignored each other. She assumed the other also had a valid, yet underhand, reason for being so high.

She knew she was in Temple Park, the district near the temple, though there had never been a park nearby. Vyolet didn't know this area very well and decided to find Jyx's address from street level. She peered down into the wide boulevard that curved through the district. Bow windows protruded into the street, with well-dressed housewives laden with wicker baskets scurrying between shops.

Vyolet gasped to see two Dreadguards standing in the centre of the street. They jabbed their skeletal fingers at each other, gesticulating along the boulevard in the direction of Nunnery Gardens. One of them waved its arms and took a swipe at its companion. Vyolet couldn't hear their death rattle communication, but they were embroiled in an argument of some sort. If they were here, then they must be looking for Jyx. The Dreadguards by the docks were no coincidence. Vyolet couldn't tell if the two below were the same ones she'd seen earlier, but the idea of there now being four Dreadguards in the Underground City didn't bear considering.

She found a building two streets over with a staple ladder embedded in its outer wall, and she dropped into the gloom between the buildings. The street sign at the end of the alley read 'Holst Alley' and Vyolet smiled. She'd found the right place after all.

A guard gargoyle perched above the door and fluttered down to hover in front of her face.

"Who are you?" it rasped.

"I'm here to see Jyximus Faire."

"I don't know you." The gargoyle narrowed its eyes and folded its arms.

"Well, you wouldn't know me, I've never been here before."

"Then how do you know how to find this Jyximus Faire here?"

"Because I was given his address." Vyolet frowned. She'd heard about guard gargoyles, but she'd never encountered one before. Then again, she rarely used front doors.

"I can't let you in if I don't know you."

"Can you let him know I'm here then? He'll come down to the door and tell you who I am."

"And leave the door unguarded? I think not! Go away."

The gargoyle flew back up to the iron support of the gas lamp and adopted a typical pose, but its eyes remained locked on Vyolet. She made no move towards the door – the gargoyle wouldn't let in her either way.

There was only one thing to try. Shadowkin practised their own form of magick, separate from the spells and sigils so favoured by the humans. Vyolet seldom used it, since her attempts at magick rarely worked, and she preferred to rely on her speed and agility to take her through the shadows. Morphing into smoke was the only magick she used with any regularity. However, there was one spell that she knew, and it was the last possibility that might actually succeed.

Vyolet positioned herself below the gas lamp. She drew a sigil inside her mouth with her tongue, and visualised its form just behind her teeth. She filled it with as much darkness as she could muster, and raised her hand to her lips, as if to blow a kiss. She blew the sigil out of her mouth, straight into the flame of the gas lamp.

The flame winked out, suffocated by shadows, and the gargoyle slipped from its perch. Its wings arrested its fall, and it fluttered upwards, calling for help. Vyolet dissolved into the darkness of Holst Alley and aimed for the keyhole of the front door.

CHAPTER 24

Eufame's choice of accommodation continued to impress Jyx at every turn. His mother answered the door and wrapped him in a bear hug. After near suffocating him, she bustled him into the apartment. A comfortable parlour and three bedrooms lay on one side of the corridor, with a well-stocked kitchen and three more bedrooms on the other side. An indoor privy lay at the end of the passage. His siblings were out, fetching goods from the market, so his mother directed him into the parlour. He sank into an overstuffed armchair beside the fireplace and removed his boots.

"Are you tired, love?" His mother came into the parlour carrying two mugs of steaming tea.

"It's been ages since I've slept," replied Jyx. He remembered the deep sleep in the box bed in Eufame's quarters, but he hadn't slept since then. He didn't even know how much time had elapsed.

"Do you think you've got time for a nap?"

"I hope so, but don't you want to know what's been

going on?" Jyx accepted a mug and his mother sat down in her rocking chair.

"Your mistress sent a couple of those Wolfkin down with a lovely old man to explain things. You'd like him, he's a bookseller. He's got a shop not far from here, actually," she said.

"Mr Rosemary?"

"Aye, that's the one. Anyway, he'd explained your mistress wanted us to have better lodgings since you'd been doing so well for her, and we got moved over here. He said you'd have come yourself but you were ever so busy."

"That's all he said?"

"Yes. Well he did say we weren't to tell anyone where we'd gone, but who was there to tell?"

"No, that's about right, Mum. She's let me pop home for a visit, but I'm expecting one of my friends soon. We've just got a couple of errands to run for Miss Delsenza before I go back to work." Jyx hated lying to his mother but if he told her the truth, she'd either panic or forbid him from leaving the apartment again. No, it was better that she assumed all was well. It was both surprising and helpful that she'd managed to miss the tales about Eufame's imprisonment so far – unless Mr Rosemary knew one or two spells to aid memory loss.

"I can see she's been feeding you at least, but you do look a little pale."

"I'm just a bit hungry. It took a bit longer to get here than I thought."

"I'll make you a sandwich." His mother stood up and bustled out of the room. Jyx curled his legs under him and snuggled into the armchair. He sipped at the tea, glad of the extra sugar she'd heaped into it. Jyx didn't need fabulous riches or untold power – he was happy with his chair, tea, and a roaring fire.

His mother returned with a ham-and-cheese sandwich, and Jyx marvelled at the freshness of the bread. Normally they came with a side order of mould. They exchanged small talk as he ate, and Jyx answered questions about the Wolfkin. His mother found the silent creatures fascinating, though Jyx couldn't work out from the description which ones Eufame had sent. He did his best to contradict any prejudice his mother might have felt towards them, but they had been clean, respectful, tidy, and strong enough to move her worldly goods, so she was inclined to think well of them.

"I know there are some folk who'd look down their noses at them, but they're a good sort in my book. Pity they get treated so badly. If I were in charge, I'd want good, strong, intelligent people on my side, not working their paws to the bone," said his mother.

"Well, indeed." Jyx finished the last of his sandwich. His eyelids drooped.

"You have yourself a nap while I sort out the kitchen. Your siblings should be back soon. It'd be nice if you got to see them before you leave."

His mother took his plate and went back to the kitchen. Jyx moved from the armchair to the battered old chaise longue underneath the window. Using his arm as a pillow, he lay down and allowed sleep to embrace him.

* * *

A hand shook his shoulder. Jyx lashed out at his unseen attacker and a small voice squeaked from the shadows. He opened his eyes and peered into the gloom.

"What did you do that for?" The person admonished him.

Jyx made out a pair of violet eyes in the darkness. His mother had turned down all of the lamps in the parlour, giving Vyolet a perfect way to sneak inside.

"I didn't know it was you, did I? In case you hadn't

noticed, I was asleep." Jyx sat up and rubbed his eyes. He stretched his back, wincing as the vertebrae popped back into position. He'd forgotten how uncomfortable the chaise longue was.

"Well you're awake now. Eufame sent me."

"All the way here? By yourself?"

"Yeah, she thought it would be faster that way. I've had a nightmare of a time, though. Look at this."

Vyolet held out her arm to show Jyx the hand-shaped burn around her wrist.

"How did you do that?" Jyx pulled her wrist closer so he could examine the mark.

"Dreadguards. One of them caught me but I managed to get away." Vyolet explained about the archives, the guards, the DWS agent, and the guard gargoyle.

Jyx smiled when she described the helpful tabby cat. "That was Bastet. She's Eufame's...well I don't know if she's a pet, a familiar, or something else, but she lives at the House of the Long Dead. I saw her earlier at Mr Rosemary's shop." Jyx told his own tale of getting to Holst Alley.

"Do you think it was the same two Dreadguards?" Vyolet asked when he'd finished.

"I don't know. I don't think so. I got along here well before you got back from the archives, so I don't know how they'd have gotten from here, down to the warehouse district, and back again for you to have seen them twice."

"So, what do we do?" Vyolet peered out of the window, her smoke-like skin becoming tangible in the dim light from the lamps outside.

"We avoid them. I'm guessing you found something in the archives then?"

"Yeah, Eufame thinks she knows where the Heart is, and we're going to go and look for it. We have to meet her at the temple."

"Why the temple?"

"There's an old chapel for a cult that's since fallen out of favour. It was blocked up but it's believed to lead into the ruins of the original city. Eufame thinks it's down there."

"I wonder what the original city was like. It's bad enough living underground in this City – imagine being even further down," said Jyx.

"Yeah, I can't picture it at all," replied Vyolet. "But we'd better get going."

"I'll have to tell my mother I'm leaving again," said Jyx.

"That's okay." Vyolet moved towards the door and dived into the shadow beside the fireplace as the door swung open. Jyx's mother stood silhouetted in the doorway.

"Ah, Jyx, you're awake. I thought I heard voices." She came into the room and turned up the gas lamps.

"Yeah, my friend's here. Remember how I said I was expecting someone?"

"Yes! Well where is he then? Let me see him. I meet so few of your friends." His mother looked around the room and Jyx realised she expected to see another boy from the Academy.

"She's behind you," said Jyx, pointing to the fireplace.

Vyolet stepped out of the shadows and folded her hands behind her back. Jyx's mother turned around and screamed.

"It's a Shadowkin!" She stared at Jyx, her mouth agape.

"Mum, this is Vyolet. Vyolet, this is my mum." Jyx stood up and moved across the room to stand beside Vyolet.

"Your friend…is a Shadowkin?" Jyx's mother shrank away from Vyolet.

"Yes. She is."

"I'm very pleased to meet you, ma'am," said Vyolet. She dipped in an awkward parody of a curtsey.

"I'm sorry but no son of mine will be friends with a Shadowkin," replied his mother.

Jyx looked at Vyolet. Tears swam in her violet eyes and she dropped her gaze. Jyx put his arm around her. His mother turned pale.

"She's a good person, Mum. She's helped me out of a few tight spots."

"Shadowkin aren't good people, Jyx. They're thieves and spies." His mother glanced at the mantelpiece, her gaze seeking out her few ornaments.

"I don't have time to argue. Vyolet came to get me because I've got an errand to run for Miss Delsenza. We can talk about this more when I get back." Jyx guided Vyolet towards the door.

"Are you bringing it home with you?" asked Jyx's mother.

Vyolet broke free from his grasp and fled along the corridor. She disappeared into the shadows by the front door. Jyx turned around in the doorway.

"Vyolet has a name, Mum. You sent me to the Academy so I'd see more of the world, and I'm glad you did because if you hadn't, I'd never have met Vyolet. Do you know how many friends I had at the Academy? Just one, and even then, he was only friends with me because he had no one else either. Do you know how many friends I have now?"

Jyx's mother simply stared at him.

"I'd hope you'd trust my judgment, and if I say Vyolet is a good person, then she's a good person. Not despite the fact she's a Shadowkin, but because of it. None of us really understand them, but based on what I've seen in the short time I've known her, then I want to get to understand them. You managed to change your mind about Wolfkin, so why not Vyolet?"

"The Wolfkin were so polite."

"And so was Vyolet!" Jyx clenched his hands into fists, blood roaring in his ears. He'd never had his mother pegged as the type to so vehemently dislike another species for no good reason. He'd thought she was better than that.

"What time will you be back?" Jyx's mother sniffed and folded her hands in front of her.

"No, no, we're not going to just pretend you weren't incredibly rude to my friend, and act like everything's fine. If you're not going to even promise to get to know her, then I won't be coming back at all."

He turned his back on his mother and stalked along the corridor. She cried after him but he'd already slammed the front door.

Vyolet sat on the top step of the staircase, her arms wrapped around her knees. She looked up at him with wet eyes, tears glistening in tracks down her face. Jyx sat beside her and put his arm around her.

"I'm sorry about that, Vyolet."

"No matter how many times humans say things like that, it still hurts, but I'll get over it. I always do."

"Eufame likes you," said Jyx.

"I know. Eufame's great, but she understands what it's like to be different, to be treated like you're a bad person just because you're not human."

"I won't pretend I know what it's like. I mean, everyone always treated me badly at the Academy because I was poor, but I was still human."

Another sob escaped from Vyolet, and Jyx hugged her close.

"I've never had a friend before," she whispered.

"Well you've got me now, and Fortis, and Bastet, and Eufame. Come on, we'll go to see her, and she'll be pleased to see you."

Jyx's front door opened behind them. His mother shuffled across the landing. Vyolet shrank away, and Jyx stood up to face her.

"Come back safely, my boy, and bring your friend with you. She's not had my cherry bakewell tart yet."

His mother returned to the apartment, and the door closed softly behind her. Jyx looked down at Vyolet.

"I think that's the closest you're going to get to an apology for now."

"She called me your friend."

"Because that's what you are. Now come on, silly, we don't want to keep Eufame waiting. She's got a hell of a temper on her!"

CHAPTER 25

The Shrine of Beseda lay at the far edge of the Underground City, its entrance hewn from the cliff face that formed one of its borders. A spiral staircase curved down into the bowels of the cliff, leading to the shrine itself. All of Beseda's disciples were women, and her priestesses spent time each day with the wronged women who came to petition the goddess. Years ago, Monte's sister had shown him an illustration of Beseda, a beautiful yet forbidding woman with the wings of an owl. She saw and knew everything, and she terrified Monte. The idea of trying to sneak into her shrine filled him with both awe and trepidation, especially as a disciple of the forbidden Lords and Ladies of Death.

Monte, Myrtle and Mr Gondavere arrived in a hansom cab, paid for by Mr Gondavere. The cab took them to Shrine Avenue, a wide street paved with white marble that led to the shrine itself. Huge night trees lined the avenue, their branches forming a twisted arch above the pavement. Their leaves glowed in the gloom, absorbing darkness instead of light. Some said night trees fed on human blood the way ordinary trees sucked up water, but Monte didn't know if that was just an old wives' tale. It certainly made people less likely to cut them down, just in case they had a thirst for vengeance.

"So, what's the plan, then? We can't exactly just walk in," said Monte.

"Myrtle will enter first, and create a diversion. While the priestesses tend to her in the atrium, you and I will sneak down to the shrine. We shall locate the catacombs, and my sources tell me that the entrance into the old ruined city lies within," replied Mr Gondavere.

"Are you sure about this, Myrtle?" asked Monte.

"Oh, it'll be exciting, dear! I don't get out much. This makes such a change!"

Monte raised an eyebrow but said nothing. He'd often heard Myrtle slip out at night when she thought he was asleep. The Lords alone knew where she went or what she did, but Monte never confronted her. He tried to avoid arguments wherever possible.

They walked down the avenue, Myrtle's arm linked through Monte's, but her gaze remained fixed on Mr Gondavere. Monte stared straight ahead so he didn't have to look at the way she kept smiling at his employer.

Two women stood either side of the doorway. They wore leather armour over linen tunics, with feathered capes hanging from their shoulders. One held a double-headed axe, the other a spear. They crossed their weapons to block the door.

"Stop!" cried the woman on the right with the axe.

The trio stopped in front of them.

"Men are not permitted in the Shrine of Beseda."

"We know. We were merely accompanying my associate's lovely wife to the door." Mr Gondavere smiled at them.

The guard with the spear grimaced at him. "What has a happily married wife to seek from Beseda?"

"It depends how happily married she is, doesn't it?" asked Monte.

Myrtle looked up at him, and naked hatred burned in her eyes.

Monte gazed back. He kept his expression placid yet unyielding, but a flicker of something flared in his gut. Monte couldn't decide if it was disinterest or defiance. The glimmer of pleasure told him it was the latter.

"Very well." The guards uncrossed their weapons and allowed Myrtle to pass inside. Monte walked away to sit on a bench beneath the nearest night tree. Mr Gondavere joined him.

"Your marriage is not a happy one, I take it?"

"Not in the slightest." Monte watched the doorway. The two guards resumed their positions, but the woman with the spear kept glancing at him. Her expression was curious, rather than hostile.

"I am surprised. Your wife is wonderful."

"Many men would agree with you." Bitterness laced Monte's words, and he fought to keep his expression neutral. He'd tried so hard to overlook her utter indifference towards him, but the more time he spent around Mr Gondavere, the less he found he could ignore it.

A commotion erupted inside the shrine entrance. The two guards raced inside. Female voices pitched and shrieked, broken by a bloodcurdling scream. Monte leapt to his feet and ran across the avenue to the entrance. He slipped inside.

A staircase to his left curved down into the darkness, and a wide, circular chamber lay to his right. Four white owls attacked a bundle on the floor across the room, and two women in feathered dresses hurled incantations at the pile of fabric. Their words burned bright in the shadows, illuminating the bundle. It was Myrtle, huddled on the floor, attempting to ward off the vicious owls. The two guards stood nearby, holding back other female petitioners.

"This is a sacred space for wronged women, not women who wrong others!" screamed one of the priestesses.

Another incantation tore open the air, and for a split second, Monte saw Myrtle hurrying through the darkened streets of Canalsditch. She visited a cottage he didn't recognise, later appearing dishevelled but grinning at the doorway. His heart plummeted into his stomach, smashing the web of apathy he'd built towards Myrtle. The scene changed to that of a midnight tryst between Myrtle and one of the other diggers in the graveyard. Tears prickled the back of his eyes, but anger washed away the sadness. A third scene showed Myrtle in the arms of a man clad in black. Monte grimaced and slipped down the stairs before he saw the face of the man. He didn't need to.

Mr Gondavere caught up with him at the bottom of the spiral staircase. A passageway would take them into the shrine, but the locked grate to their left was of more interest to Mr Gondavere. Darkness lay beyond, and the scent of grave dirt and wet stone drifted into the stairwell. Monte glared into the darkness.

"This must surely be the entrance to the catacombs. Somewhere in there lies the entrance to the ruined city," said Mr Gondavere.

"There's nowhere else for us to go. We certainly can't go into the shrine itself," replied Monte. His thoughts strayed to the attack upstairs, and he hoped the owls had finished off Myrtle. The hope scared him. Before Myrtle, he'd never wished anything bad on anyone. He shoved his fists into his pockets to stop his hands from shaking.

Mr Gondavere produced a long, thin skeleton

key from inside his case. He waggled it inside the lock, and the grate swung open with a squeal. They slipped into the darkness and closed the grate behind them. Two cloaked women came out of the shrine and appeared in the stairwell. Monte pressed himself into the shadows.

"I could've sworn I heard something out here," said one of the women.

"Sounded like the gate but it looks locked," replied the other.

The first woman rattled the gate.

"It is locked. We must be hearing things."

They retreated into the shrine, and Monte let out the breath he'd been holding.

"Come along, my good man. Time waits for no man." Mr Gondavere's voice grew faint as he walked away along the corridor.

Monte followed, keeping one arm outstretched to his right and the other in front. He trailed his fingers along the wall, tracing wet stones thick with moss. He blinked but it didn't help. The shadows were impenetrable. Flashes of the scenes from the shrine kept lighting up the darkness.

"There's a corner coming up, Monte. Once we're around it, I'll strike a light so we may see." Mr Gondavere's voice was closer this time.

Monte's fingers brushed the wall in front of him, and he followed the wall to his right until it met another wall. He marked the path of the corner and moved along the passage.

Pale blue light flared in front of him, and Monte gasped to see flames flickering from Mr Gondavere's hand.

"What manner of goblin nonsense is this?" he asked.

"A parlour trick I learned from a mage, nothing more."

"It looks like marsh fire," replied Monte. He'd seen similar flames in the graveyard, burning above graves that he could never find if the fires flickered out. No matter how far he walked towards the flames, he remained the same distance away from them. Legends abounded among the gravediggers of individuals driven mad by the 'marsh fire'.

"I can assure you, it's merely a trick." Mr Gondavere's voice skated on a knife edge, and Monte decided to drop the subject. He'd file it away with all of the other things he wanted to ask about.

They walked in silence along the corridor. Huge slabs of stone made up the walls, and a shallow vault served as a ceiling. Monte fought to keep his thoughts on the task at hand. He hadn't even known this place existed yesterday, and now here he was, exploring it.

"I must say, I rather thought you would be more emotional about the demise of your wife," said Mr Gondavere. "She was a beautiful woman."

"We hadn't been happy for a while. I tried, she didn't." Monte thought again of her spectacular garden, the focus of her main efforts in life. The visions he'd seen upstairs turned the thought sour, the blooms shrivelling in the light of her deceit.

"At least she served a noble purpose. When I asked her to create a diversion, I believed she would feign a fit, or some such. I had no idea the priestesses would fall upon her in such a way."

"Would you have kept your hands off her if you had?" Monte couldn't stop the words coming out of his mouth, speaking them aloud before he'd even realised his mind could form them.

Mr Gondavere stopped and turned around. The flames cast flickering shadows across his face that distended and contracted his features, giving him the fluid appearance of a goblin.

"It is true that your wife was most accommodating. It has been a long time since I have been spoken to kindly by a woman. That is all I will say on the matter."

"Exactly who, or what, are you?"

"Your employer, for the time being, at least." Mr Gondavere continued along the corridor.

Monte glared at his back. He dug his nails into his palms to stop himself flying at such a strange man. Or creature. How could Myrtle...with *him*? Monte bit his tongue to keep himself from retching.

The corridor opened into an anteroom. Brick pillars held up the vaulted ceiling, and marble pillars marked a doorway in the opposite wall. A marble slab formed a lintel, bearing the inscription, 'Behold the Empire of Death. Tread carefully or not at all.' Mr Gondavere ignored the inscription and walked beneath the lintel. Monte performed the respectful salute of the gravediggers and passed into the catacombs.

As a gravedigger, he'd seen hundreds of coffins, and plenty of bodies wound in burial shrouds, yet he'd seen few dead bodies openly on display. The catacombs shocked him into silence. Bones were piled on either side of the long, low passageway. Grinning skulls leered at him among smooth thighbones. Monte had expected coffins resting in loculi, not human remains in the open.

"Do you know the history of these catacombs?" Mr Gondavere's flickering blue flames lent the skulls a fleeting form of animation, their empty eye sockets following Monte's progress.

"No, sir," replied Monte. The shock of the sight had forced a modicum of respect out of him.

"These were once followers of the Lords and Ladies of Death. They had magnificent tombs, full of statuary and the noblest forms of funereal art. When the Lords and Ladies were cast down by Brigante Delsenza, the tombs were torn open, the statuary dispersed, and the art sold off. The bones were thrown in here to be forgotten."

"Who's Brigante Delsenza?"

"She is the oldest of the Delsenza clan. Descended from banshees, they command powers over the dead, and the Veil. Her youngest sister is Eufame, the erstwhile necromancer general. The whole clan despised the Lords and Ladies of Death, seeing them as parasites, not the noble patrons of the dead that they are." Mr Gondavere held himself straighter as he spoke.

Monte tried to reconcile what Mr Gondavere said with what he knew of the Lords and Ladies of Death. If he was honest, that was very little. He'd had no patron deity as a child, believing in the concepts of home and family instead. He only adopted the Lords and Ladies when he found work as a gravedigger. He believed them to be forgotten beings who guided the dead across the Veil and into the realms beyond. Given the necromancer general had the power to cross the Veil and speak with the dead, giving them a voice even after death, why would the Delsenza clan tear them down? There was more to the tale than Mr Gondavere was letting on.

"Keep your eyes peeled, Monte. One of these gates must lead to the ruined city." Mr Gondavere pointed at the gates set into the walls at regular intervals between the piles of bones.

"How will we know which one it is?"

"It'll be marked in some way. Hold your hand out."

Monte held out his hand. Mr Gondavere passed the flames into his palm with a whisper. Monte stared at the flickering flames that burned orange when they made contact with his skin. They didn't burn, or give off any heat at all – they simply tickled. Mr Gondavere whispered into his hand to create more blue flames of his own.

"You take this side and I'll take that side." Mr Gondavere inspected the nearest gateway. Monte held up his hand and inspected the stone around the gate on his side.

They made their way along the passageway, inspecting each grate. Monte tried to ignore the skeletons piled on either side of the doorways and yelped when his free hand made contact with a skull. He looked down, expecting its jaws to clamp down upon his fingers, but it simply looked up at him with empty eye sockets.

"I have found it!" cried Mr Gondavere.

Monte hurried across to the gate where Mr Gondavere jabbed a finger at a small mark scraped into the stone.

"It's a heart!"

"Exactly! What else can it mean, if not the Heart of the City?"

"Isn't that a little easy?" asked Monte.

"Not in the slightest. First someone would need to gain access to the shrine, and then they would need to get into the catacombs, not to mention being able to locate the correct gate." Mr Gondavere produced the skeleton key again, and the gate swung open at his touch. "Come along, man! You will be the first human to set eyes upon the ruined city in an age!"

Mr Gondavere plunged into the darkness. Monte ignored the dread bubbling in his stomach and followed.

Chapter 26

Jyx and Vyolet followed the back streets of Temple Park, keen to avoid the main thoroughfares and the loitering Dreadguards. Jyx couldn't get over the difference between the district, and the one in which he'd grown up. No street urchins lurked in the alleys and no trolls lumbered by. It wasn't the City Above, but it wasn't the slum he was used to.

Before long, the temple loomed before them, flaming brackets hanging from its cracked columns. They followed the narrow street along its side, passing between groups of people heading to the entrance. Vyolet dissolved in and out of view, melting into the shadows when the groups were too large. Jyx pulled up his hood and walked as quickly as he could. He'd feel much safer with Eufame or the Wolfkin around. The Eufame fragment in his mind wiggled in response.

I have got to be more confident in my abilities, he admonished himself as he darted after Vyolet. *Just not too confident.*

They turned the corner into the courtyard. Columns lined the walls on three sides, and the main temple building took up most of the fourth wall. Benches dotted around the courtyard held petitioners of all ages and races. Children played in the fountain at the courtyard's centre and peddlers shuffled from bench to bench, holding out their wares. Three overweight men in the blood red uniform of the council guard loitered near a meat seller. The juices from their skewers dribbled down their stubbled chins. Jyx frowned. Why were the council guard in the Underground City at all, let alone the Temple?

"Look!" Vyolet's voice drifted from a shadow to Jyx's left. Two hooded figures lurked in the shadows near the back of the courtyard, the cloaks barely disguising muscular arms and wolf-like snouts. They were accompanied by a third figure, tall and stately in a black cloak. Jyx and Vyolet slipped through the throng towards them.

"Ah, so Vyolet got the message to you!" The tall figure turned towards them as they approached. Eufame's cold eyes glittered in the depths of the hood. The splinter in his mind pulsed, happy to be so near the necromancer general.

"Yes, she found me, okay, but there are Dreadguards in the Underground City," said Jyx. He pushed down his hood.

"I know, we've seen them. Luckily my sister's magick does not extend this far Underground, or I couldn't have cloaked us. Though I see you've found a way to cloak yourself, Jyx. I can smell the ghost of a mirror enchantment on you," said Eufame.

"I met Mr Rosemary," said Jyx.

"I know, Bastet told me. She told me she'd met you too, Vyolet," said Eufame.

"She fixed my ankle after I twisted it, but I didn't know who she was at the time."

"But you trusted her anyway. That's enough for

my Bastet." Eufame's eyes narrowed, and Jyx realised she smiled within the hood.

"Why are the council guard down here? Are they looking for you?" Jyx sneaked another glance at the guards, but the steaming meat kept them occupied.

"Oh they've got nothing to do with us. They're probably sizing up this place for the Crown Prince's plans. Judging by the look of them, they've been underground for a while. They're no threat," replied Eufame.

"We haven't a moment to lose, mistress. Already the others have found a way inside." A familiar voice echoed inside Jyx's mind. Validus inclined his head so Jyx would know which Wolfkin was which.

"They have? Damn it. We'd better hurry up." Eufame strode away and through the main entrance of the temple. Vyolet dissolved into smoke and secreted herself inside the shadows of Jyx's hood before he followed Eufame and the Wolfkin.

* * *

Desperate people thronged the temple square, peeling off in groups to visit their chosen chapels. The temple school must have finished for the day since no children clustered on the far side of the square. Jyx looked at the lectern and rows of benches with some affection. He'd first learned the value of books sitting on those hard pews.

"The entrance is somewhere over here," said Eufame as they reached the quiet far corner. She whispered a few words and flung her arm wide, as if she cast a net into a stream. The magick hummed at the edges of Jyx's hearing, and tiny silver sparks glittered around them. He sensed a stronger version of his own mirror enchantment.

"How will we find it?" asked Jyx.

"I don't actually know. I'd ask the stones, but I've never had much of a fondness for earth magick."

"I have," said Jyx. Just before Eufame selected him as her apprentice, he'd been studying geomancy in secret at the Academy. He'd learned a lot in between, but he was sure he remembered the basics.

"How far did you get with it?"

"I once had a conversation with the stone lintel above the front door of my mother's old building. I'd forgotten about that until now, probably because it was such a dull chat," replied Jyx.

"Excellent. Can you ask these stones if they know where the entrance is? You should be able to tell by their replies which ones are older, and the younger stones are likely to be newer. They're the ones that will cover the entrance."

Jyx blanched. He wasn't sure he could remember the sigil. Eufame pushed back her hood, her cold eyes bright with expectation. Vyolet remained in the shadows of his hood, a comforting presence behind him. Validus nodded to encourage him.

He knelt on the floor and chose a stone at random. He drew what he thought was the right sigil in the air over the stone and whispered the incantation.

"*Mecum loqueretur, lapis, volo enim fabulam.*"

Nothing. Jyx frowned. He moved along and repeated the sigil and incantation over the next stone. Again, nothing. Was it the right incantation or had he misremembered the sigil? He closed his eyes and thought of the geomancy textbook, mentally turning the pages. There it was, conversing with earth materials. According to his memory, the sigil and incantation were both right.

"If you're expecting to get a word out of those two, then I wouldn't bother."

Jyx looked around to find the source of the voice. "Where are you?" he asked.

"Three along to your right, and two up."

Jyx counted along to the right stone. Its edges glowed green, humming with the power of his incantation.

"Why won't those two talk to me?" he asked.

"They're too new. We've been here for years, but they're a more recent addition. They think themselves above us, as if they're the most vital part of this entire structure," replied the stone. "It's all utter nonsense, of course."

"Of course, anyone with eyes can see that you're all important," replied Jyx.

"Exactly! But such socialist thinking is beyond that lot over there. Of course, there are a lot of things beyond them, that's essentially why they're there."

"Is that right?"

"It is. What did you want to speak about with them?"

"It doesn't matter now, you've answered my question. Do you think I'd be able to persuade them to move out of the way? We need to get through."

"Oh they won't move for you, my boy."

"Why not?" asked Jyx.

"They're too lofty for such things. Fear not, however. They will move for us."

A faint green glow rippled through the stones, apart from a patch of stonework that the glow would not touch. Jyx wasn't surprised to see that the patch was the size and shape of a narrow chapel doorway.

The untouched stones vibrated, slowly at first, until they joggled and shook against each other. The cement between them ground into dust and Jyx stepped back to allow the stones to move towards him, jiggling out of their spaces and dropping to the ground. Jyx held his sleeve over his mouth so he wouldn't breathe in the dust.

"There, that's rid of them. It's amazing what you'll find down there," said the stone he'd been speaking to.

"You've been ever so helpful! I'm very grateful," said Jyx.

"Not at all. It's been nice to have a conversation

with someone again. Do stop by if you're in the area again."

"I will," said Jyx. He muttered the stone speech incantation in reverse and the green glow faded from the stones.

"Very nice, Jyx. Your abilities really are coming along well, and without instruction. Most impressive." Eufame stood behind him and peered over his shoulder.

"Before we go down there, can I ask you something?"

"I'm sure you can ask something – whether you will or not is entirely up to you."

Jyx shot her a pained look. "You're not setting me up for something again, are you?"

"There is little I can do to convince you that I am not, except to tell you that no, I am not setting you up for anything. You are here as my apprentice, even if I have essentially asked you to 'go rogue' on my behalf," said Eufame.

She gestured at the rough doorway in the wall, and Jyx passed through. Vyolet climbed out of his hood and formed her usual self out of a pillar of smoke. The Wolfkin followed and lit torches they produced from beneath their cloaks. Eufame stepped inside last and paused to cast another enchantment over the doorway. Passers-by would see an intact wall and no masonry lying on the ground.

"Will that last long enough?" asked Jyx.

"It'll last as long as I want it to." Eufame took the lead and plunged into the darkness.

Narrow steps led down into the abandoned chapel and Jyx followed the Wolfkin's flickering torches. Vyolet scampered on ahead, unafraid of the oppressive darkness in the stairwell. Validus lifted an old torch out of a bracket on the wall and lit it using his own flame. He handed it to Jyx.

"Now you have your own means of seeing, Master Faire."

"Thank you," replied Jyx.

The flame sizzled and sang as it burned, its warmth a reassuring presence near his face. Water dripped in the darkness and the stones smelled of ancient incense. The stairs led into a long, low room, its black walls decorated with white figures. At first Jyx thought they were similar portraits to those found on the walls of the House of the Long Dead, but as he looked closer, he saw that they differed immensely. Where the figures in Eufame's vault were stately, and drawn flat with the heads of animals, these figures were carved into the stone like woodcut illustrations. Some were short and squat, and others were tall and skeletal.

"What are these? They're horrific." Vyolet stood back from the wall, her eyes wide and her nose wrinkled up.

"They're portraits of the Lords and Ladies of Death, the cult that inspired the construction of this chapel. Do you see anything that unites all of the figures?" asked Eufame.

"They've all got fangs," replied Jyx, examining a tall woman in an old-fashioned dress.

"Indeed. They were parasites, before Brigante banished them to a twilight realm," replied Eufame.

"Who's Brigante?"

"My oldest sister. She has even less patience for the Lords and Ladies than I do for the politics of the City Above. I rather miss her, actually. She has a tremendous talent for shape-shifting."

"Even the Wolfkin could not tolerate the excesses of the Lords and Ladies." Validus pointed at a portrait carved into the wall. An impossibly tall woman dwarfed a cowering Wolfkin, her fangs bared.

"This one's interesting though." Vyolet pointed to a small illustration, almost easy to miss in the shadows in the corner. A male figure, with a round belly, short legs and huge beard, stood beneath a tree. The other

Lords and Ladies bared their fangs and wore expressions of cruelty and arrogance, but this figure looked behind him, fear clouding his eyes. Vyolet pointed to a haze beyond the tree.

"What's that?" asked Jyx.

"It's a Shadowkin. I've seen this type of figure before. Kids sometimes paint them on walls in the City," she said.

"Interesting." Eufame peered at the illustration again.

"I guess they didn't like us," said Vyolet.

"It's worth investigating when this is all sorted out. Your people have a fascinating history that should be reclaimed," replied Eufame.

She straightened up and led them through the low vaulted room. More chambers branched away from the room at the back and they hurried through the maze of short corridors and square rooms. Jyx couldn't work out what any of the empty rooms might have been used for, but he'd never ventured into the chapels above either and had no point of reference.

They followed Eufame into the smallest room at the furthest point from the chapel. It was the only furnished room they'd seen so far, with an empty bookcase standing against the wall opposite the door. A cold breeze moved around the room though Jyx couldn't work out where it was coming from. There were no vents in the walls and the cold persisted even when they closed the door.

"This has got to be the entrance to the ruined city. Why else would it be cold in here?" asked Eufame.

"Why did this chapel have an entrance to the city, and none of the others do?" asked Jyx.

"None of the other chapels are below ground. This is the only one. Though I rather suspect the followers of the Lords and Ladies also liked having a back door," said Eufame.

Validus eased past Jyx and took hold of one side

of the bookcase. Fortis took the other and they edged it to one side. A grate was embedded in the wall and freezing air blasted into the small room from the darkness beyond.

"Excellent work, my dears," said Eufame.

She touched the lock with her fingers and it sprang open. The gate swung inwards, its hinges screaming in protest.

Eufame turned to them all and smiled. "Well then. Into the breach, eh?"

CHAPTER 27

A long corridor led away from the catacombs, so narrow that it forced Monte to turn sideways. He inched along the passage, following the downward slope until it opened out onto a landing. An iron balustrade surrounded two sides, and a staircase led down from the third side, clinging to the rock wall. Monte peered into the darkness, but their flames didn't illuminate much beyond the outlines of some buildings at the bottom of the stairs.

"Welcome to the ruined city, Monte," said Mr Gondavere.

"I didn't even realise this was here."

"No one ever does. That's the beauty of it."

"You speak like you've been here before." Monte followed Mr Gondavere down the fifteen crooked steps to a street paved with cracked stones. Black moss bloomed between the slabs, sending tendrils crawling across the pavement.

"It's a magical place, is it not?" said Mr Gondavere.

Monte narrowed his eyes. Mr Gondavere could have been one of the councillors with an attitude like that. Well, two could play at that game.

"Why is it so cold? I thought we'd be warmer because we're even further underground." Monte stared into the darkness beyond the circle of light cast by the flames in his palm. Was something moving out there? A phantom of Myrtle danced before his eyes, her mouth stretched wide in a taunting grin. He screwed up his face to block her out.

"This isn't a place of life, Monte. This is very much a place of death," replied Mr Gondavere. "Specifically the Lords and Ladies of Death."

Monte shivered. He'd always pictured death as cold, and fathomless. It was rational, and pragmatic. He saw it every day – it was just as natural as drawing breath. But here in the ruined city, it felt oppressive, and vengeful. He'd always called on the Lords and Ladies of Death in times of trouble, assuming that they were his only choice as an undertaker. Perhaps he should have remained an atheist after all.

"Brigante Delsenza banished the Lords and Ladies, but she couldn't send them just anywhere. The entrance to the alternative realm is down here," said Mr Gondavere.

"How do you know all of this stuff?" Monte wasn't entirely sure he wanted to know the answer.

"I have my sources." Mr Gondavere smiled, and his teeth glittered in the light from the blue fire in his palm. Was it Monte's imagination, or were they longer, sharper somehow?

"You never tell me anything," said Monte.

"I pay you to help me, Monte. That is all." Mr Gondavere stopped at a crossing. He looked up each of the streets in turn, before selecting the street to the right. Large buildings loomed out of the darkness. They were low, with night trees growing out of them through broken windows. Marks daubed on the door looked like numbers, but not any numbers that Monte could read. Some of the walls lay in fragments, piles of black bricks scattered across the street, and others had roofs open to the air, turning the empty houses into courtyards.

Monte was used to the small cottages and crumbling tenements of the Underground City, with its narrow alleys and crowded streets, and the canals and palazzos of the City Above had been an eye opener. Yet the ruined city followed a third style, with wide streets, low houses and plenty of space. He peered through shattered windows and into houses, staring at the upended furniture and broken belongings. What had happened here?

"What are we looking for?" asked Monte.

"A tomb. The Heart of the City lies down here, Monte. Once we have located it, then the power of the City is mine."

"What will you use it for?"

"Had you asked me that question before we ventured into the Shrine, I would have avoided answering it, but I see no harm in telling you now. After all, you'll never find your way out without me." Mr Gondavere turned and smiled at Monte, his fangs glinting in the low light. "I will use the power of the Heart to recall my brothers and sisters, and not even Brigante Delsenza can stop me."

A wave of fear crashed over Monte and the cold settled in his gut like an icy stone. If Mr Gondavere had brothers and sisters who had been banished, then that meant only one thing. Mr Gondavere was related to the Lords and Ladies of Death – and here he was, alone with him in an ancient city that most people didn't believe was real.

"I don't think we need to worry about Brigante Delsenza, sir." Monte fought to keep the wobble out of his voice. He'd served Mr Gondavere well so far – perhaps if his employer believed he sought the same things then he could still get out of this alive.

Mr Gondavere turned to look at him and his heart fluttered.

"Brigante is the least of our worries, Monte. Her sister, on the other hand…"

"Eufame Delsenza isn't likely to make an appearance, is she, sir?"

"According to my sources, she is indeed on her way, accompanied by two Wolfkin and her apprentice. She thinks she has hidden their presence, but none can truly hide from the Lords and Ladies of Death. Come, we must hurry."

Mr Gondavere led them down another street and Monte peered into broken houses as they passed. Graffiti covered the back wall of the courtyard on his right. Tall, thin figures were inscribed in white paint, shrinking away from an indistinct haze beside them. Monte swung his light away before Mr Gondavere noticed. His employer stopped suddenly at a crossroads. A wide boulevard lined with cobblestones and weeds crossed the narrow street.

"Ah! I had entirely forgotten this avenue. If memory serves, this leads to the Tombs of Kings, and it is there that we shall find the Heart of the City," said Mr Gondavere.

Monte nodded and followed Mr Gondavere onto the avenue. Something skittered in the darkness to his right, and Monte gulped. This wouldn't end well at all.

CHAPTER 28

A stairwell led down into darkness on the other side of the gate. Jyx had expected total darkness, but two tiny lights bobbed along some distance away. It looked like marsh fire – but why would there be marsh fire in a ruined city?

"Damn it, looks like we aren't the first to reach the city." Eufame peered over Jyx's shoulder into the shadows.

"It's beautiful down there," said Vyolet. She gazed down into the city below, her eyes huge. Jyx envied her ability to see in the dark and made a mental note to look up charms he could use in future to do likewise.

"Some of your people used to live down here, Vyolet. For a long time they were the only ones who knew it was still here. But then they found ways to work with the humans, and now they're scattered throughout the Underground City instead," said Eufame. "I wouldn't be surprised if the actions of my sister also played a part in things."

"Why?" asked Jyx.

"When Brigante banished the Lords and Ladies of Death to another realm, that realm needed some kind of access point. The entrance is somewhere in the ruined city. The Shadowkin didn't want to be anywhere near that, and who can blame them?"

Fortis leaned beyond Jyx and took back the lit torch. He extinguished it with a wave of his hand and Jyx stared up at the bulk of the Wolfkin. His eyes struggled to adjust to the new darkness.

"That's a good point, Fortis. We don't want to advertise our presence if we can help it," said Eufame.

Fortis and Validus stepped onto the stairs. They nodded to each other and began their descent. Jyx looked beyond them to the tiny bobbing marsh lights.

"Exactly who is down there?" he asked.

"I'm not sure of his name yet, but I'm pretty sure we don't want him getting his hands on the Heart of the City. He has someone with him, a human of some kind. I don't think the human is overly fond of him, though. That may, or may not, work in our favour." Eufame stepped onto the stairs and followed the Wolfkin into the darkness below.

"How can she see?" asked Jyx.

"She's not human, remember. Hold my hand and I'll lead you." Vyolet slipped her hand into Jyx's and led him down the stairs.

Total darkness enveloped them at the bottom. The ground below his feet felt like cobblestones grown slippery with moss, and he shuddered at the way the shadows lay across his skin.

"We're in a wide street, Jyx. The houses are all a single storey, and a lot of them look like something bad happened here. Broken windows, walls that have caved in – there are even trees growing out of some of the roofs," said Vyolet, keeping her voice low.

"Have you ever been down here before?" asked Jyx.

"No, but I remember the stories about it. The Elders always forbade us from coming down here," replied Vyolet.

Jyx allowed her to lead him, though the shard of Eufame in his mind made it easy to follow the necromancer general through the dark streets. He focused on his hearing instead of his useless sight, listening for the soft footfalls of the Wolfkin, and the swish of Eufame's robes. Vyolet was like silent smoke beside him. It was no wonder people employed the Shadowkin as rogues, spies and thieves. How different the Underground City might have been if the humans had worked with them, instead of against them.

"Vyolet?" Eufame's voice sounded up ahead.

The Shadowkin hauled Jyx after her. Jyx smelled the cold edges of Eufame's cloak and guessed she stood beside him. The scent of warm leather told him the Wolfkin were also nearby.

"I need your help." Eufame's voice sounded near Jyx's right side.

"My help?"

"Yes. The street signs are all in your tongue, not mine."

"Oh, I see. Do you know what I need to look out for?" asked Vyolet.

"The Tombs of Kings," replied Eufame. "I know they're at the edge of the ruined city, tunnelled into the walls, I just don't know where."

Vyolet let go of Jyx's hand. He stifled a yelp.

"Jyx?" Eufame's voice sounded closer.

"I can't see. Vyolet's been leading me," replied Jyx.

"Oh, I quite forgot. Here, hold still." Eufame's hand clamped over Jyx's eyes, her skin icy against his. She muttered something under her breath. When she removed her palm, the world swam into view. Dim outlines of buildings appeared in the shadows, and the white streak in Eufame's hair glowed in the darkness beside him.

"I've passed on a little of my sight to you, so you can at least find your way. I can't have you blind down here," said Eufame.

Vyolet took up her position at the head of the party, accompanied by Fortis. Eufame came next, followed by Jyx, and Validus brought up the rear. Being sandwiched between the necromancer general and a Wolfkin brought a measure of security to Jyx, even if he couldn't shake the feeling that something was watching them from the shadows. He'd seen books on mental acuity, and psychic magick, in the library at the Academy, but he'd always dismissed them as nonsense. Considering the fact he carried a sliver of Eufame in his mind, he now knew such things were real. Still, it didn't help to berate himself for being an idiot at the Academy.

Up ahead, Fortis raised his head and sniffed the air. He let out a tiny yip and a low growl. Validus responded in kind behind him. A shiver ran down Jyx's spine. Something skittered in the street to their right. Sounding like claws on stone, it echoed among the buildings. It was still far away, but the fact it was there at all made Jyx's stomach clench.

Eufame replied with her own bark, and the party pressed on, their brisk walk verging on a slow jog. Jyx didn't stop to ask why Eufame wasn't facing down the threat. Either it was too far away to be a problem, or she was hoping to find the Heart first. He didn't want to consider the third alternative – that Eufame couldn't tackle whatever it was herself. And if she couldn't defend them with the help of two Wolfkin…

For the first time in his life, Jyx wished he'd shown aptitude as a soldier, not a mage.

"Down here," whispered Vyolet. She disappeared around a corner into the darkness. They followed, and found themselves in a long corridor. Rounded arches punctured the walls, and Jyx peered into the shadows beyond. Were these tombs?

"She's in here. I can feel her," said Eufame. She kept her voice low, and Jyx jumped to hear it puncture the silence.

"What was out there?" asked Jyx.

"Bloodhounds." An edge of frost sharpened Eufame's tone.

"What are they?" Jyx tried to remember all of the books he'd read, and he'd never come across anything called a Bloodhound before.

"Something you should pray you never meet," said Vyolet. "I've heard stories about them, and they never end well."

"There is someone else here." Validus's voice echoed in Jyx's head.

"Who?" asked Jyx.

Before Validus could reply, Eufame broke into a run and stormed ahead. Jyx ran to keep up, his boots slapping on the flagstones. She plunged along the corridor towards the tomb at the end. Lights flickered into being in the darkness of the tomb, and a figure stepped forward through the arch. He held a blue flame in his palm that fluttered against his skin. Eufame stuttered to a halt, and Jyx bumped into her back. She held her arms wide, both to steady Jyx and to hold him behind her. The warmth of the Wolfkin lapped against his back.

"Ah, so the necromancer general has decided to grace us with her presence," said the man. The blue flames in his palm cast a sickly glow across his face. Jyx screwed up his nose. The stranger had more teeth than Jyx was comfortable with, and they were sharper than they should be. He wore black from head to foot, including a wilted flower in his lapel. He might have looked like an Underground City dandy, were it not for those teeth.

"And you are?" asked Eufame.

"Horatio Gondavere, though you may call me Mr Gondavere. I assume you have come here for the same reason that I have?"

"I came here to show my student the tombs," replied Eufame.

Jyx marvelled at the ease with which the lie rolled off her tongue, but was it really a lie? He was her student, and she was showing him the tombs.

"Do not lie to me, necromancer. You came to locate the Heart of the City." Mr Gondavere narrowed his eyes and pursed his lips. The expression was an ugly one, but at least it hid his awful teeth.

"And if I did?"

"Then I should have to introduce you to some friends of mine." Mr Gondavere placed two fingers into his mouth and blew. A piercing whistle echoed around the corridor, producing blue sparks where the sound struck the stone walls.

Familiar skittering came along the corridor towards them. It was the same sound Jyx had heard outside, only much closer. The sound of claws on stone. Sharp claws, at that. He paused to wonder where Vyolet was, but he couldn't see much. He hoped she hid in the shadows of one of the tombs. He didn't know a lot about Shadowkin, but he'd come to see them as stealthy and quiet, not strong fighters like the Wolfkin.

Fortis dropped into a crouch, holding his paws up in a boxer's stance. Validus stood with his legs wide, the muscles of his thighs taut as he braced himself. Jyx willed them to draw their weapons, but instead they bared their teeth. The corridor echoed with their fearsome growls. Jyx shrank against Eufame, surprised that she didn't turn to face the threat.

"Do you not intend to aid your Wolfkin?" asked Mr Gondavere.

"They aren't my Wolfkin, and they're more than

a match for anything you might have conjured up," replied Eufame.

"Even Bloodhounds?" Mr Gondavere smiled.

Jyx's stomach clenched to see the row of teeth again. He turned to look behind him. Shapes emerged from the dark, throwing themselves against the Wolfkin. Snapping jaws clattered around the Wolfkins' arms and legs and vicious claws flashed in the darkness. Fortis and Validus howled and lurched into the attack, pushing back the Bloodhounds. Jyx tried to make out features, but the strange creatures were too dark to see clearly. Only their blood red eyes stood out in the shadows. A shudder behind him prompted Jyx to turn around. He looked up into Eufame's face, and naked terror rippled through him. Fear shone in the necromancer general's eyes.

Chapter 29

Vyolet edged past Eufame and Jyx, unseen in the shadows of the corridor. She stared at Mr Gondavere. She'd never seen one of the Lords of Death before, though she wasn't entirely sure she was looking at one now. He was too short, too human-like, to be a true Lord. Jyx trembled to see his mouthful of teeth, but Vyolet merely grimaced. She'd seen worse among the patrons of the Flee Market.

Between Eufame and Mr Gondavere, she watched the Bloodhounds approach. Their sinewy bodies and dark fur gave them away among the shadows they tried to hide in. She glanced at the Wolfkin and winced when they pushed themselves into the Bloodhound attack. Still, it threw the Bloodhounds off guard, and the Wolfkin forced the creatures further up the corridor.

They're pushing them away from us.

She didn't have time to worry about the Wolfkin. There was nothing she could do against Bloodhounds. Her uncles would have been useful, able to shape weapons from the shadows, or maybe her grandmother, with her ability to phase and fight simultaneously. No, the Wolfkin were good warriors, and she was better suited to discovering why Mr Gondavere blocked the doorway.

She looked at the arch behind Mr Gondavere. He seemed very keen to keep Eufame and Jyx away from it. Vyolet concentrated hard, turning her very essence as dark as she possibly could, and inched towards the doorway. She hugged the wall, keeping herself in the darkest shadows. Mr Gondavere hadn't looked at her once, so she could only assume he couldn't see her.

He can't be a full Lord then. If Mama's stories were right, then they used to hunt us. We were the only thing they feared.

Mr Gondavere raised his arm towards Eufame, and Vyolet seized her chance. She ducked and slipped under his elbow.

The other arches all led directly into tombs, but this doorway took her into a short passage. A cloak of shadows hung from the ceiling and to the outside view, the tomb beyond lay in darkness. Vyolet slipped through the cloak and gasped. Dim light filled the tomb up ahead. The raised voices of Eufame and Mr Gondavere faded, drowned out by the low hum of the cloak's magick.

Vyolet hurried on, too impatient to consider the sorcery involved in the cloak. Wall niches lined the passageway and held coffins in various stages of decay. She peeked through a gap in the nearest coffin where the lid and the sides had grown apart. All she could see was a bony shoulder blade, wrapped in rags.

She reached another archway, lower than the first, and peered inside. A stone figure rested against the wall. It hugged its knees to its chest, its face hidden by a mane of limestone curls. A broken spear and a plumed helmet lay on the floor beside her. A man knelt on the floor, hunched over a pile of rocks.

Flames danced in his palm and he held them close to the rocks. He peered at one stone after another. Vyolet narrowed her eyes – at least now she knew the source of the dim light. But who was he? He wore the clothes of a gravedigger, but the flames marked him as some kind of magic wielder.

"Oh it's no use, I'll never be able to fit these back together," said the man. His accent gave him away as being from Canalsditch.

So not exactly a sorcerer or a mage then.

She gazed at him. He tried to fit the stones together, turning them this way and that to find the edges that belonged to one another. Beads of sweat clustered across his brow, and his fingers twitched.

Vyolet gauged the distance to the shadows in the corner, in case she needed a speedy getaway, and stepped forward into the dim light cast by the man's flames. He looked up and fell backwards onto his bottom. He scrabbled across the stone floor of the tomb, careful to hold up his palm to keep the flames going.

"You're a Shadowkin!"

"I am. Who are you? And why are you here?" asked Vyolet.

"I could ask you the same thing!" he replied. His hand trembled and the flames in his palm performed a jerky dance.

"Fair enough, I suppose. I'm Vyolet. And you are?"

"Monte McThwaite. Why is a Shadowkin down here? Are there more of you?"

"Why is a gravedigger from Canalsditch in here?"

Monte stared at her. Vyolet stared back. Years of having the people of the Underground City staring at her made it easy to challenge their looks. Most turned away, guilty at having been caught, but not Monte. There was curiosity in his gaze, not fear.

"Oh, you have no idea what it's been like. I met him in the pub, and he offered me a job, and it seemed like a good idea, what with the money he was offering and everything, and it seemed exciting at first. But then he took my Myrtle, and dragged me down here, and no I don't know how to get away from him without just doing what he says. He wants to bring back the Lords and Ladies of Death, and I don't think I can stop him!" Monte's shoulders sagged and he dropped his gaze.

"The man outside?" Vyolet jerked her thumb towards the archway behind her.

"Yes. Mr Gondavere. I think he's one of the Lords and Ladies of Death – or at least he's related to them somehow."

"I thought as much. He looks like the drawings I saw when I was little, but he's not as tall or thin as them. He's a bit too human," replied Vyolet.

A grin spread across Monte's face. Was that relief in his eyes? Vyolet cocked her head and peered down at him.

"What?" she asked.

"I don't even know who you are, or even why you're here, but it's just so nice to have someone to talk to that's not him," he replied.

"Most people won't talk to Shadowkin," said Vyolet.

"I don't care what race you are, at least you're not like him." Monte pushed himself to his feet, keeping the flames away from the floor. "Is he still out there?"

"He was exchanging barbs with Eufame, and he's called Bloodhounds on the Wolfkin. I wanted to help them, but I thought it was more important to know what was going on in here." Vyolet listened hard but the sounds of the fighting were distant. Maybe the Wolfkin forced the hounds outside. Unless she pulled down that cloak in the corridor, she couldn't hear anything.

"Eufame Delsenza is here?"

"Yes. She's looking for the Heart of the City," replied Vyolet.

"Well she's going to be a bit disappointed then." Monte pointed at the assorted stones and rocks on the floor.

Vyolet gasped. "Mara was right!"

"Who's Mara?" asked Monte.

"One of the Wolfkin. She told us the Heart was broken, but Eufame seemed to think we could find a way around it," replied Vyolet.

"An old woman warned me the Heart was broken, but I didn't know what she was talking about," said Monte. "Though given all the fighting between the Cities, I can't say I'm surprised at all, more shocked it didn't break sooner."

"Is that why Mr Gondavere is here?" asked Vyolet.

"Yes. He wants to use it to re-open the realm that Eufame's sister banished the Lords and Ladies of Death to. I don't know about you, but I think that's an awful idea. I always thought the Lords and Ladies of Death just looked after people on the deathbeds, speeding them to wherever they were supposed to go next, but then I met him," said Monte. "I only came with him because I didn't really know what he was going to do. He certainly isn't going to let me just quit a job like this."

"Why did you take the job in the first place?" asked Vyolet.

"Same reason you take any job. It paid better than the one I had."

A loud crash penetrated the cloak of shadows. Vyolet started, and Monte scrabbled to his feet. Something came along the passageway towards them.

CHAPTER 30

The noise of the Wolfkins' battle receded down the corridor as they pushed the Bloodhounds into the darkness. The barks and snarls of the burly warriors chilled Jyx. He'd grown so used to Validus's calm eloquence inside his head.

"You see, Ms Delsenza, there's not really any way that this situation can play out in which I will not walk out as the victor." Mr Gondavere smiled again.

A high-pitched squeal rattled against the stones. Jyx gasped, but when he looked at Eufame, confidence had replaced the fear in her eyes.

That mustn't have been a Wolfkin then.

"Exactly who are you?" asked Eufame. "You're not one of the Lords and Ladies of Death. If you were, you'd be rotting with the rest of them. Were you the runt of the litter?"

Mr Gondavere scowled. His left eye twitched, and a faint red flush crept up his neck from beneath his collar. "You think you're so clever, don't you? Everyone's been too scared to stand up to you, and now you think you own the place."

At her side, Eufame drew a tiny sigil in the air. Jyx noticed her fingers spelling out the characters, but Mr Gondavere was too focused on staring her down. A faint scent hung in the air, like the smell of the sky before a thunderstorm. Dust motes flickered white in front of Jyx's eyes.

"If you bring back the Lords and Ladies, you won't own a thing. They will burn through the Cities like locusts, leaving you absolutely no one to rule over, and they'll treat you as badly as they did before Brigante intervened. So I'm offering you the opportunity to step aside, and disappear. Go back to the shadows. Hang around the bars of Canalsditch – do whatever you want, but move aside," replied Eufame.

Mr Gondavere sneered. He raised his arm and hurled a bolt of red energy towards them. Jyx ducked, but the bolt collided with the almost imperceptible white shield in front of Eufame. The ball of energy sizzled and dropped to the floor, where it seeped into the cracks of the stones.

"Really, Mr Gondavere. You must learn the rules of engagement." Eufame's fingers worked again.

"You are not getting past me!" Mr Gondavere brought up both hands and threw two bolts. Both of them hit the barrier, although a spiderweb crack raced across the white shield in front of Jyx. The smell of burning flesh hung heavy in the air. Eufame frowned.

"You're not that clever, necromancer." Mr Gondavere held up his hands. Red mist gathered around his fingers, coalescing into barbs and thorns. The energy sizzled and crackled, emanating waves of anger and hate. Jyx stared at Mr Gondavere. The red mist grew thicker and the colour drained from his already-pale face.

Jyx was torn between the desire to watch and

learn, and the impulse to run and hide. Blood magick was beyond him. He'd never managed to read the single book about it at the Academy, kept as it was under lock and key in Dean Whittaker's office.

"I've faced worse than you, Gondavere."

Eufame waved her hand and the shield disappeared. She pushed back her sleeves to reveal the dark red tattoos that snaked up her arms. Jyx had seen her call on their power before, when she faced Queen Neferpenthe in the courtyard of the House of the Long Dead. New additions occupied the spaces between the swirls. The black runes replicated some of the markings Jyx had seen on the walls of the House. Her tattoos pulsed white, filling the corridor with the searing heat of lightning. A funeral bell tolled in the recesses of Jyx's mind.

She's drawing on the power of the Veil itself.

Mr Gondavere drew back his left hand and hurled a handful of glowing red spikes at them. Eufame pushed Jyx forward and he scrambled under Mr Gondavere's outstretched arm. Eufame screamed and the tattoos spat forth twisting snakes of white energy. The red spikes collided with the white plumes, and the howls of both weapons filled the corridor, echoing against the stone.

"Go!" Eufame shouted at Jyx.

Mr Gondavere turned and raised his right hand. The words of the old spell sprang to Jyx's lips. It was one of the first he'd ever learned and drawing the sigil was as natural as drawing breath. Seconds later, green flames erupted at the hem of Mr Gondavere's coat. They licked upwards, leaving charred rags in their wake. Jyx darted through the archway and into the corridor before. Mr Gondavere roared after him but a bolt of energy turned the air white. With Eufame occupying Mr Gondavere's attention, Jyx ran along the passageway.

Halfway along, the air grew thick and wet, but

an instant later he emerged into a dimly lit passage-way. He turned around. A rippling cloak of shadows hung from the ceiling, hiding whoever hid in the tomb beyond. The cloak bore the same dead flesh smell as Mr Gondavere, and Jyx repeated the flames sigil where the shadows met the floor. The green fire tore up the cloak and the shadows screamed as they burned.

Flickering lights lay ahead, and Jyx ran towards them. Mr Gondavere was guarding this tomb for a reason, and Jyx suspected he knew why. The Heart of the City must be down here.

A man stood in the centre of the room, clad in the clothes of a gravedigger. Vyolet stood beside him. The fear on her face dissolved when she recognised Jyx, and she ran across the tomb. She wrapped her arms around him. Her skin was warm against his, and he resisted the urge to sniff her hair. He knew she'd smell of gun smoke.

"Who's this?" he asked when Vyolet disentan-gled herself.

"Monte. He's from Canalsditch."

"What's he doing down here?"

"He came down here with Mr Gondavere, and he can speak for himself, thank you very much," replied Monte. "Who are you?"

"Eufame Delsenza's apprentice. Jyximus Faire, sir." Jyx bowed. Bent at the waist, he noticed the collection of rocks on the floor. A statue sat pressed against the wall, a broken spear on the floor by its feet. The carving of the beautiful war-rior in Eufame's room sprang to mind. It seemed like months since he'd been in the House of the Long Dead.

"That's the Heart of the City, Jyx. Or at least it was," said Vyolet.

"It was a statue?" Jyx knelt on the floor. He picked up two of the fragments.

"Yeah. Monte thinks it's useless now. How can you mend a broken heart like that?"

"It's quite easy, actually. You just need to persuade the stones to get back together." Jyx grinned at Vyolet. He'd often wondered if geomancy was a waste of time, but this was the second time in as many hours that he'd needed it.

"Can you do that?" asked Monte.

"I can. Right. I'll need to concentrate."

Monte moved across to the doorway to keep watch. Vyolet knelt beside Jyx, ready to disappear into his shadow if anyone came in. Jyx closed his eyes and rifled through his mental library. First he'd need to actually talk to the stones. He aimed his finger, and drew a perfect circle on the floor in green light. He added the relevant sigils around its edge and placed each of the fragments within its perimeter.

"*Et ego loquar de lapidibus, ego quaero pro auxilio.*"

The sigil glowed and earthed itself with a low hum. Tiny sparks ran in circles around the edge of the circle. Jyx smiled at Vyolet. He'd made a connection with the flagstones, at least. Now for the fragments.

"*Nunc ego loquar ad fragmenta.*"

The fragments lay inside the circle. The circle continued to pulse with green light, but the stones didn't move.

"What's wrong?" asked Vyolet.

"Are they supposed to be doing something?" asked Monte.

"Shush, both of you! I don't understand why it isn't working. I need to think." Jyx stared at the stones. Had he missed out a clause? The last time he did that, he resurrected a mummy horde that devoured council members and killed Wolfkin. Having said that, he could do with resurrecting the Heart of the City right now.

He clapped his hands to clear the air and tried again. "*Nunc ego loquar ad fragmenta.*"

The stones inside the circle skittered around, but still didn't glow green. They just wouldn't respond to him.

"Oh no, I just remembered! We were told you'd need to know the Heart of the City's name before she'd respond to you. Perhaps that's the problem now?" asked Monte.

"How am I supposed to know her name?" Jyx stared at Monte. He'd always just known her as the Heart of the City. He'd never stopped to consider that she might have an actual name.

The Eufame shard in his head wriggled. He didn't hear her voice, but his gaze moved downward, as if a hand directed his head towards the floor. The circle pulsed, quietly humming in front of him. Understanding snapped its fingers in his mind.

Jyx placed his fingertips on the edge of the circle. "Hi, stone floor. Can you hear me?"

"Of course we can hear you. We're not deaf, you know," replied the flagstone nearest Jyx's knee.

"Oh thank you! I'm sorry, I'm not usually so bad mannered, I'm just a little stressed," said Jyx.

"We can see you're in a spot of bother, son," said the flagstone nearest Vyolet.

"Can you help me?"

"What is it you need? We can't persuade the Heart to get back together, I'm afraid," said the first stone.

"Do you know the Heart's name? When she was a warrior?"

"Of course we do! Everyone down in the Ruined City remembers her. Oh, she was glorious. Such a sight to be seen! I remember when she'd ride down the boulevards in her chariot, her hair flying and her spear held high. Oh how everyone would cheer," said the second stone.

"How could you remember that? You were in here with me," said the first stone.

"Oh hush your nonsense, you jealous old fool," replied the second stone. "We can each see what our brethren sees, remember?"

"You're all connected?" asked Jyx. Geomancy was proving to be a lot more interesting than he'd first thought. It stood to reason that all of the stones would share a consciousness. After all, water and air did – why not earth?

"Indeed we are. I must say, this is so nice to be having a chat with a mage again. It's been a long time," said the second stone.

"He's not a mage, you idiot. At least not yet. He's an apprentice. We shouldn't really be talking to him."

"If he's mastered the ability to talk to us, then he's more than an apprentice, and we should give him some respect, you idiotic slab of flooring." The second stone wriggled, as if it made a rude gesture at its companion.

"Don't listen to those two old women. She's called Hari-Ma'hara. She was always very approachable, if I remember rightly. Well, approachable for a warrior goddess, anyway," said the stone nearest to Monte.

"Thank you so much! You've been very helpful!" replied Jyx.

The three stones glowed once, and fell silent. Jyx rearranged the fragments in the circle and held his hands over them. "*Nunc ego loquar ad fragmenta*".

Mr Gondavere burst into the tomb. Blood ran down his face from a cut above his left eye, pooling in his eyebrow. "You fool!"

"Do it, Jyx!" The Eufame shard screamed in his mind. Jyx looked for her behind Mr Gondavere, but the doorway remained empty. He paused. Should he wait for her?

"I said do it!" she shouted again.

"*Hari Ma'Hara, Nunc ego loquar ad fragmenta, placere adiuva me et congregabit.*"

The fragments of the Heart jittered around in the circle. Mr Gondavere lurched towards Jyx, his hand outstretched. Crackling red energy twisted around his fingers. Jyx turned his head away and squeezed his eyes shut. The sound of crunching stone and the squealing of rocks grating against each other, filled the air. A sickening thud, of flesh against stone, prompted Jyx to open one eye and look up.

The statue leaned across him, shielding him with her body. She held up a shield on her right arm, a broken spear in her left hand. Mr Gondavere leapt around, nursing his left hand. He howled, issuing curses in a language Jyx didn't recognise.

The stones in the circle rearranged themselves into the shape of a heart. They glowed beneath Jyx's outstretched palms.

"Speak, and I will listen." A female voice, deep but rough around the edges, rang out in the chamber.

"Why did you just do that?" asked Jyx.

"I could not let someone injure the mage who knows my name before I discover what he wants," replied the voice.

"He's no mage." Mr Gondavere straightened, bruises blooming all over his left hand. Red energy coiled around his right hand.

"Leave him alone, sir. He's only a boy," said Monte.

Mr Gondavere grimaced. He raised his right hand and flung a bolt of angry energy at the gravedigger. The statue threw the remains of her spear and it pierced the bolt, carrying it across the tomb to the far wall. The spear absorbed the energy and burrowed into a crack between two stones.

"Pick on someone your own size!" Vyolet stepped forward, placing herself between Monte and Mr Gondavere. Her skin darkened, turning her the colour of fresh charcoal, and her eyes flashed indigo in the dim light. Dark grey clouds swirled around her feet. Jyx gasped to see the power pulsing through his Shadowkin friend.

"A Shadowkin!" Mr Gondavere's grimace disappeared. His eyes widened and his mouth formed a rough 'o'.

"You're damned right I'm a Shadowkin, and now I'm an angry Shadowkin!"

CHAPTER 31

Jyx stared at Vyolet. Clouds of charcoal smoke drifted across the floor, and Mr Gondavere shrank back towards the wall. The statue of Hari-Ma'hara lowered her shield arm.

"I would have the young mage speak." The weight of Time itself hung heavy at the edges of her voice.

"Spare us all the indignity, Honoured One." Mr Gondavere clung to the wall behind him, held at bay by the rippling shadow currents at his feet.

"Speak ill of my friend again and I'll slap you," said Vyolet. Black sparks danced in her eyes. Monte stood behind her, hand outstretched as if to stop her, but too terrified to intervene.

"I should be the one commanding the Honoured One, not you! You're just a boy with a pet freak and a mistress too stupid to know her time is over!" Mr Gondavere leered at them each in turn.

"None command me," replied Hari-Ma'hara. She stood stock still beside Jyx, but a fragment of her heart rolled across the floor into his hand. He glanced down at it. Did she mean for him to have it? She'd intervened once, but he wasn't sure if she'd do it again. No, he and Vyolet would need to do something about Mr Gondavere, especially given his insults.

Jyx conjured the sigil he needed in his mind's eye and superimposed it over the fragment of rock.

"You see, Honoured One? He does not even defend himself, or others. He merely plays with stones. He is not worthy of you. But I? I can offer you wondrous things in return for your help," said Mr Gondavere.

Jyx glanced up at Hari Ma'Hara. Was that his imagination, or did the statue just roll its eyes?

"These silly children need to be taught their place," said Mr Gondavere.

Jyx threw the stone before he'd even taken aim, his magick correcting its flight. It sailed across the room and struck Mr Gondavere on the forehead. The rock hit his oozing cut dead centre and sent a fresh stream of blood towards his eyebrow.

"You little bastard!" Mr Gondavere screamed and lurched towards Jyx. He stepped into the shadows swirling across the floor and howled. Another howl answered, distant yet strangely familiar. Jyx willed Validus and Fortis to return. He'd need their help before the night was through.

Vyolet's shadows turned deepest black where they touched Mr Gondavere. They swarmed upward, licking at his clothes as fire might consume wall hangings. He twisted to escape but the shadows held him fast. Jyx turned his head away but the statue planted her hand on his scalp and forced him to watch.

"It is in such moments that you will find yourself, young mage. Do not look away when you inflict pain on another, even if that other deserved it," said Hari-Ma'hara.

The shadows reached Mr Gondavere's waist, obscuring all view of his lower half. He plunged his hands into the mass, trying to push it away, but the shadows caught him and pulled him deeper. Jyx glanced at Vyolet. She stared, open mouthed.

She's not even controlling them anymore.

The shadows gave a final pull and Mr Gondavere's screaming form disappeared beneath the black waves. The darkness bubbled and frothed for a moment.

"What....what was that?" asked Monte.

His voice broke the spell. The shadows dropped to the floor, empty and diaphanous like cobwebs in morning dew. They flowed along the flagstones, following cracks to the walls. Mr Gondavere was gone. The fragment of Hari Ma'Hara's heart lay on the floor where his feet had been.

"What an odious man. Tell me, gravedigger. How did you come to be in his employ?" asked Hari-Ma'hara.

"It's a long story, and I fear there are more important things afoot, m'lady," replied Monte. He reached out and placed a hand on Vyolet's shoulder. She continued to stare at the spot where Mr Gondavere had stood moments earlier, but curled her fingers around Monte's hand.

"You are wise, gravedigger. Mage, I would know your business with me," said Hari-Ma'hara.

"Please help us, m'lady. My mistress, Eufame Delsenza, is out in the corridor – she came to seek your aid. The Cities are at war, and she's tried to do her best to hold everything together but the Crown Prince is trying to get rid of her so he can clear the Underground City out. He thinks it's a slum and oh, my family live down here and we're not bad people really, but I don't know how to stop the City Above and their council," said Jyx. The words tumbled over one another in a hurry to be said.

"The youngest Delsenza? She is here?" Hari-Ma'hara gazed down at Jyx. He twisted and looked up into her face. The statue wore a fierce expression, and he could see what the flagstones meant earlier. She would have truly been a fearsome sight in her chariot, thundering along the boulevards of the original City.

"Yeah, but I don't know why she hasn't come in," said Jyx. "I'm worried about her."

"Your concern for your companions is touching, young mage," replied Hari-Ma'hara.

Jyx looked up at her, convinced he would see sarcasm or disdain on her stone face, but the corners of her mouth flicked upwards.

"They're my friends," replied Jyx.

"It has been many years since I involved myself with the affairs of humans, but you make me curious. I will see the youngest Delsenza and have her explain herself."

Jyx led Hari-Ma'Hara out of the chamber. The grinding of stone on stone set his teeth on edge. He didn't dare remind her that she'd left her heart behind. They might have stopped Mr Gondavere from using it, but he was still far from persuading her to help the Cities.

The Eufame shard in his mind gave a sharp tug, and Jyx winced. His mistress wasn't happy. He just hoped she wasn't hurt.

Jyx peered into the shadows up ahead. Vyolet squealed and ran past him, dissolving into darkness. Jyx broke into a trot and followed her up the passage.

He gasped. Eufame lay on the floor of the corridor. She was half propped up against the wall, and a huge chunk of rock lay across her legs. Dust covered her bloodied hands and arms. Her hair hung around her face, now even paler than usual. Vyolet knelt on the floor beside her, running her fingers along the edge of the rock.

"Ah, Jyx. There you are. I don't suppose you could help me out?"

"What happened?" Jyx ran up the corridor and

knelt beside Vyolet. Up close, it looked even worse. The rock had missed Eufame's torso but her legs must be shattered beneath it.

"That idiot tried to bring the ceiling down. He only managed a chunk but it was enough to keep me stuck here. I watched what happened through your eyes, Jyx. I'm very proud of you both." Eufame looked at Vyolet, a ghost of a smile hovering around her lips.

"We can talk about it later, we need to get you free." Jyx didn't want to think about how much pain she must be in.

"The young mage has some talent with geomancy." Hari-Ma'Hara caught them up. She leaned over Jyx to look down at Eufame.

"The Heart of the City herself," said Eufame.

"I am Hari-Ma'Hara. My heart remains in the tomb for now."

Jyx ran his hand along the chunk of rock. He pushed against the stone with his consciousness, searching for its pulse. The rock offered no resistance or answers. He drew a sigil over the rock and tried again. The scent of dead flesh that had clung to Mr Gondavere wafted up from the stone. A knot formed in his stomach.

"I don't think I can move this. It's too heavy for me, and it won't be able to move on its own," said Jyx.

"What do you mean?" asked Vyolet.

"Most stones pulse with some sort of life force, like they're just waiting for someone to start a conversation. Like the ones in the chamber," said Jyx.

"And this one?"

Jyx couldn't answer. The rock pinning Eufame was utterly silent. He looked at the necromancer. Maybe she had a plan, or she'd be able to work out a way to get her free. She shook her head. Jyx's bottom lip trembled. Eufame may have once sentenced him to the Perpetual Death, but she'd done a lot for him. She'd trusted him, and now he couldn't help her.

Jyx did the one thing he didn't want to do. He burst into tears.

CHAPTER 32

"Oh, come now, Mr Faire. There's no need for tears," said Eufame.

Vyolet's own bottom lip trembled but she bit down hard on it. Shadowkin didn't cry. Shadowkin got things done. If she could make Mr Gondavere disappear, she could help the necromancer.

She looked up at the goddess. Hari-Ma'Hara leaned over Eufame, concerned etched into her stone features. "Can you help her, m'lady?"

"I cannot. Not in my current state," she replied.

A howl, long and triumphant, echoed through the ruined City. Its dying notes drifted along the corridor towards them.

Vyolet broke out into a grin. "I know two mighty warriors that can help!"

She jumped to her feet and broke into a run, dissolving into the shadows to move more quickly along the passage. She flew past the tombs as though her feet had wings. Vyolet burst out into the City. Patches of blood glowed in the dark, splattered across the stone floor and the walls across the street. A dead Bloodhound lay in a heap in the gutter. Vyolet resisted the urge to spit on it as she passed.

She listened to the shadows as she ran. One of the Wolfkin howled again, louder and more forceful this time. The darkness told her to head east, so she threw herself in that direction and kept running. Spatters of Bloodhound blood formed a loose trail to follow.

The Wolfkin rounded a corner and jogged towards her. Vyolet phased out of the shadows and into a more solid form. The Wolfkin stopped when they saw her. Fortis had a mess of nasty scratches across his muzzle and Validus moved with a limp. Both of them were covered in cuts and bites, but they were alive.

"Quick! Quick! You have to come quickly!"

"Who howled earlier?" asked Fortis, his paws forming the sign language.

"Mr Gondavere. It's a long story, but you have to hurry. Eufame's hurt," said Vyolet.

Validus and Fortis broke into a run. Vyolet dissolved into shadow and propped herself under Validus's arm to support him. His gait hitched on one side from his limp and Vyolet didn't want him hurting himself further. They retraced her route and she spotted two more dead Bloodhounds on the way back to the tombs.

They tore down the corridor, but Vyolet hid behind Fortis. Maybe she had been gone too long. Maybe the broken necromancer would have gone beyond the Veil by the time she fetched help. Maybe –

"Ah, my dear associates! I can't begin to express how glad I am to see you both!" Eufame's voice wavered, but Vyolet broke into a grin to hear it.

"Wolfkin! Oh, it has been an age since I have seen Wolfkin!" Hari Ma'Hara's statue broke into a wide grin.

Validus paused to bow, but Fortis knelt at Eufame's side. Jyx stepped back to move aside. He looked at Validus, who nodded at him.

"Validus says he thinks they can move the stone," said Jyx.

"Hang on a minute!" Monte suddenly ran back along the corridor towards the Heart's tomb.

"What on earth is he doing?" asked Eufame. Annoyance knitted her brows together.

Validus and Fortis ran their paws along the seam between the rock and the floor. They wriggled their toes but neither could get their claws into the gap. It was too small.

"Right! This might help!" Monte reappeared clutching Hari Ma'Hara's shield. He waved it at the goddess. "I hope you don't mind, m'lady."

"Not at all. Anything to help."

Monte shoved the edge of the shield into the gap. Vyolet rushed around to his side of the rock. Monte, Vyolet and Jyx pushed down on the shield, and the rock lifted an inch. Fortis and Validus dug their toes into the gap, lifting the stone higher as they worked more of their paws into the space. Eufame wiggled her fingers and a thin veil of white light spread along the underside of the rock.

Monte stepped onto the shield, throwing his weight down hard. The rock lifted higher and the Wolfkins' muscles strained. The rock rose a foot, and then two. Hari Ma'Hara stepped forward and offered Eufame her hands. The necromancer took them and the goddess pulled her out from beneath the rock. Eufame's feet were clear when the Wolfkin dropped the rock. The crash reverberated along the corridor, and it pitched Monte off the shield. He stumbled forward into Jyx and Vyolet's open arms. Hari Ma'Hara set Eufame down on the floor.

"Ah, that's better," said Eufame. She rubbed her thighs and winced.

"Is it painful?" asked Jyx.

"Yes, but with four older siblings who have a taste for torture, I've endured worse."

"Will you be all right?" asked Vyolet.

"I may need some assistance." Eufame looked up at the Wolfkin. They nodded, and ushered Vyolet, Jyx and Monte aside. Fortis laid his battered front paws on Eufame's left leg, Validus on her right.

A deep, low humming filled the air. The hairs on Vyolet's arms stood on end, wafting to the faint music swirling at the heart of the humming. The two Wolfkin swayed in unison. A white glow beneath their paws chased away the shadows around Eufame. She lay back against the wall, her eyes closed and a half-smile playing about her lips. The hum grew louder, matching the growing intensity of the white light. Monte slipped his hand into Vyolet's and she yelped. The Wolfkin ignored the interruption. Vyolet looked up into Monte's face. Terror and wonder fought in his expression.

He's never really seen real natural magick before. Come to think of it, neither have I.

She knew her own dark shadow magick, and she'd seen what Jyx could do, but this simple display of something ancient and primal by the Wolfkin captured her heart. Her soul danced with the Wolfkin, and she longed to join in.

A moment later, a third voice joined the chorus. Vyolet looked at Jyx. His face bore the same serene expression as Eufame, and he swayed in time with the Wolfkin. Green tendrils snaked from his fingers towards the Wolfkin's paws, staining the white light a pale mint colour. Vyolet peered at his hands. The green light came from Hari Ma'Hara, her hand on his shoulder and pouring energy into Jyx from deep inside the stone.

It's all connected. They're all joined. Ancient stone and Wolfkin lore.

A tear escaped from Vyolet's eye to be excluded from the magick. It rolled down her cheek and fell. It hit the stone floor and a peal of thunder rumbled around the Ruined City. Jyx and the Wolfkin howled together and the light faded. Vyolet looked down at Eufame.

"I say, that was a stellar working!" The necromancer broke into a smile, and for the first time she was radiant with pride and gratitude. Vyolet couldn't help but smile back.

"Did it work?" asked Monte.

Fortis stood up and steadied Jyx. Validus stood and held out a paw to Eufame. She bent both knees and raised one leg, then the other. Still grinning, she took the outstretched paw and stood. "I'd say that worked, wouldn't you?"

"I've never seen magick like that before," said Vyolet. She looked at the floor.

"We'll talk later," said Eufame. A sharp nod marked an end to the conversation.

"I have never seen such loyalty. Not in many long years," said Hari Ma'Hara. Her grating stone voice echoed in the corridor. "I have missed so much."

"I can show you what you've missed, if you'd like?" asked Eufame.

Hari Ma'Hara nodded. "I cannot help you until I know what needs to be defeated."

"Then let's go somewhere we can make ourselves more comfortable."

CHAPTER 33

The Wolfkin led the group out of the tombs and across the boulevard to a ruined building. A night tree grew out of the floor, its branches erupting through the remains of the shattered roof. Eufame stepped over the corpse of the Bloodhound and clambered over the broken wall into what must have once been a shop. Empty floral baskets littered the floor. Perhaps it was once a florist, purveying blooms and offerings for the nearby tombs.

"You're moving well," said Jyx.

Eufame laughed. "I'd hope so, after the magick you lot did."

Validus and Fortis helped Hari Ma'Hara over the wall. She knelt on the floor in the centre of the room, and Eufame sat cross-legged in front of her. Vyolet and Monte stayed outside in the street. Jyx perched on the edge of the hole in the wall.

"I don't let just anyone into my head, but I can't exactly refuse a goddess, and you need to see what's been going on in your absence," said Eufame.

Hari Ma'Hara nodded. They both leaned forward. Hari placed her stone hands on either side of Eufame's face. Eufame repeated the gesture, resting her long fingers on the goddess. They stared into each other's eyes.

The Eufame shard in Jyx's mind wriggled. A shadow cut across his vision and he yelped. He could see Hari Ma'Hara and Eufame on the floor in front of him, but at the same time Hari Ma'Hara swam in front of his eyes, as seen from Eufame's perspective. Her stone face leaned close, her eyes impenetrable. The shade cloaked his sight and Jyx plunged forward into a velvet cloak of darkness.

For a few moments, nothing happened. Jyx floated in time and space, and his memory strayed to his time spent beyond the Veil. The Perpetual Death at least equipped him for the weightless, and powerless, sensation currently keeping him afloat. His buoyancy held panic at bay, though his mind cycled through the sigils he knew for conjuring light.

Before he could use any, figures melted out of the darkness. Dim light brightened his surroundings. The edges of buildings solidified and Green Dragon Alley appeared, hazy behind the gauze of Eufame's memory. A small figure curled on the ground among the detritus, scrawny legs visible between two tall men. Clad in the blood red uniform of the council guard, they laid into the figure with a flurry of kicks. A low rumbling, like stone on stone, rolled around inside his head. Jyx cried out and the picture faded.

A new image appeared. Council guards herded Night Ladies and young servant girls into a warehouse near the Golden Lamb. The Night Ladies strutted and preened, tossing insolent looks to the guards, but they wrapped their arms around the servant girls as they disappeared inside. Terror burned in their eyes behind their brave expressions. A handful of council guards rubbed their hands together and exchanged lascivious glances. They followed the girls inside. The doors slammed shut behind them, and the image faded.

More pictures followed in quick succession. A journalist spying on the Crown Prince enjoying a tryst with a woman who was not the Princess. The Crown Prince ordering the execution of the journalist before his exposé could be published. Council guards beating up more inhabitants of the Underground City. Guards stealing stock to take to the City Above before torching the ruined businesses. Eufame arguing with council members. More violence against women and elderly people. A Wolfkin in shackles, pelted with fruit in the grounds of a City Above mansion. Money changing hands between Dean Whittaker at the Academy and a council member. Gentlemen from the City Above visiting the Underground City to gawk at its citizens. The Crown Prince demanding the presence of the Royal Line at his coronation. Shadowkin sent to the House of Correction without trial.

The final memory burst into life, this time accompanied by sound. Eufame and a Wolfkin – Jyx thought it might be Validus – strode through a grand entrance hall. A portrait of the Crown Prince hung above an ornate fireplace, and small coats-of-arms studded the pillars to either side. Seeing a nearby door ajar, Eufame darted inside. The gauze of memory fell away and Jyx gasped. A scale model, carved from wood, dominated a table at the centre of the room. At one end stood at Underground City as it currently was. In the middle was the Underground City as it would be. Completely razed. At the other end was the new Underground City – a pleasure palace for the wealthy in the City Above, free from the changing weather patterns and hostile neighbours that plagued the upper citadel.

The world went black.

CHAPTER 34

Jyx moaned. A headache clustered behind his eyes and set off tiny explosions of pain when he tried to move. He cracked open his eyes. Eufame peered down at him. Vyolet peeked over her shoulder, her face pale with concern.

"Are you all right there?" asked Eufame.

"My head feels all wrong," replied Jyx.

Validus helped Jyx to his feet. Monte held out his arm, and Jyx leaned on it. The coarse fabric of his jacket comforted Jyx in its utter banality. Such material reminded him that above him, life went on in a place where people bought bread, dug graves, and wore such ordinary, normal clothes.

"Of course it does, it'll feel a bit odd for a while. Not many people get to splash about inside the memory of a banshee and live to tell the tale," said Eufame.

"I was impressed by your disruption of the Crown Prince's plans for his coronation," said Hari Ma'Hara.

Her mouth crunched upwards in the approximation of a smile.

Heat flooded Jyx's cheeks and he looked away. Vyolet sniggered behind him and he wished he'd learned a sigil to banish blushing.

"Your efforts were commendable, if rash, young mage," said Hari Ma'Hara.

"He played his part beautifully. And look at him now! My successful little rogue. He broke me out of the House of Correction, you know. Along with this charming young Shadowkin," said Eufame.

Hari Ma'Hara smiled at Jyx. It was his turn to snigger when Vyolet's dark grey cheeks turned black.

"I hate to interrupt, and all of this is very sweet after the day I've had, but what do we do now? Mr Gondavere might be gone but that doesn't mean the problems up there have. Do you know how many empty businesses I pass on the way to work?" said Monte. He shivered at the mention of his former employer's name.

"Monte has a point. What will we do now?" asked Jyx.

"I have seen what you have tried to prevent. The City Above has grown corrupt, and unwieldy. The twin Cities were supposed to rise above the ashes of this Ruined City. One was not supposed to subjugate the other. The council cannot be allowed to continue unchecked," replied Hari Ma'Hara.

"So you'll help us?" asked Eufame.

"I shall, but I require something of you, first. Particularly your mage."

"What do you need?" asked Jyx.

"My heart is still broken. I cannot fulfil my role without it. You have some skill in geomancy, and I would trust you to complete your earlier magick," replied the stone goddess.

Jyx nodded. Fortis lifted him over the broken wall, and he ran towards the catacombs. His eyes had adjusted to the gloom in the Ruined City, and he stumbled over rocks and other debris in the dark corridor. Something black, like a stain within the shadows, flew past him towards the tomb.

He reached the chamber. Vyolet stood beside the fragments of the Heart.

"What shall we do?" she asked.

"I think I'll try and heal it in here. It'll be easier to carry a whole Heart than risk dropping a couple of fragments carrying it back through there," replied Jyx.

"Good thinking."

Jyx knelt and redrew the spell circle with green light. He added the sigils to its boundary.

"*Et ego loquar de lapidibus, ego quaero pro auxilio.*"

The fragments bounced and rattled across the floor, including the piece that struck Mr Gondavere. They gathered themselves in the centre of the circle. The sigils glowed dark green, the colour of the glass bottles kept by the apothecaries.

"*Nunc ego loquar ad fragmenta.*"

Unlike last time, the fragments turned green, pulsing with an inner glow. Jyx wrinkled his nose. The green light smelled of wet moss on stone. He'd smelled that scent before, right when Hari Ma'Hara put her hand on his shoulder when they healed Eufame.

"What's wrong?" asked Vyolet.

"I've never known magick to have a smell before, but it's like I can smell Hari, even though she's not here."

"Well her heart is." Vyolet kept her small feet away from the green circle of light.

Jyx nodded. "*Find viam reversi sunt.*" He held his hand over the fragments. "*Vos postulo ut cooperantur.*"

The smaller pieces bounced and tumbled around one another. The fragments fused together, sending green sparks skittering across the floor.

"*Tamquam ceciderunt in unum!*"

A throaty chuckle reverberated around the room. The laugh sounded like heavy stone rolling along a rocky path. The larger fragments collided with one another, their edges fusing where they made contact. They rattled among the smaller fragments, coalescing into a recognisable shape. The smell of wet moss grew stronger, but Jyx held his panic at bay. He could ask Eufame about the new magickal development later.

A tiny green explosion lit up the room, staining the shadows black. Jyx blinked hard to clear the after glare. He looked up at Vyolet. She'd thrown down the goggles she wore in the City Above to guard her eyes. A wide smile lit up her face.

"You did it, Jyx!"

Jyx looked down at the circle. Lying at its dead centre was a perfectly formed stone heart. The circle and its sigils faded, winking one by one out of existence. Jyx pushed himself to his feet. Vyolet launched herself across the tomb and threw herself on him for a hug. She laughed in his arms, and he couldn't help but laugh in reply.

"No wonder Eufame needed your help! She's brilliant, but she couldn't do that," said the Shadowkin.

"I know...who knew geomancy was so useful, eh?"

Jyx and Vyolet giggled, but the laugh faded on their lips. Jyx gazed into the purple depths of Vyolet's eyes. Suddenly very aware of her arms around his neck and her face inches from his, he felt a flush creep up beneath his collar. Vyolet blinked hard and released Jyx. She stepped backwards and looked down at the Heart.

"We'd better get it back to them then, Jyx."

Jyx gulped and nodded. He gathered up the skirt of his robe, and Vyolet helped him lift the Heart into its makeshift sling. Vyolet pulled the broken spear out of the wall and they hurried out of the tomb.

Jyx reached the group in the abandoned shop before Vyolet. He held up the stone, still wrapped in his robe. Hari Ma'Hara's stone face lit up.

"You have done me a great service, young mage," she said.

She plucked the Heart out of its fabric nest and slammed it into her chest. Eufame and the Wolfkin shielded their eyes from the brilliant green light that shone from the statue. Jyx covered his eyes and grabbed Monte's hand, placing it over Monte's face to stop him from staring.

"I have your spear," said Vyolet. Jyx cracked open one eye. The green light faded to a faint glow, as though Hari Ma'Hara shone from within like an ancient stone star. Vyolet held out the broken spear to the goddess.

"Can it be mended?" asked Jyx.

Hari Ma'Hara took the spear from Vyolet. She wrapped her hands around the break and whispered to the splintered shaft. The air around the broken wood shimmered and danced. The magick smelled of sawdust and sunlight. Hari Ma'Hara unwrapped her hands to reveal a solid spear.

"It looks as good as new!"

"Jyx, you of all people should know that almost anything can be mended!" said Eufame. Annoyance coloured her tone, but a faint smile played around her lips.

"We do not want to hurry you, but we should ascend to the Underground City. Who knows what has transpired in our absence?" said Validus.

Fortis relayed the message to Vyolet, who repeated it aloud for Monte's benefit.

"He has a point, Hari. Ready to leave the Ruined City?"

"As ready as I'll ever be."

The makeshift company left the broken shop, clambering over shattered walls and made their way towards the staircase. No one mentioned the Bloodhound corpses lying on the cobbles.

CHAPTER 35

They reached the staircase, and Validus helped Hari Ma'Hara climb the stairs. Jyx thought the healing of her Heart might have turned her back into a living goddess, but apparently the Hydra's curse was permanent. Still, the return of her Heart, whole and bursting with pride and love for the Cities, gave her a new lease of life. The regular beat of the stone organ sounded like the *tick-tock* of Time itself.

Vyolet led the way into the old chapel of the Lords and Ladies of Death. She pointed out the wall paintings to Monte. He shuddered to recognise shades of his former employer in the figures on the wall.

"It is likely that the Dreadguards may have traced us by now," said Eufame.

"Will they be waiting outside?" asked Jyx.

"It's possible."

"There is another way out," said Monte. "But it's through the Shrine of Beseda."

"Is that how you got down here?" asked Eufame.

"Yes. My wife…created a diversion and we slipped downstairs. There's an entrance right beside the shrine itself. We don't actually have to go into the shrine itself, but I don't think the priestesses will be happy to see us come up the stairs." Monte's voice caught at the mention of his wife.

"They shall bow before me," said Hari Ma'Hara. "They know who I am."

"Then it's settled. The Dreadguards won't be expecting us to come out of the Shrine if they think we went into the Temple. Monte, lead the way."

The group followed Monte into a side passage. Bones piled on either side of the long, low passageway and skulls grinned at them. Gaps between the heaps of smooth thighbones led to grates, speaking of a network of corridors beyond the catacombs. Jyx forced himself to look ahead, keeping his gaze locked on Monte's back.

They passed under an archway and reached a gate at the end of the corridor. Eufame peered through the bars. Jyx closed his eyes and let the shard of the necromancer in his mind take over. A wide anteroom opened out on the other side of the gate. A priestess in a feathered headdress guarded a room to their left – presumably the shrine. A spiral staircase curved up into the darkness on the right.

Eufame tickled the lock and the gate sprang open. The priestess gasped and lowered her staff, dropping into a defensive crouch.

"It's all right, priestess. We're just passing through." Eufame strolled out into the anteroom.

Jyx grabbed Vyolet's hand and pulled her through the arch after him.

"You have men with you. They are not permitted in here," said the priestess.

"I have one man, and a mage on the cusp of manhood. I also have a Shadowkin, two Wolfkin, and the Heart of the City." Eufame smiled, and a chill ran down Jyx's spine. The frost in her tone betrayed Eufame's annoyance at the interruption.

Hari Ma'Hara stepped through the gateway, and the flickering torchlight animated her stone features. The priestess dropped to her knees, and her staff clattered to the floor. She bowed her head.

"May we pass?" asked Hari Ma'Hara.

"Indeed you may," replied the priestess.

Hari Ma'Hara headed for the stairs. Eufame and Monte followed her, and Jyx and Vyolet hurried after them. They climbed up into the darkness, but the warmth of the Wolfkin behind them reassured Jyx. Cries of fright, and then supplication, rang out in the chamber above.

"I'm guessing they've just seen Hari," said Vyolet.

"I'd be scared of her if I hadn't already met her," replied Jyx.

"I wonder what Eufame wants her to do."

"We'll find out soon enough." Jyx tried not to think about Eufame's most recent grand scheme, the one that had ended in a bloody battle at the House of the Long Dead, and his imprisonment in the Perpetual Death.

Jyx and Vyolet climbed up into the chamber. Eufame and Hari Ma'Hara were already at the door to the temple, and three priestesses knelt on the floor. Monte stared at them. Jyx crept up to him and steered the gravedigger towards the door.

"Monte? What's the matter?"

"My wife... She died here," said Monte, a dull heaviness flattened his tone.

"Oh, I'm so sorry to hear that," said Jyx.

"She died because she wasn't honourable." Monte sniffed and pulled his sleeve out of Jyx's grasp.

A soft paw on Jyx's back steered him out of the welcome space within the temple. A narrow boulevard stretched through the gardens in front of the shrine, and a large black coach sat at the end of the path. The crest of the House of the Long Dead was emblazoned on the door. Four glossy black mares stamped on the cobblestones, straining against the harness. The figure that sat on the driver's bench clasped the reins firmly in a curled paw.

"Interesting. I didn't order any transportation," said Eufame.

"Is it safe?" asked Jyx.

"I am quite sure that it will be so. There are forces afoot, and for once they do not work against us," said Validus.

They reached the coach. Fortis helped Hari Ma'Hara inside. Jyx peered through the window.

"There's only room for four," he said.

"I believe I can help with that mathematical problem," said an unfamiliar voice. Jyx turned around. A tall man in a battered grey wizard's hat leaned against the wall. He took a bite out of a bruised apple.

"Crompton Daye! What are you doing here?" asked Monte.

"Your employer owed me a favour," said Crompton. His eyes twinkled in the shadow cast by his hat.

"You gave a favour to Mr Gondavere? Pfft. I'd have thought better of you, Crompton," said Eufame.

"Simmer down, E. It all worked out for the best, didn't it? Besides, I sent them to someone else who knows more about such things than myself," said Crompton.

"You know him?" Jyx gestured at the wizard.

"Oh, everyone knows Crompton Daye. Well, it's been a pleasure seeing you again, but we're working to a deadline," said Eufame.

"I know, I know, but I just wanted to offer Mr McThwaite here a new job."

"I'm going back to gravedigging. At least I know what's what when I've got a spade and a patch of earth to work with," said Monte.

Jyx was pleased to notice his hangdog expression had faded.

"Listen, my friend. You've seen far too much for gravedigging to be satisfactory anymore, and you'd be a lot more help to me and my associate." Crompton pushed himself away from the wall and strolled across to the coach.

"Your associate?"

"You know him better as Bucklebeard. He's got to go away to take care of a few things and he needs a hand doing an inventory of his shop. Mostly books and such, but all kinds of archaeological treasures. Needs a clever man who's seen a thing or two. He asked if I knew anyone who could help, and I had a feeling you might be in the market for new employment. Especially in the City Above," said Crompton. He smiled.

Monte turned to look at Eufame. Excitement burned in his eyes. Jyx wasn't surprised. He didn't know who this Bucklebeard was, but any job offer than included books was a winner in his view.

"Go. You'll be fantastic at it," said Eufame.

"I'm not abandoning you?" asked Monte.

"Not at all. Bucklebeard is an interesting chap. You'll enjoy working for him," said Eufame.

"This isn't goodbye, Monte. We'll come and visit," said Jyx.

Monte nodded, and moved to stand with Crompton. Validus helped Eufame into the coach, followed by Vyolet and Jyx.

"What about you and Fortis?" asked Jyx.

"We will meet you at your destination."

The horses let out an unearthly cry and the coach lurched away from the kerb. Its wheels clattered on the cobblestones, sending sparks flying in all directions. Jyx waved at Monte until they left the boulevard and pulled into the street. Urchins fled at the carriage's approach, and housewives yelled curses in their wake.

"Where are we going?" asked Jyx. His teeth rattled with every jolt of the coach.

"The council chambers. Hari has an appointment with the Crown Prince, and he should be there right about now," replied Eufame.

"But that means going through Lockervar's Gate." Jyx couldn't imagine the guards just opening the gate to let them pass. True, it was possible that Eufame's sister hadn't broadcast details of Eufame's escape. The guards might not even know there were Dreadguards in the Underground City.

"It does. But just trust me," said Eufame.

Familiar closes and alleys flew past on either side. The coach sped through the streets and onwards onto the approach to the Gate. The massive arch dominated the northern wall of the Underground City. Only Jyx's Academy sigil had granted him free passage in his old life, when he passed through the Gate every day to go to school.

Jyx leaned out of the window. The usual line of applicants snaked along the wall. A woman with a baby gesticulated at the Gate while the guard made a show of making notes in a ledger. Another guard left his side and lifted the great barrier between the Cities. He nodded at the coach as it passed. Jyx stared in wonder but movement in the shadows caught his eye. A familiar siren winked at him and disappeared into the throng moving along the street.

"I told you we wouldn't have any problems," said Eufame.

"How did you arrange that?" asked Jyx.

"I have my methods," replied Eufame.

"Magick?"

"No, a network of employees. Far less taxing on the nerves."

The coach rattled and bumped through the streets of the City Above. The roads were wider here, and less congested. The pedestrians wore finer clothes, and Jyx spotted one grand lady walking a dog. But despite the elegance, no one spoke to one another. People passed each other in the street as if no one else existed.

"It's a sad place, to be sure," said Vyolet. She gazed out of the window, her mouth pressed in a grim line.

"My mother would hate it here. She likes chatting to her neighbours, and seeing how people are getting on. My aunt would hate it even more – imagine leaving the house and never speaking to another soul unless you had to!" replied Jyx.

"This is not how the City was," said Hari Ma'Hara. Her brow furrowed and her mouth turned downwards.

"How was it in your day?" asked Jyx.

"It had its problems, as all cities do, but the rich and poor were not so separate. The rich would often hold charitable drives to fund enterprises for the poor, or they would find odd jobs on their estates to let the poor earn a living," replied Hari Ma'Hara. "It wasn't perfect, but people knew their neighbours. Children could play in the street, safe in the knowledge that their community would look after them."

Jyx recognised the fine buildings of the Justice Quarter. At the edge of his perception, a dark, menacing bulk hunkered in the shadows. His skin crawled to be so near the House of Correction again.

"Is it wise to be riding around in a coach bearing your crest?" asked Jyx.

"It's not bearing our crest now. It changed to that of my sister when we crossed through the Gate. It's only temporary, though, but it'll last until we reach the council. After that, it hardly matters what's on the coach," replied Eufame.

Jyx shivered. He'd never heard anything less than absolute confidence in Eufame's voice before.

"Fear not, young mage. The council shall have to answer to me," said Hari Ma'Hara.

"Indeed, Jyx, and I still have friends among the council. Not everyone was in favour of the Crown Prince's plans," said Eufame.

The coach turned into a street to their right, and Jyx allowed himself a small sigh of relief. Any road that took them away from the House of Correction, even only by a small margin, was a good road.

Jyx stuck his head out of the window. A massive building sat across the end of the road, blocking any further progress. Its white stone and tall, narrow windows glinted in the sunlight. Beautiful gardens flanked its gargantuan wings, set behind tall iron railings topped with spikes. Two hooded figures blocked the gate. Paws peeped out of their wide sleeves, curled around the halberds favoured by the council guards. A familiar tabby cat sat beside the pillar to the right of the gateway.

The guards stepped aside to allow the coach to pass. Eufame nodded at them and the coach crossed from the cobblestones onto the smooth stone surface of the council driveway.

"Well then, my dears. It looks like we'll be paying the council a visit very soon. There's no going back now."

CHAPTER 36

The coach rattled to a halt, and a door opened, its hinges squeaking in protest. Vyolet slipped her goggles over her eyes so the daylight in the City Above wouldn't blind her. Travelling in the coach had knocked her queasy. She breathed in through her nose to a count of four then held her breath for another four beats, and breathed out through her mouth to a count of eight. The simple relaxation technique was one of the few things she remembered about her mother.

"Ah, Vyolet. What do you think of the council chambers?" Eufame steadied Vyolet with a cold hand on her shoulder.

An enormous white building squatted at the end of a circular gravel drive. The windows glared down at them, screaming under the weight of the sunlight. Sculptures twisted and cavorted in niches along the upper floors.

"It's bigger than I was expecting. It's like a palace," said Vyolet.

"It was, once upon a time. In fact, the Crown Prince lives in that wing." Eufame pointed to the huge bulk of the east wing.

"Why?"

"He likes to be close to the council. He doesn't really trust them."

"Does anyone trust anyone else up here?" Jyx stared up at the white building.

"Not really, but we're going to use that to our advantage if we have to."

Vyolet gazed up at the entrance doors. They towered two storeys above her and their black surface shimmered. She'd only ever seen night iron once before, forming a safe in the Underground City. Only the Shadowkin knew how to both make and disenchant it. The doors must be at least two centuries old. Vyolet suppressed a grin. The council probably considered themselves safe behind them.

Two council guards stood either side of the doors. The group approached them, and they lowered their pikes.

"Ah, she graces us with her presence at last, Waldo," said the guard on the left.

"Good, you were expecting me then," replied Eufame. Her lips curved in her most bone-chilling smile.

"There are some people here want to see you, actually."

"Take me to them, then."

"Nah, sorry. They'll come out to see you," said the guard, Waldo.

Eufame narrowed her eyes and glared at the guards. "You clearly know who I am."

"Yeah, we do, but you don't frighten us anymore. You're just a criminal," said the other guard.

"It's all right, we'll just find another way in," said Jyx.

Vyolet stepped out from behind him, and the

guards rushed towards her, their pikes stopping only an inch or so from her chest.

"What did you bring a bleedin' Shadowkin for? Don't you know what they're like?" asked Waldo.

"She's a hundred times more efficient than you'll ever be," said Eufame.

A howl echoed along the driveway. Eufame threw her head back and unleashed an answering howl, clear but underscored with menace.

"What the hell are you doing now? Waldo, go and get the chief," said the other guard.

Waldo turned to leave but his companion grabbed his arm. He stared over Vyolet's shoulder, the colour draining from his face. She turned to look behind her. Two familiar figures raced up the driveway, discarding council guard uniforms as they ran.

"And now bloody Wolfkin!"

The two unfamiliar Wolfkin charged, their cloaks flapping open to reveal House of the Long Dead armour beneath. Waldo and his companion scattered, neither of them seemingly keen to be caught in the cul-de-sac of the doorway. One ran towards one wing, and the black Wolfkin followed. Waldo ran the other way, and the white Wolfkin gave chase.

"Right, now that's out of the way, we can go inside," said Eufame.

"Did you know the guards on the gate were on our side?" asked Jyx.

"No, but I suspect that's why Fortis and Validus left us to ride in the coach. They must have passed the message on to Bastet, who in turn alerted the Wolfkin at the House. The real guards are no doubt nearby. It's not just Jyx that can make sleeping sand," replied Eufame.

"The doors are of night iron," said Hari Ma'Hara. During the fracas, she'd walked up to them, and held her stone hand against their shimmering surface.

"They are. Luckily we have an expert with us who will help us get through that little obstacle," said Eufame.

"I don't have a clue what to do with night iron. I've never even seen it before! Professor Abjucat always said it was just a myth," said Jyx.

"I didn't mean you, Jyx."

"Shadowkin used to make night iron, many years ago. They don't make it anymore. My mother always said we wouldn't make things for people that didn't appreciate us," said Vyolet.

She approached the doors, one hand held over her heart in a Shadowkin gesture of reverence. A memory flashed in her mind, her mother making the same gesture before a copy of an old text she'd liberated. She frowned. People considered the Shadowkin to be heartless thieves, but they knew the value of the things they encountered. The humans only knew the price.

"Do you know how to disenchant it?" asked Jyx.

"I've never seen it before, not up close," replied Vyolet.

"Trust yourself, Vyolet. Shadowkin have their own magick. We've seen glimpses of yours so far – this night iron should be child's play for you," said Eufame.

Thoughts of the black smoke engulfing Mr Gondavere flickered before her eyes. She blinked hard to wash them away.

She laid her hand on the metal. It vibrated beneath her palms, singing a song that spiralled and swooped through her mind. Her mother used to sing this song when she couldn't sleep as a child! She hummed the tune, but the words wouldn't come. Had she ever known the words, or was it simply the melody she remembered?

The night iron changed its vibration, the movements slowing at her touch. Vyolet pursed her lips and whistled, the tune coming more easily. The shimmer dulled when she hit the higher notes and the melody galloped towards a crescendo. Vyolet opened her mouth and the final top C note broke free from her throat. The night iron let out an audible sigh, and the door swung open.

"Bloody hell," said Jyx.

Vyolet turned to look at him. Jyx stood open-mouthed. Eufame beamed, her face glowing with pure pride. Hari Ma'Hara strode across the courtyard and laid a heavy stone hand on Vyolet's shoulder.

"Your kind will be despised no more, Vyolet, and you will have the opportunity to learn more about your gifts."

Tears pricked the back of Vyolet's eyes, and she was grateful for the goggles.

"Come along, everyone. We have a council to depose." Eufame strode past Vyolet and slipped through the open door. Hari Ma-Hara took Vyolet's hand and led her into the atrium.

They didn't get far. Eufame stopped just inside the door and Vyolet didn't wait long to find out why.

A semi-circle of council guards stood in the middle of the vast entry chamber. They didn't concern Vyolet, not with the Wolfkin nearby.

What did concern her was the six Dreadguards looming behind them.

CHAPTER 37

"Eufame Delsenza, you are under arrest for your escape from the House of Correction, a crime which is compounded by your original crimes which saw you thus imprisoned," said a council guard. The purple band around his upper arm marked him as the head guard.

"My sister couldn't come to arrest me herself?"

"You know that she cannot leave the House," replied the head guard.

Jyx stole a glance around the atrium. Vast chandeliers hung from the ornate ceiling, embedded in central plasterwork confections. Frescoes lined the upper walls, their paintings depicting scenes of history from the City Above. The inclusion of the infamous murderer Waverley Tyrell made Jyx shudder. He much preferred the carvings in Eufame's chambers.

"Fine. I'll come with you. On one condition."

Jyx stared at Eufame. Why was she making bargains with the council guard? The Dreadguards mur-

mured between themselves, a chilling sound like bells tolling underwater.

"We do not strike deals with criminals, Delsenza," said the guard. A note of unease quivered in his voice.

"I hate to pull rank on you like this, and personally I can't abide those rule-quoting know-it-alls that seem to memorise obscure regulations, but technically speaking, I have not yet been tried for any crimes, making me as yet an innocent party under investigation. I was held in the House of Correction due to the temper tantrums of your employer, not through the legal process," said Eufame.

The shard in his mind burned white with fury. Jyx looked down at her arms. Her sleeves rested in the crooks of her elbows, revealing her pale forearms. The familiar blood red tattoos curved and snaked upwards from her wrists. A faint glimmer of white traced their outlines.

"Okay, so you're not a criminal, but –"

"I wasn't finished, you disrespectful clown. As I had not been formally sentenced, I did not technically escape from the House of Correction, and therefore you have no grounds on which to arrest me, aside from not notifying anyone of my departure from said House. Not to mention the fact that I am still a full member of the council, and you will address me as such!"

The white static crackled around Eufame, and the air smelled of ozone and wet metal. Jyx looked around for a weapon but saw nothing. His magick wasn't strong enough to win a physical fight, and he couldn't hold off the Dreadguards on his own. Unless he could persuade the marble of the floor to help, he'd have to rely on Eufame.

Hari Ma'Hara stepped forward. Her stone feet left indentations in the floor.

"I have had enough of this. Fetch your so-called Crown Prince." Hari Ma'Hara glared at the guards.

"And who, or what, are you?" asked the head guard.

"You may not address me by my real name, for you are not worthy to speak it, but you may have heard of me as the Heart of the City."

The outstretched pikes dipped and the council guards stepped back, bumping into the Dreadguards.

"What are you doing here?" asked the head guard.

"Fetch your Crown Prince. I shall speak only with him." Hari Ma'Hara took another step towards them.

"He's authorised us to deal with this," said the head guard.

The Dreadguards swarmed past the council guards.

"What do we do?" asked Jyx.

"What you do best," replied Eufame.

Jyx fell to the floor and scribbled a geomantic sigil on the marble. Would the Council Palace have wards in place to prevent magick? He hoped not. Panic seized his mind and everything but geomancy disappeared from his memory. The veins in the marble flickered green before Jyx could finish worrying.

"Can you help us?" asked Jyx. Surely desperation would trump the need to speak in the language of magick?

The Dreadguards were feet away from Eufame. The marble slabs heaved upwards. Those closest to Jyx stood up, forming a shield of veined rock between him and the guards. The Dreadguards skidded to a halt, thrown backwards by the bucking of the slabs beneath their feet. The council guards hung back, open-mouthed and staring at the rebellious floor.

Nearby, Vyolet let out a cry. Black clouds billowed around her feet, sending tendrils of shadow across the roiling marble. The Dreadguards inched away from the dark probes. One of Vyolet's vines reached a Dreadguard. It let out an unholy squeal when the shadow brushed its skeletal foot. They huddled together, waving their hands as his mother did when she wanted to shoo mice.

Eufame held her hands apart. White sparks fizzed and crackled in the space between her fingers. She moulded the blinding ball of energy, drawing it outwards. She formed a dazzling scythe, so bright it hurt Jyx's eyes to look at it. He'd seen her create energy scythes before; last time, it defeated Queen Neferpenthe. Could she do the same to the Dreadguards?

Hari Ma'Hara stepped over Jyx's marble shield. She swung her spear in a wide arc, sending ripples through the air. The shockwave hit the council guards, knocking them onto their backs.

"Do you need any more of a demonstration?" asked Eufame.

"We've got Wolfkin outside," said Jyx.

Eufame nodded.

"Oh yea Gods, just go upstairs. We don't get paid enough to deal with this," replied the head guard. He wheezed and clutched his side. Jyx winced. The guard would have a nasty bruise across his back in the morning.

The Dreadguards unleashed an impenetrable stream of chattering at the head guard. Jyx tried to block out the sound of their unearthly speech. They sounded as if someone had shaken a bag of bones nearby.

"You can do what you want, but we give up. Between this lot and Wolfkin, I'd rather face the Crown Prince," said the head guard.

Jyx helped Vyolet to climb over his marble shield. Vyolet gestured with her hands and her black tendrils raced across the floor. They flowed and rippled like smoke, forming an undulating ring around the Dreadguards.

"That should hold them in place," said Vyolet.

"Good job, Vyolet. Dreadguards tend to be more

inclined towards their responsibilities than council guards," replied Eufame. The head guard snorted, but his wheeze stole most of his derision.

Jyx and Vyolet followed Hari Ma'Hara and Eufame across the atrium. Eufame bounded up the stairs three at a time, and Jyx ran to catch up. As his feet sank into the soft carpet, a memory of the quicksand at the edge of the Academy's grounds teetered at the edge of his mind.

A corridor opened off the landing at the top of the stairs. A huge stained glass window dominated the end of the passage, depicting a tall figure wielding a white scythe. Twisted forms cowered at her feet.

"Is that you?" asked Jyx.

"No, that's Brigante fighting the Lords and Ladies of Death. Vyolet, you may want to take refuge in Jyx's hood until you're needed."

Vyolet nodded and a moment later the scent of gun smoke drifted out of his hood. Eufame gestured at the double doors beside the window. Hari Ma'Hara threw open the doors, and Jyx and Eufame followed her inside. A large oval table took up half of the room, and a model of a razed Underground City occupied the other half. Thirteen chairs surrounded the table, but only eleven were occupied by councillors. A squat man sat at the far end of the table. A narrow coronet perched on his head, balanced on his wig of golden curls. A gold chain of office hung around his neck and an array of gaudy rings clung to his fat fingers. Watery eyes peered out between the fleshy mounds of his pale face. Jyx shuddered. The Crown Prince looked nothing like the tall, willowy young man in his official portrait.

"Delsenza! What are you doing here?"

"I've brought a most esteemed guest to meet you, your Highness," said Eufame. She bowed to the prince, but winked at a dark-haired councillor to her left. A vague smirk hovered at his lips, and he gave an almost imperceptible nod.

"You are the Crown Prince?" Hari Ma'Hara's grating stone voice brought silence to the council chamber.

The Crown Prince pouted. "I am. And you are?"

"The Heart of the City."

The Crown Prince turned white and the pout dropped from his lips. He sat forward in his chair. Six of the councillors stood up so fast they knocked their chairs backwards. The remaining five looked past Hari Ma'Hara at Jyx. Two of them smiled at him. Jyx managed a weak smile in return, but his stomach roiled.

Do they know who I am? Do they know what I did to the Coronation Procession?

"Your Eminence!" The Crown Prince finally found his tongue. He clambered out of his seat and waddled around the table. Jyx looked down at him and frowned.

"Why do you wish to destroy the Underground City?" asked Hari Ma'Hara.

"Who told you that I wanted to do that?" The Crown Prince let out a high-pitched giggle and fluttered his fingers at the stone goddess. She pointed at the model on the other side of the room.

"Your plans would appear to be most conclusive," said Hari Ma'Hara.

"Your Highness, the Heart has come here to lodge a complaint. See, you can't touch the Underground City as she's sworn to protect the Twin Cities. You can't really have the Twin Cities if one of them doesn't exist." Eufame flicked a tiny figure across the courtyard of the model's council building.

"Don't be a fool, Delsenza. Of course the Underground City will still exist. Just not in its current form." One of the councillors scowled at Eufame.

"Turning a slum into a pleasure palace is not acceptable. Where do you propose to put the Underground City's inhabitants?"

"They will be offered alternative accommodation elsewhere," replied the councillor.

"Not good enough." Eufame wagged her finger.

The Crown Prince glared at the necromancer general. He stamped his foot, annoyance sending a mottled blush across his cheeks. He rounded on the councillor.

"It wasn't supposed to be like this! There weren't going to be any inhabitants because Mr Gondavere was going to deal with that for me! He was supposed to make her help me, not that idiotic dead talker!"

Eufame chuckled at the Crown Prince's description of her. Jyx glanced at Hari Ma'Hara. The goddess wore a terrible expression, fury and disgust chasing each other across her stone features. A faint green glimmer rippled around her, pooling in the cracks of her torso. Sparks flickered at the corners of her eyes. Jyx took a step back, glad that Vyolet rested safely in the shadows of his hood.

"Mr Gondavere was working for you all along?" Jyx frowned.

"And who are you? Why is there a commoner in my chamber?" asked the Crown Prince.

"What's the matter, your Highness? Don't you like to meet your actual subjects? The ones you would have happily thrown to the Lords and Ladies of Death if your stooge had succeeded in reaching our friend here first?" Eufame stormed across the room and towered over the Crown Prince.

The Crown Prince spluttered in reply.

"I have heard enough. I am no pawn in a political game," said Hari Ma'Hara.

Before the Crown Prince could utter another word, Hari threw back her head and let out a fearsome scream. The green magick resting in the stone exploded outwards, filling the room with energy far too powerful to look at. Jyx squeezed shut his eyes, feeling the shockwave of Hari's sorcery push up against his skin. Warm and cold at the same time, the magick surrounded him, but no fear accompanied the light, only safety, and security. The solid power of earth and stone folded him into its green embrace, and Jyx allowed himself to sink into the weightless void between the worlds.

Chapter 38

Jyx struggled to focus. Soft lights bobbed and swirled around him. Was this the world beyond the Veil? He didn't care. The Perpetual Death would continue, and maybe he'd have another dream like the one he'd just had – the one in which he rescued Eufame from the House of Correction and helped to resurrect an ancient goddess. If he strained his ears, he could even hear Eufame now.

"Jyx! Jyx, are you awake?"

Why would he be awake beyond the Veil?

Pain exploded across his face, throbbing in a handprint on his left cheek. His eyes flew open, and a familiar grimace rested inches from his nose.

"Ah, finally! I was beginning to wonder when you'd wake up!" Eufame moved back and hauled him up into a sitting position.

The remains of the room lay broken around him. Velvet drapes hung in tatters before shattered windows. The table rested on the floor in two halves, scorch marks running along its split edge. The five seated councillors huddled around one half, examining each other for injuries. The other six councillors and the Crown Prince were nowhere to be seen. Only six pairs of smoking riding boots, and one pair of ridiculous jewelled slippers, proved they'd ever been there.

Eufame helped Jyx to his feet. Hari Ma'Hara stood nearby.

"Where's Vyolet?" asked Jyx.

"She's fine. I rescued her from your hood when you passed out. She's gone downstairs to fetch the Wolfkin," replied Eufame.

"What happened?"

"Hari here did her thing. She burned through the corruption that was threatening the Twin Cities."

Hari nodded and smiled.

"These councillors survived because they want the cities to work for everyone," said Eufame. She pointed at the remains of the council.

"I must say, Eufame, I didn't quite expect that to be so...spectacular," said one of the councillors.

Eufame laughed. "No, that was better than I ever could have hoped for!"

"What about the Crown Prince?" asked Jyx.

"Well it turns out we don't have one anymore," replied Eufame.

Jyx gulped. "I didn't think it was going to lead to murder." He stared at a scorched handprint on the wall.

"Oh, come on now, they weren't murdered at all. If they'd been innocent, they would be here now. But they weren't. You saw what they had planned for the Underground City. If Mr Gondavere had gotten to Hari first, we'd be knee deep in the Lords and Ladies of Death now, and half the City would already be lost," said Eufame.

"I should return to the Ruined City," said Hari Ma'Hara.

"Must you go so soon?" asked one of the councillors.

"Yes, it'll take a while to form a new council. I think

any applicants should have to get your seal of approval before we'll allow them anywhere near a position," added another.

"They have a point," said Eufame.

"Then I shall stay. For a time. Until things are settled."

The councillors smiled, relief shining in their eyes.

Vyolet's voice drifted into the room. "Eufame?"

"Ah! Vyolet has returned. Let's see how things stand downstairs."

* * *

In the atrium, the council guards knelt on the broken floor, hands held behind their heads. A ring of Wolfkin guarded them with vicious pikes. They all wore different armour, including the sigils for the House of the Long Dead, the Academy, and even the House of Correction. Vyolet never thought she'd see so many Wolfkin in one place, and so soon after Hari's fury. Had they known beforehand what would happen?

Eufame and the others came down the stairs. Vyolet gestured to a spot where the Dreadguards had been. Black scorchmarks covered the floor.

"Did Hari's magick kill the Dreadguards?" asked Vyolet.

"I doubt it." Eufame reached the bottom step of the stairs and pointed at the night iron doors. They stood wide open.

"Will your sister be angry with you?" asked Vyolet.

"For a while, but she'll get over it. Naiad's a stickler for rules, so she'll be more furious that I left of my own accord. The Crown Prince probably invoked some ancient piece of legislation that she wanted to abide by," replied Eufame.

Hari Ma'Hara nodded to the Wolfkin and strode to the door. Jyx scampered after her.

"Come on, Vyolet. It's a brave new world now.

If we can manage it, the council and I want to reverse the legislation against the Wolfkin and the Shadowkin. You'll be able to do whatever you want," said Eufame.

Vyolet looked at the black stains on the floor, ghosts of the shadow tendrils she'd made just an hour earlier.

"Can I learn magick?" she asked.

"Of course you can. Question is, would you rather learn at the Academy, or with me?"

"Isn't Jyx your apprentice?" asked Vyolet.

"Oh I think he'll be a mage in his own right before long. He's learned more by doing than he ever would have learned at the Academy. Make no mistake, Vyolet, I can't teach you to be a necromancer, but we can certainly explore that Shadow magick of yours," said Eufame.

"Then I'll come with you," said Vyolet. She didn't even need to think about it. A life spent hiding in the shadows, filching food, or stealing secrets for people who thought she was no better than vermin? Or a life learning what she was really capable of? It wasn't a difficult decision.

"Excellent choice, Vyolet! Let's get you to the House of the Long Dead. I need to see what damage the council guards have done in my absence," said Eufame.

They followed Jyx out of the front doors. Hari Ma'Hara already sat in the black carriage, deep in conversation with a Wolfkin who stood nearby. Her series of barks and yips sounded even more alien in her grating stone voice. Jyx climbed in beside her. Vyolet pulled down her goggles to step outside into the gathering dusk.

Darkness pooled in the alcoves either side of the doors. A tiny movement to her left drew Vyolet's attention to two figures lurking in the shadows. She peered at the taller figure, making out feminine curves strapped beneath leather armour. White sigils covered the gauntlets and the patterns reminded Vyolet of the tattoos on Eufame's arms. The figure's hood obscured the upper portion of her face, but she held one long, white finger up to her lips. Vyolet looked at Eufame then back at the figure. She nodded and climbed up into the black carriage behind the necromancer general.

The figure in the shadows watched the coach leave the grounds and smiled. Her wizard companion jangled the buckles in his beard.

"I wish you'd told me about your scheme earlier. I'd have stalled the gravedigger for longer," he said.

"Relax, my dear. I knew my little sister could handle it all."

TO BE CONTINUED...

Did you enjoy *The Necromancer's Rogue*? Don't forget to leave a review on your favourite retailer's website – even if it's only short. It helps readers find better books to read from online stores.

Thank you!

At the start of this book, I promised you an exclusive prequel story. So if you enjoyed this book, and you want to get to know Eufame Delsenza a little better, then join my mailing list to receive *The Skeleton in the Floor*!

Find out exactly *how* a skeleton ended up embedded in the floor of the House of the Long Dead. Meet her first apprentice, Faro Pixenby. Enjoy more intrigue, betrayal, and powerful magick!

Go to;
http://www.icysedgwick.com/skeleton/
to get your free copy.

You'll also get one monthly email (I'm not a spam factory, after all) containing a free short story, book recommendations, and other cool stuff I think you might like.

Don't worry that I'll just bombard you with "BUY MY BOOK!" That isn't my style.

But if you sign up, you'll also get the chance to join my review team, which means you get free copies of my books before they're released, and all you have to do is pop a short review on Amazon!

MEET THE AUTHOR

Icy Sedgwick was born in the north east of England, and is currently based in Newcastle. She had her first book, the pulp Western adventure, *The Guns of Retribution*, published in September 2011. When she isn't writing or teaching, she's working on a PhD in Film Studies, knitting, exploring graveyards, or watching history documentaries.

CONNECT WITH ICY!

Website:
http://www.icysedgwick.com/

Twitter:
https://twitter.com/IcySedgwick/

Instagram:
https://www.instagram.com/icysedgwick/

Facebook:
https://www.facebook.com/miss.icy.sedgwick/

Pinterest:
https://www.pinterest.co.uk/icysedgwick/

G+:
https://plus.google.com/+IcySedgwick/about

Printed in Great Britain
by Amazon

11354787R00158